Those Captive Blues

Linda Holmes-Drew

Linda Holmes-Drew

Copyright © 2017 Linda Holmes-Drew

All rights reserved.

ISBN: 1974679594
ISBN-13:9781974679591

Dedication

First and foremost, to my husband, David, for his amazing patience with my writing and rewriting. To my children who believe in me, Lynn Jarrett, my editor, and dear friend whose help is immeasurable, and Tanya Provines for creating my cover.

Last but certainly not least, to the blue-eyed man who inspired me to write this series. He'll never be forgotten. Also to my sweet cousin, Joyce who is lingering at Heaven's gate. She and I shared the same love for this man.

Hugs and love to you all.

Linda Holmes-Drew

Missing You

Today it rained
Like tears
From angels filled with pain.
Dark clouds
Like sorrows
Rolled across the skies.
A chill
Like caresses
Touched my soul in vain.
Thunder
Like heartache
Brought remembrance to my eyes.

--Linda Holmes-Drew

Chapter 1

The day'd started as a muggy, unseasonably warm one. Dark angry clouds rolled across the sky. My dogs and my horses, even my cows, had seemed very restless when I'd gone out to check on 'em. It'd rained a little on and off, but that'd done little to improve the heaviness in the air. I tried to calm that uneasiness that continued to claw at the pit of my stomach. Somewhere along the way, I'd developed that sixth sense my Nanny had always told me about. She said God had give it to women 'cause men would never take the time to listen to it! Well, I'd learned a long time ago to pay close attention to that naggin' feelin'.

I looked out the upstairs window as the wind began to howl. It was gettin' mighty dark for the early afternoon. I hadn't seen a sky like that sense I was just a little kid, but I remembered it real well. Who could forget those deep black clouds with hints of green rollin' across them mountains. Daddy'd rushed us all down to the old root cellar where we ended up spendin' the whole night. The next day we found trees tore up all around the mountain side. Some of the neighbors had even lost the roofs off their houses.

Light hail suddenly began to hit the window. I rushed downstairs to find my boys who'd been playin' in the kitchen floor. I grabbed jackets to protect 'em and dragged 'em out the back door. We didn't have a root cellar, but I knew the only place on the property where we'd be safe. My heart was poundin' in my chest as I struggled to carry my twin three-year-old boys across the yard and up the hill to the small cabin. I opened the door and put the babies inside the room.

"You boys stay right here. I gotta try to go let the horses out so they can run for cover."

I rushed out into the pourin' rain and about halfway across the pasture, large hail began. I paused and decided I needed to be with my babies more than the horses. Just as I turned to go back, a huge hailstone smacked me on the cheek. It stunned me for a second, as another one whacked me on top of my head. I ran as fast as I could while the hailstones continued to pummel my body. I charged into the cabin just as the hail, rain, and wind stopped.

Dead silence. A gate creaked in the distance as it barely swung back into position.

The smell of an old musty, mildewed cellar drifted into the room. Every instinct I had, screamed! I slammed the door shut and worked frantically to pull the old armoire away from the wall. It'd been years since I'd opened it, but after several tries, the hidden door finally began to release.

"C'mon boys! Hurry!" I yelled, as the babies hurried quickly across the room. I grabbed the lantern inside the door and lit it as I heard the wind outside begin to scream. It took all my strength to pull the ancient door shut.

"Mommy?" Little Eli's voice was shaky. "What's happenin'? Where we at?"

"It's okay, honey. Hold hands and follow me." I led 'em down the tiny box-lined trail that opened into the old cave.

I shuddered at the smell of the evil place. But I had little to no choice . . . it was the safest place for my kids and myself. We didn't get many twisters up on the mountain but occasionally, there'd been a few. It was soundless inside the cave, so I didn't have no idea what was happenin' out there. I prayed my animals would be okay. My horses and dogs were my main concern now that we was safely sheltered. I'd be devastated if anything should happen to any of 'em. We'd been through so much together. It'd be like losin' family. There was just too many memories attached to 'em.

I found a couple of old boxes and made seats for the three of us.

"Mommy, what happenin'?" Jonny asked.

"It's a bad old storm out there and we come here until it's over. We're safe baby." I told him as I tried to calm myself down.

"We campin', Mama?" Eli asked.

"Somethin' like that. Do ya want me to tell ya a story?" I asked.

"Mama?" yelled Jonny. "What 'bout Boots and Roz? They're ascared too! I wanna go get 'em." He demanded with his tiny hands on his hips.

"They'll be okay. They're in their secret hidin' place. They know where to go." I prayed that I was right but in truth, I didn't have no idea where they was.

I held my babies and told 'em stories 'til they fell sound asleep. I thought about goin' out to see what was happenin', but was too afraid to open the door. I decided to wait awhile and be sure it was over. I wandered out into the main cave. I took the lantern and edged toward the scene of the most horrific experience of my life.

In the dim light I found the place where I'd been held captive for so long. The heavy eyebolts was still in the wall where the chains had been. Cautiously, I turned toward the opposite wall. The eyebolts was still in that wall too. I bent over and picked up a large rock, the same rock that had finally brought freedom. Freedom for me as well as for him.

I backed away as if somethin' was movin' toward me. I suppose that in a way it was. The memories was so strong that they seemed to have a life of their own. I'd spent well over three years tryin' to put it all behind me. There was times I still cried and times that my broken heart still ached so bad I could hardly breathe, but that was somethin' I tried desperately to forget.

"MOMMY!" Screamed one of the babies.

Everything disappeared at the call of my baby. I ran back to where they'd been sleepin'.

"It's okay, honey. I'm right here." I snuggled 'em and they went right back to sleep. Eventually, I fell asleep myself.

It wasn't a peaceful sleep. I could hear the shreakin' voice of the black hooded rat-man when he'd told me he would cut me into pieces. The harsh whisper of the black hooded vicious one as he slammed my head on the metal table where he had me tied. I saw the bundle he dropped across from me as he rolled it out onto the floor. I could see the thatch of silver blonde hair and the bloody face it belonged to and I awoke with a jolt. Sweat trickled down my face and neck. My breath came in heavy gasps.

Surely the storm was over by now. I needed to get out of that damn place. I took the lantern and slipped down the path to the old door. Cautiously, I pushed on the handle that Toby had installed several years ago. After a few good shoves, it started to move. I opened it slightly and peered into the cabin. Thank God, it was still there. I went to the door and looked outside. Several large trees from the grove in front of the main cabin were in the back yard and scattered in the pasture. My heart stopped as I saw that a large section of the barn was gone. My horses, Pride, Patton, and Promise, had been in there. Oh God! My boys, I'd always called 'em, they didn't even have a chance. I started off the porch, but I remembered that my babies was alone in the dark cave. I hurried back inside and gathered 'em up and carried 'em out and laid 'em carefully on the bed. I put the lantern out and closed the door to that evil part of my past.

I finally got the boys to the house and on the couch in the livin' room. They slept right through it.

I slipped out the front door and ran to the barn. I halted at what was left of the door. I waded through mud and icy slush from the hail and stepped cautiously inside the door. Hay was strewn from top to bottom and the side and back walls was gone. With horror and fear, I turned to the stalls. Huddled in the back of one was two of my precious boys, Pride and Promise. Their eyes were wild with fear and their nostrils flared. I looked around frantically for Patton, but he was nowhere to be found. There was blood on the side of the stable where his stall had been, but nothin' more. I turned quickly towards the other two horses. I spoke softly to 'em and tried to pet 'em, but they was far too terrified. I wasn't sure what to do. I'd never seen 'em so afraid. I gave 'em some fresh feed and water and went back toward the house to give 'em a chance to settle down.

When I neared the house, my dogs, Boots and Roz, come scurryin' out from under the porch. I was so happy to see 'em, I could've bawled! They was shiverin' and sure 'nuff scared, but unharmed. I hugged 'em and reassured 'em and they finally took off for a drink of water.

I made my way up the steps, took off my mud-covered shoes, and stepped inside just as I heard a truck come speedin' up to the grove. It didn't come up to the house. However, it wasn't long before two figgers come runnin' up the drive. My very best friends, Floy and her husband, Toby, rushed up the steps.

"Lilah, are you alright? Where's the babies?" Toby gasped. "How much damage did ya get? There's a ton of trees we had to dodge to get up here. That's why we had to leave the truck down the drive . . . several trees across it. Oh, hell! Look at that barn! The horses! Are the horses okay?"

I flinched as the realization hit home. "No. Patton's gone." I whispered as tears began to roll down my cheeks. "Pride and Promise won't let me near 'em and there's blood . . . blood in Patton's stall. He's gone Toby! The horse he always rode is gone! Just like him . . . just gone!" I wept.

"Honey, are ya okay?" Floy wrapped her arms around me. She pushed my hair out of my face. "Where is this blood comin' from? Are you hurt?"

I didn't have no idea what she was talkin' about, but she grabbed a rag and wet it.

"Let me wipe your face and neck. You're bleedin' pretty good."

I hadn't realized that the hailstones had cut my head and cheek. I guess I was pretty scared myself, 'cause I barely remembered bein' hit. Floy put some bandages on the cuts and we sat down at the kitchen table.

"Where's the baby?" I asked.

"She's with Mama. She was at the house when the storm hit. We could see the twister when it went over the mountain toward your place. We headed up here right away, but we had to work around a dozen trees to get here. I'm just so thankful you didn't get it any worse than you did. It could've took everything!"

"It took enough, Floy. It took Patton . . . Patton." I sighed a ragged sigh that reached to my soul. "I've gotta find him so I can bury him proper, here where he lived."

"We'll find him, honey. Come on and let's get the boys up to bed. Okay?"

She helped me get the babies changed into their pajamas and tucked into bed. We sat downstairs and talked for a long time before they left. Toby'd gone down to the barn and checked on the horses again. He was pleased to tell me that both Pride and Promise had taken sweet feed from his hand and seemed to have calmed down quite a bit. That was good news. I would spend time with 'em tomorrow.

After they left, I got a glass of tea and went out on the front porch. The air was cooler and smelled so clean. I sat down in Nanny's old rocker and watched the sky. It was still lightnin' off in the distance, but the rain had stopped and everything was quiet . . . except for the frogs that was still singin' for rain.

Just then, the clouds cleared enough for the full moon to show its face. For the hundredth time, I remembered what he'd told me once. "I looked up at that moon every night and asked him to keep a watchful eye on ya 'til I could get back." he had said.

"Mr. Moon?" I asked out loud, "Please keep a watchful eye on him . . . until he finds his way back home." I felt a single tear make its way down my cheek and roll down my neck. At least it had narrowed down to one tear . . . for years, it'd been rivers.

I closed my eyes and allowed myself, against my better judgment, to remember. I could feel his kisses, feel his silky, silver-blonde hair as I ran my fingers through it. I could smell that unforgettable cologne, and always, always, I could remember those hypnotic, crystal blue eyes. My heart pounded in my chest and my body began to ache for him.

"STOP!!" I cried out before I realized it. I jumped out of the chair and walked down the steps onto the wet gravel. I wanted to run . . . I needed to run! I knew I couldn't. I had babies, his babies, to tend and I couldn't leave 'em alone. My nurse and friend, Dee, had taken a few days off to go see her family. Most times when the memories became too intense, she would watch the boys so I could run or ride the horses until I had eased the pain. Turnin' around, I went back inside and got ready for bed. It'd been a horrible, bittersweet day!

****

I opened my exhausted eyes and lay quietly in my bed. It was daylight. I looked at the clock and realized that it'd been daylight for a while. I sat up quickly and looked around. Crawlin' from beneath the blankets, I went to the window and peered outside. For the first time in years, my old rooster had failed to wake me with his insistent crowin'. I'd often threatened to make chicken soup or dumplin's out of him when he'd woke me up just before daylight. He was nowhere to be seen. There were only a handful of chickens roamin' freely around the yard. Some of 'em looked like they'd had a rough night, but the old rooster wasn't there.

I got my housecoat and slippers and went in to check on the boys. They was cuddled together and sound asleep. So peaceful, so beautiful was these identical little boys that I could still scarcely believe that they was actually mine. The babies that I didn't believe I could ever have, and yet, there they was . . . perfect little replicas of their Daddy. Eli's little hand grasped the cuff of a powder blue shirt, while Jonny rested his little blonde head on the opposite sleeve. My hand shook as I reached to caress the collar. With an unwillin' heart, my mind wondered back to the night he'd left.

I'd sat in the floor of our bedroom in shock and disbelief. Chad had quickly packed his belongin's and turned to me with a tear-streaked face.

"I don't know that I can ever come back, honey. But I can't say I never will. I only know that I love you with everything that's in me. I'm so sorry." Then he'd turned and walked out the door. I heard the door close and in a couple of minutes I heard the truck start and leave. There was a hole in the pit of my stomach that I knew would never heal.

Several weeks after he'd left, Floy and I decided that it might make things a little easier if we cleaned, rearranged, and painted my bedroom. As we pulled out Nanny's old chair from the corner, I spotted somethin' blue in the floor. When I picked it up, I immediately recognized the powder blue shirt that Chad had often worn. I touched the embroidered initials with my shakin' hand. TCB, Thomas Chadwick Barrett, he'd told me. A name so branded in my memory that I doubt I could ever be able to forget. When the boys was born, they'd been so tiny I'd wrapped the two of 'em in the shirt that still held the scent of their Daddy. I sat and rocked 'em quite often while they snuggled inside it. Over time, they'd become so attached to it that they hardly ever fell asleep without it. I wondered if they sensed the importance of it and that it belonged to someone very significant in their lives.

I stood up and slipped out of the room and quietly eased the door shut. I went down the old stairs that held so many memories of family and friends from generations past. How I loved that old house. When Nanny left it to me with all the land and her holdings, I'd been in a state of shock. My Nanny and I had an amazin' relationship and I missed her so much. Sometimes I could feel her presence in every room in the house. Today, it seemed exceptionally strong.

I finished breakfast and the babies was still not awake. I went out on the front porch with my last cup of coffee and sat in the old rocker. I stared down to the barn . . . or at least what was left of it. I needed to get dressed and go let the horses out in the pasture. My heart ached at the thought of what Patton must've gone through in his last moments. I'd bought him and Pride when me and Floy made a trip to Lexington a little over four years ago. They caught my eye right off and I instantly fell in love with 'em. That'd been the first time I'd laid eyes on Chad and I didn't even know it until he told me later.

"Mommy? Where you hided?" I heard one of the babies call.

Pulled from my painful train of thought, I hurried inside to see who was awake.

"Mornin', sweet baby. Did ya sleep good?" I asked as I scooped little Eli up and spun him around.

"No." He firmly stated. "The wind blowed and that bear cave was scary!"

"You had a bad ole dream. That storm's gone far, far away." I paused for a second. "Eli, why did you call it a bear cave?"

". . .'Cause that's where a bear used to live afore he got killed," he said casually as he squirmed down and headed toward the kitchen.

I stood there as chills ran up and down my back. There was absolutely no way he could've known about that bear. Why would he say that . . . where could he have heard such? Maybe it was somethin' I'd read to him or he'd seen on TV . . . that had to be the answer. I tried to shrug off the uneasiness that I'd started to feel.

Shortly after lunch, Toby and his cousin come with chain saws to remove the trees and stumps that was scattered around the cabin.

"Hey, Lilah. This here's my cousin from Mississippi. Remember, I told ya he was comin' to spend a couple of weeks with us. He got in last night. Lilah, this is Seth . . . Seth, Lilah. Did ya get any sleep last night? How 'bout the boys?" Toby chatted on.

"I slept okay. The boys slept like little logs. How 'bout you guys? Did ya'll get any rest?"

"Hell, you know me, Lilah. I could sleep through an earthquake! After Nam . . . bein' home . . . nothin' wakes me up very easy."

"That's good Toby. I guess there's a lot of vets that sure can't say that." I turned to his cousin, "It's nice to meet ya, Seth. Toby's talked about ya a lot. He thinks there ain't much his big cousin can't do."

"Aw, I don't know about all that, but we been close all our lives." He reached out his hand, "and it's sure a pleasure to meet you, ma'am. He didn't lie a bit . . . you're prettier than the wildflowers in early spring."

I shly shook his outstretched hand. With a very red face, I thanked him and stepped back inside.

"I never said all that stuff, Seth!" I heard Toby mumble. "You're so full of bull . . . you know what!"

I heard Seth snicker as he and Toby began to scuffle.

As soon as I got inside, I turned and peeked out the window. They was walkin' toward the barn. Seth was several inches taller than Toby and had a more muscular build. The biggest difference was his near-black hair, but his soft gray-blue eyes caused him to strongly resemble his younger cousin. Perhaps, he was even . . . better lookin'.

I scolded myself as I turned and went to see what my busy little boys was doin'. The phone rang.

"Hello." I answered.

"Hey. How ya doin'?" It was Walter, my ex-husband.

"I'm good . . . and you?"

"Aw, I'm fine. Just wanted to make sure that nobody got hurt yesterday in that twister."

"No. Some damage to the barn and lost a few trees, but we're okay." I couldn't bring myself to mention Patton. "Toby and his cousin's takin' care of it."

"Do ya think they might need any help?" He asked.

"I don't really know, Walt. They're just gettin' started."

"If it's okay with you, I'll come on out and see."

"Ya don't have to . . . but whatever ya think."

"Alright, I'll see ya' in a little bit." He hung up.

I didn't know what Toby would think. Him and Walter'd never got along, but since Walter'd started to straighten his life up, Toby had tolerated him a lot better.

Walter and me had got married way too young. He'd been far from ready to settle down and his drinkin' and skirt chasin' had landed him a divorce before he knew it. After my kidnappin', he'd kinda come to realize that life wasn't the free-for-all game he'd once thought it was. He'd since apologized for all that'd happened when we was together and seemed to be makin' a big effort to reform his life. We was casual friends, but nothin' more.

I'd just hung up the phone when the front door opened.

"Dee, you're home!" I was excited. She'd started as my nurse after my accident several years ago and had become like family. When the babies was born, I called and asked her to move in permanently and work as my full-time nanny for the boys. It was especially nice that she'd become one of my very closest friends.

"I heard about that twister comin' over the mountain and I just couldn't get home fast enough! How's my little termites?" she asked.

"They're fine. That storm nearly give me a heart attack, but we're good," I told her.

"Sure a lot of trees ripped down along the road. I saw the barn when I pulled up. I'm just glad everyone's alright." She sighed.

"Not everyone, Dee. We lost Patton." I said flatly.
She stood there a minute as she let the information sink into her head.

"You mean . . . Chad's horse . . . the one he always rode?"

"Yeah. We ain't found him yet. He's just . . . gone." I whispered as I dropped in the chair.

"I'm so sorry, honey. I know that horse meant so much to ya. You guys had some great rides on him and Pride.

"Chad never got to ride Promise, ya know . . . the one I got him that Christmas. He was just a little colt then. I guess now he is big enough, I ought to send him to Mr. Burrows and have him broke to ride. I'd always held out hope that Chad would . . . might . . . . I guess I'll call Mr. Burrows tomorrow. Would you like a glass of tea?" I asked as I got up and headed toward the kitchen.

****

The chainsaws ran pretty much all mornin'. Toby and Seth cut the trees into logs and stacked 'em in the back by the woodpile to be split later. I stood in the back doorway and watched out the screen door as they worked. Memories of Chad come floodin' back into my head . . .

again. There'd been a time when I'd stood in that same spot and watched as he'd worked to split and stack the wood. The muscles had rippled as his perspiration-covered body had swung the splittin' maul again and again. His silver-blonde hair had blowed freely in the mornin' breeze and rested casually across his deeply-tanned face.

I sipped my very hot cup of coffee and stepped away from the door. It seemed harder lately to keep my memories in check. My mind'd been occupied with the boys for so long, it'd become easier to let go of a lot. If that storm hadn't drove us into the old cave, maybe it all wouldn't have come rushin' back the way it was. A sudden bangin' on the back door startled me so bad that I dropped my cup.

"Um . . . Lilah?" It was Seth. "I didn't mean to scare ya. Toby wanted me to ask ya for a couple of glasses so we can get a drink," he said as he come inside and grabbed a towel from the table and began to wipe up the coffee I'd spilled.

"Don't worry about that, Seth. I'll clean it up," I told him as I struggled to get the cup from under the table.

As I stood up and turned, my foot slipped on the wet floor and I fell forward. Seth had just stood up too, and I landed right in his arms. Our faces were only inches apart. We was both shocked at the sudden uncomfortable position that we'd found ourselves in. I regained my balance and backed up quickly.

"I'm so sorry, Seth. My foot slipped and I . . . I lost my balance," I tried to explain.

"No problem, Lilah. I'm not complainin' in the least." He blushed as he spoke.

"Well . . . uh, here's ya some glasses."

He stood there for a minute, then turned quickly and went out the back door. I hadn't been that close to a man in years. I was shocked at the way it'd affected me. I suddenly needed to sit down and take a deep breath. My heart pounded at the recollection of those strong muscular arms and the natural fragrance that came from his overheated body. *NO . . . never again! Never again!!* I scolded myself for what I was thinkin'.

The rumble of a truck comin' up the drive, and the commotion of the dogs out front, caught my attention. I got to the door just in time to see Walter climb out of his battered old pick up.

"Man, that storm did do a number on that old barn didn't it? Are the animals alright?" he asked.

I hesitated a couple a minutes. "No." I answered. "I lost that old rooster, and . . . and Patton's gone. We ain't found him yet."

"Aw sugar . . . I'm really sorry to hear that. I'll be glad to help ya look for him when ya get ready." He answered sincerely.

We walked down toward the barn where Toby and Seth was workin'. I saw Toby when he glanced our way. He turned and said somethin' to Seth and I could only imagine what it was.

"Toby, Walter come out to help. What do ya want him to start on?" I asked, tryin' to make it a little more comfortable.

"Hell, I don't know. He can pull that sheet iron down, I guess." He said as he turned his head where Walter couldn't see him roll his eyes.

"Sure." Walter answered. "Where do ya want me to stack it?"

Toby was tellin' him their plans as I turned and started back up to the house. Pride and Promise had seen me in the yard and came gallopin' across the pasture, so I walked over to the gate and went inside the corral.

"My beautiful boys." I called out as they trotted up to me.

They was a little more settled, but still jumped at the slightest loud noise. I reached for Pride and he come closer and rested his head on my shoulder as I wrapped my arms around his neck. Again the tears started to flow. They run down my cheeks and I felt him quiver as they dropped onto his neck. I knew he was sufferin' the loss the same as I was. We comforted each other for a few more minutes before I turned back toward the house.

Chapter 2

It'd been several weeks since the big storm when I recalled that I wanted to get Promise to Mr. Burrows to be broke to ride. It was way past time. I'd waited long enough. After almost four years, I was pretty sure that Chad wasn't returnin' to me. I tried to convince myself that since he knew about the boys, he'd have returned by now.

I picked up the phone and dialed the number.

"Hello?" Someone answered.

"Hi. Can I speak to Mr. Burrows, please?" I asked.

"Oh, I'm sorry, but Jim Burrows has moved away. Several years ago in fact."

"I didn't know, I have a young horse I was wantin' him to break for me." I was sure she could hear the disappointment in my voice.

"Well, my brother has taken over his business, if you would like to speak with him," she answered.

"Can I make an appointment with him? I'd like to meet him face-to-face before I make any decisions."

"Sure, let me get my book and pen."

I set up a day and a time and was anxious to meet him.

As I hung up the phone, I heard a car pull up in the drive. I no sooner got out of my chair than little Laurel come runnin' in the door.

"Hi, Aunt Lilah. Me and Mama come to see ya! Where's Eli and Jonny?" She grinned as she hugged my neck.

"They're upstairs in the playroom. Ya can go on up." I told her. Floy, come in the door right behind her.

"I'm sorry about that. I try to teach her to knock, but she thinks she lives here!" I could tell that she was frustrated with her daughter.

"Now you know good and well that this is a open door to you and your family. I love that little stinker like she was my own." I hugged her and we sat down at the table.

"Are ya busy? I didn't think to call first." She asked me.

"No," I answered as I handed her a glass of tea and made one for myself. "I just tried to call Mr. Burrows to see if he'd be able to break Promise pretty soon. I found out he ain't there no more."

"So now what ya gonna do?" She asked.

"I'm not sure. I made an appointment to meet the man who took over his business. I ain't made no commitment yet. I want to meet him and see what kind of person he is before turnin' my little horse over to him." I told her.

"Sounds like a wise idea to me. What's his name?"

"I think she said Tyler, Ross Tyler. Have ya ever heard of him?" I asked.

"I'll ask Toby when we get home."

"I hope he's good with horses, 'cause I don't have a clue where to go if he ain't." I told her.

We visited for a couple of more hours before her and Laurel headed back home. As usual, Eli and Jonny proceeded to have a fit 'cause they wasn't ready for their best friend to leave.

"I'll be right back!" Laurel yelled over her Mama's shoulder as she was carted out to the car.

****

I drove into Bigby and parked the car in front of the office of Ross Tyler. I was a little early, but I just hated to be late. I went inside.

"Hello, may I help you?" asked the middle-aged woman behind the desk.

"Yeah, I'm Lilah Parker. I got an appointment to meet with Ross Tyler."

"Sure Miss Parker. I'll let him know you're here." She answered.

I sat there a minute 'til she come back out. She stood in the door and motioned for me to go on in.

"Miss Parker? Come in and have a seat. I'm Ross Tyler. I took over Jim's business and I understand that you have a horse that you need broken to ride." He smiled broadly.

Ross Tyler was a tall man, about 6 feet, maybe a little more. He seemed warm and friendly enough, and I liked him right off.

"Do ya have a lot of experience in breakin' horses?" I asked.
"As a matter of fact, I have very little experience in that field. I'm the owner of the "Split T Farriers Company." But, I do have several employees that are excellent in all fields of shoeing and breaking." He

answered. "Let's go out and meet them and I'll show you around the place."

We went out the back door and into a park-like area of beautifully kept grounds that impressed me right off the bat. Farther away were the stables where they kept the horses and did their work. As we neared the stables, I noticed how well kept all the buildin's and work areas was. Several older men was busy supervisin' younger guys that I figgered was bein' trained.

"Miss Parker, this is where we teach our younger employees what we want and how we want it done. If it will make you more comfortable, we would be glad to have one of our more experienced trainers work with your horse." He spoke softly as if to not distract the others.

"Mr. Tyler, I think this'll work just fine." I held out my hand.

"No, just call me Ross, please," he said as he took my hand and held it for a second.

"Okay, Ross. I'm Lilah. I'll get my horse here whenever ya say." I smiled back at him.

"Great! How about Saturday afternoon? About 5 or 5:30?" He asked.

"I'll be here." I replied.

I felt good on the way home. I felt pretty sure that this was a good place for Promise to learn his manners. I was lookin' forward to gettin' started with him.

****

The kids and me had just come in from plantin' a few more things in our little garden and the phone began to ring.

"Hello?" I answered. "Hello?"

I could hear nothin' but static. My heart skipped a beat in my chest. Almost every Christmas Eve I received a very brief call about midnight. It would be Chad, but I could hardly hear him for the static in the line. What could be wrong that he'd be callin' me in the spring? The line suddenly cleared, "Hello, Lilah?"

"Yeah."

"It's me, Toby. What's the matter with your phone?" He asked.

I sat down. I didn't know if I was glad or dreadfully disappointed.

"Yeah, Toby?" I asked.

"Hey, Seth's back in town and we thought we might all get together and go out to eat. Kid free! How does that sound?" He laughed.

"Sure. Sounds good. What time?"

"Aw . . . about 6:00, I guess."

"Okay, I'll meet ya at your house. See ya then." I answered and hung up.

My hopes had just soared like a big old eagle for a minute, and then crashed like a big old plane. I comforted myself with knowin' that at least it wasn't no bad news.

At 5:00, I was dressed and ready to head out to Toby and Floy's house. Dee was watchin' the boys and was fixin' their supper.

"I won't be too late." I told 'em as I went out the door.

It'd been a long time since I'd gone out socially without my babies, and I felt like I was forgettin' somethin'. Well yeah, I was, two little bodies and a big old diaper bag full of everything from drinks to snacks to spare clothes and toys. This was gonna be nice.

I pulled up and got out in front of Floy and Toby's house. I still felt a little strange every time I went there. The house they lived in was where I grew up with my Mama and Daddy and a whole bunch of brothers and sisters; that is, until I went up to the cabin on the mountain to take care of Nanny.

I was 13 then, but I spent a lotta time runnin' up and down that mountain road between the two places. When I was 18, I married Walter Cullwell. My family was fit to be tied, but I was determined. Before I could turn around twice, I'd run his sorry butt off and was back on the mountain with my Nanny. After Nanny'd passed away, I inherited everything she had -- land, cabins, and a sizeable amount of money. Mama and Daddy moved off to Arkansas with all the kids and Toby had bought Floy their house. Chad and me had a ball fixin' it up while they was on their honeymoon.

The front door opened.

"We heard ya drive up. What the heck ya doin' out here?" Floy asked.

"Just tryin' to remember to forget a whole lotta things. Sorry." I walked inside.

"Lilah, you remember Seth?" Floy more or less reintroduced us.

"Yeah, sure I do." I smiled at him.

"How could I forget." Seth smiled that gorgeous smile.

I felt myself blush as I recalled what had happened in the kitchen right after the storm.

Floy's Mama was there to watch Laurel, and we were all free for the evenin'.

We had a hard time decidin' whether to go to Shoemaker's Café in Mason or to one of the little cafés in Dover or Bigby. We finally decided to go to a new place outside of Bigby. There was just way too many memories in some of the old places.

****

We sat down and ordered our meal and I found myself really enjoyin' the conversation. It was a really nice place that served Mexican food and had great music to go with it. I looked around the pretty large crowd, but didn't see anybody that I knew. It didn't surprise me much. It'd been a long time since I'd been out.

"So, did ya meet the horse trainer?" Toby asked me.

"Yeah, he seems like a really nice guy. I'm takin' Promise over there Saturday evenin'." I explained.

"How ya takin' him?" He asked as he took a chip and dug into the salsa.

"In that horse trailer I bought a few years back."

"Well, I figgered that, but what ya gonna pull it with darlin'?" He grinned.

"I don't know. I guess I didn't think it out, did I?" I thought about it for a minute. "Do ya think your truck will pull it?" I asked.

"No, I know it won't. Chad was the only one . . . I mean . . . hey, Seth, will yours do the job?" He asked.

"Sure it will. I'll be glad to help ya out, Lilah." Seth smiled and winked at me. If he only knew how that simple gesture struck at my heart.

I agreed and we continued with our meal. Toby turned up his glass to finish his tea when I noticed his face go pale.

"Toby? What's wrong?" I asked.

He just continued to stare behind me. Of course, I turned to see what had his attention. Sittin' behind us about three tables back, was a very unlikely family. I swallowed hard and turned back to Floy.

"What?" She asked as she took another chip.

I motioned with my head and she looked over my shoulder. She stopped mid-chew. She looked at Toby whose soft gray eyes was flamin'.

"Well," she snickered, "I can't imagine a more perfect couple. Don't you think, honey?" She looked back at her husband.

I noticed some of the anger had died in his eyes, but he was still plenty upset. It didn't surprise me any, seein' as how it was Chad's old stalker, Danna, and Jamie, who'd brought about the accident that caused Floy to have the baby so early. It was interestin' how the child they had was black-haired and black-eyed, just like Jamie. Danna had declared her desperate love for Chad and Jamie was so jealous of me and Chad that he almost caused a huge catastrophe. It was at the same time Danna turned up pregnant. Floy was right . . . they really deserved each other and they both looked miserable. It always amazed me how Floy had such a natural ability to soothe things over at the drop of a hat.

Seth glanced over his shoulder and then back at Toby. "Anything need takin' care of cuz?"

Toby sat there a minute, "Naw, I think that stuff Floy's always talkin' about, karma, has already done its job. Let's get out of here."

We got in the car and started toward town. Of course, my mind wandered back to the time when Danna had been such a pain in my butt. I'd been sure that Chad was involved with her and I'd put myself through hell. All along, it'd been me that he was in love with.

"Uh Lilah, what do ya think about maybe stoppin' at King's and seein' what's goin' on?" Toby asked, a little unsure.

"Oh, Toby . . . I ain't so sure that's a very good idea." Floy elbowed him.

I knew how much Toby had always loved to dance and it was about the only country dance place still in business.

"Well, sure." I answered. "It might be fun. It's been a long time."

****

We parked and went inside. Nothin' had changed but the people. For a brief moment, I couldn't seem to breathe. The music, the lights, and even the smells of cologne, perfume, and liquor brought back a flood of memories . . . unforgettable memories. All I could do for a long minute was just stand there, paralyzed.

"Lilah? Are you okay?" Floy asked as she took my hand.

"Yeah, yeah, of course I am. It's just been awhile." I almost whispered.

The music hadn't changed much and the dances was the same. I followed Toby, Floy, and Seth to a table and sat down. It wasn't long before I found myself lookin' in every corner and at every cowboy standin' at the bar. I knew in my heart that I wouldn't see what I was lookin' for, but that didn't stop my eyes. Floy and Toby got up to dance while me and Seth sat in silence.

"Ya look real uncomfortable Lilah. Is it me? Would ya have rather went on home or somethin'?" he asked me very nicely.

"No Seth, it ain't got nothin' to do with you. It's just ghosts from my past that refuse to stay buried," I told him.

"I'm sorry. Did ya lose somebody recently?"

"No! I didn't mean it like that. It's just that . . . well . . . a few years back, I used to come here all the time. It's where I met Chad, the babies' daddy, and this is just a bittersweet place for me."

"So . . . what happened to this, Chad, if ya don't mind me askin'?" Seth asked in a very sincere tone.

"I . . . uh, well, I don't really know. I think his life was just too complicated, maybe to the point that he couldn't control it. One night he just told me he had to go."

"Go where? Did he know about the babies?"

"No. He didn't know. I didn't even know. Where he went? I have no idea," I answered.

"I'm really sorry. I can tell ya got your heart broke. I been there myself. Okay, enough of this. Would ya dance with me?" He asked as he held out his hand.

I was glad to get off the subject, so I took his hand and followed him to the dance floor. It was a relief that the band was playin' a nice slow song. I wasn't sure I was ready to try the two-step yet. Seth pulled me in close and put his arm around me. He was wearin' the new cologne that Floy had got Toby. I think it was called "Polo." It was very nice, but not nearly as nice as the one Chad had always wore. Seth was taller than Chad and very muscular . . . a very attractive guy. The song ended and we walked back to the table and sat down.

"Thank ya, Lilah. Would ya like somethin' to drink?" He asked as he leaned across the table so I could hear him over the noise.

His handsome good looks and strikin' gray eyes held my attention. "Yeah sure. Just a beer I think."

He smiled and nodded his head as he headed for the bar. I noticed that he walked with a slight strut, but not an arrogant one. He had beautiful black hair that feathered perfectly. He was sure 'nuff a eye-catcher. It was then that Floy and Toby returned to the table.

"I saw ya dancin' with my cuz. He's a good guy, Lilah. He'll do anything for anybody, but he don't take no crap from nobody neither. Ya'll look real good together." Toby teased.

"He's a good dancer. I like him." Was all I could say. The truth was that I wasn't lookin' for nothin' romantic. I just wanted to have a relaxin' evenin'. However, Seth made a relaxin' evenin' even more pleasant.

We danced several more times and I was startin' to feel right at home on the old dance floor. As Seth and I was dancin' to a slower song, someone tapped him on the shoulder and asked if he could cut in for the rest of the dance. Seth, bein' the gentleman he was, nodded and stepped aside. I looked up into the liquid black eyes that belonged to my very sexy ex-husband.

"Walt? I didn't know you still come out here." I said with surprise.

"I don't usually. I just come out with Jerry and a couple of other guys. Nick lets me come in as long as I don't get drunk and stupid like I used to do. I have two beers and then Coke for the rest of the night. I was surprised when I saw you come in with Seth." He smiled.

"No, I'm not really with Seth. We all just come as a group. We went to eat at that new café over by Bigby, then decided to stop by and relax a little." I explained.

For the life of me I didn't know why I'd felt the sudden need to explain anything to Walter. However, after many years of anger and hate, we'd managed to develop a semi-friendly relationship. We passed Floy and Toby on the dance floor and I saw Toby give us the evil eye. Toby still refused to believe that Walt had give up his old hen-house ways.

The song ended and we walked back to the table where Seth quietly waited.

"Thanks Lilah, you guys have a good time." Walt nodded to Seth and walked away.

I looked at Seth and he gave me a cute little smirk.

"What?" I asked.

"I think your ex still has a thing for you girl. He's got that look in his eye." He teased.

"Well, you must have been lookin' at his eyes more than I was, 'cause I don't see one thing that I'm interested in where he's concerned. He cooked his goose with me a long time ago. We're just very, very casual friends at best." I said.

The band began a new song and Seth took my hand and I followed him out to the floor. As we danced, I noticed the gentle way he held me even though he had large, rough hands, the hands of a real workin' man. I liked that. We danced straight into the next song, but about halfway through it, Seth was tapped on the shoulder again. He nodded and stepped away again. *Are ya kiddin' me?* I thought to myself. I was pulled into a pair of strong, muscular arms and whisked away.

I stumbled at first, then regained my balance and looked up at the tall man who held me. He wore a black and white pinstriped shirt and a black western sport coat. His black hat, pulled low on his forehead, cast a shadow on his face. He had beautiful lips and a cleft in his chin, but other than that I couldn't hardly see him. I was sure that I didn't recognize him. When the song ended, he stepped back and held my hand gently.

"Thank ya, Miss Parker. That was very nice and I did enjoy it so much."

The voice sounded familiar, but I couldn't put a face to it. I took a step back and tried to look under the brim of that hat. He obliged by pushin' it to the back of his head. My eyes met with sparklin' blue-green ones and the very handsome face of Ross Tyler.

"Mr. Tyler!" I was surprised. "I didn't recognize ya underneath that hat," I said excitedly.

"Just Ross, please. I saw you come in with a group and I had hoped for the opportunity to say hello. The dance was just icing on the cake. Are you with your fiancé . . . husband?" He asked.

"No. Just my friend's cousin. He's visitin' for a few days," I explained. "Thank ya for the dance," I told him as I walked back to my table where Seth sat, again, with that silly little smirk.

"Am I gonna have to get an appointment to finish a dance with you? Seems to me like I'm here with the belle-of-the-ball!" He grinned. We stayed for a couple more hours and then called it a night.

****

It was a day or two later when Toby and Seth come back to finish a few things on the barn. I caught myself findin' one reason after the other to go down there. I always got a little smirk from Toby and a charmin' smile from Seth. I didn't understand why I couldn't stay away from that damn barn . . . or maybe I just didn't want to admit that it was Seth that I was havin' such a hard time stayin' away from and not the barn. In all the time Chad had been gone, I hadn't even looked at nobody else, let alone felt such an attraction to 'em.

"I brought ya'll some water," I said flatly. I knew it was just an excuse to make yet another trip down to the barn where they was workin'. "I'll make some tea when I make lunch after awhile."

"Thank ya, Lilah," Toby answered.

"Yeah . . . thank ya," Seth said as he reached to take the glass.

His fingers wrapped over mine and I felt a tingle that made me catch my breath for a second. I knew without a doubt that in spite of myself, I was becomin' more and more attracted to him and I wasn't at all sure I liked it.

Chapter 3

It was slightly warmer than usual for a late spring night. The kids was in bed already and Dee had gone to stay the night with a friend in Bigby, so I found myself relaxin' on the front porch with a glass of fresh lemonade. The sounds of the night creatures was beautiful and for a moment I felt like I was back with Nanny. She used to tell me that the night sounds was like real fine music to her ears. I had to admit, I believed she was right and nothin' was more calmin' than those night sounds, the stars, and the moonlight in the Appalachians. Off in the distance, I heard a wolf howl . . . probably callin' to his mate.

I was pulled back to reality by the nicker of a horse nearby. I realized it hadn't come from the barn and my eyes suddenly focused on movement down the driveway. I could see the shadow of a horse and rider comin' my way. Since I wasn't expectin' company, and certainly not at that late hour, I moved toward the door. I always kept my shotgun propped against the wall . . . just in case of a critter or unwelcome guest. If the past had taught me anything, it was to always try and be prepared.

"It's just me, Lilah." I heard someone call out from the dark. I was pretty sure that I recognized the voice.

"And exactly who is *me*?" I answered with a giggle.

Seth rode up to the porch and stopped. He wrapped one leg around the saddle horn and leaned over it. I was surprised by the way he looked just sittin' there. The light from the front door spotlighted him like a rodeo star. His black hair framed a tan face with beautiful blue-gray eyes and a sexy little smile. Topped off with his white summer cowboy hat and a dark blue open neck western shirt . . . he certainly had my attention. He was the crownin' touch to the spirited, golden palomino he sat upon so easily.

"Well, ya could get down off that beautiful creature and come sit with me," I told him. "When did ya get her? She's really gorgeous!"

"I come across her a couple of weeks ago and I just couldn't get her off my mind. Next thing I knew . . . I went back and got her." He grinned as he slid easily from the saddle and made his way up the steps.

"I can sure see why. She's perfect . . . deep gold with that long, light blonde mane and tail! She suits you . . . you make a beautiful couple!" I teased him. However, I was serious about how gorgeous the horse was. I'd never seen anything like her, and I guess if I was totally honest, I was becomin' somewhat serious about Seth too. So many things about him reminded me of Chad. His beauty was matched only by his soft southern ways and he had a gentleness in almost everything he said. Like Chad, I don't think he had any idea about how good-lookin' he was or the effect he was havin' on me.

He sat in the rocker next to mine and stretched out his long legs and gave a big sigh.

"What's wrong?" I asked him.

"Oh . . . just work. Never endin' questions with no answers. Sometimes I think I should just retire and find a place like this and just kick back and take life a little easier."

"So why don't ya do that?" I asked him.

"I think it's called . . . obligations. Things I signed on for and I got to complete before I can even think about anything else." He answered as he took his hat off and laid it on his knee.

"What is it that ya do?"

"Well . . . it's kinda hard to explain. To cut it short, I look into things that other people want or need to know the details about." He said as he laughed.

"So you're a private investigator?"

"No. I don't like that title at all. It's nothin' that grand. Let's say for instance . . . somebody's lookin' into buyin' a piece of land and they want to know its history. I check into it and just let 'em know. Not a big deal, but I'm still obligated for a few more 'look sees.'"

"I bet it's interestin' findin' out all that stuff," I said as I handed Seth a lemonade.

"Yep, sometimes." He sighed. "Hey, ya wanna go for a ride tomorrow? We could pack a lunch and eat up on the mountain."

How many picnics had I had on that mountain with Chad? It was hard to remember, but I could never forget the amazin' lovemakin' we'd shared up there. Well, that was then and it'd been a long time ago.

"Sure. I'd love to . . . I'll put us a lunch together."

"Does that mean I have to leave now?" he asked with a chuckle in his voice.

"Well, heck no. That just means we have plans for tomorrow." I smiled back at him.

We spent the next couple of hours talkin' about the ranch and the horses. We talked about Floy and Toby and their little girl, but I couldn't help but notice that he said very little about his own life. I tried several times to turn the conversation toward him and his family, but he always slid past it and come back around to somethin' else. I finally let it go as I figured he just didn't want to talk about hisself. We fell into a comfortable silence as we watched the late night start to settle in the great mountains. As I sat there, I felt somethin' softly land on the big toe of the foot I had propped on the porch railin'. Seth and I both stared as the end of my toe lit up into a soft green glow. It was a very unexpected visit from one of the lightnin' bugs from the meadow grass. I moved my toe back and forth and still the little critter sat comfortably without takin' flight.

"I guess he likes ya." Seth whispered. "Can't see as how I blame him."

"I don't think I've ever seen one do that," I told him as the tiny insect glowed again.

"You're just a regular little twinkle toes aren't ya?" We both laughed out loud and the little bug flew away.

After another half hour of simple chatter, Seth stood up and put on his hat. "I guess I better get headed back down the mountain. What time do we want to take that ride?"

"How about 11:00? We can eat and then just ride the trails."

"Sounds good to me." He stood there lookin' into my eyes like it was the first time he'd ever seen me. I was caught up in the sparkle of his soft blue-gray eyes as he leaned toward me. I braced myself for the first kiss I'd had since Chad had left. I was both surprised and disappointed when he simply gave me a hug and a gentle kiss on my cheek.

"Tomorrow." He whispered as he stepped down from the porch and climbed gracefully back into the saddle.

I watched as he started down the dusty driveway. The moonlight caught his white hat and broad shoulders as he rode into the dark shadows of the trees that lined the way down the path and into the night.

****

I'd just finished saddlin' Pride when I heard Dee yell from the house.

"Phone call, Lilah!"

I rode Pride up to the cabin, slid out of the saddle, and hurried up the porch steps.

"Hello?" I answered.

"Hey, it's me. I'm headin' that way in just a couple of minutes."

"Okay. I'm ready except for gettin' our picnic lunch basket from the kitchen. Dee made it back in time to watch the boys, so I'll be ready when ya get here." I told him.

"See ya in a bit." He said as he hung up the phone.

Sure enough, it was only a short time before he came into view. I was standin' on the porch waitin' so he could help me load the basket. I saw him comin' up the drive and stopped where I stood. Seth was wearin' a turquoise blue shirt that could've been spotted for miles. It looked especially great with his black hair, beautiful eyes, and white hat. I felt my heart flutter for a minute before I took a deep breath to calm down a bit. *Mercy!* I thought to myself. *You need to pull yourself together, Lilah.* I sensed that I was openin' up the perfect chance to make a down right fool of myself.

He pulled up right beside me and leaned from the saddle.

"Thought ya might like this." He semi-smiled as he handed me a wild rose that he'd most likely picked along the roadside. But it was beautiful and smelled like heaven.

I fumbled for words for a minute. "Thank ya Seth. How did ya know that these are probably my most favorite flower in the world?"

"Lucky guess I reckon." He smiled and that one dimple in his cheek gave him the look of an ornery, yet innocent, child.

We loaded the basket and rode off across the pasture toward the mountains. The sun was bright and the pastures was green. What more perfect settin' could anyone ask for? There was no need to hurry since we had all day, so we let the horses walk at a normal pace as we guided 'em toward an old trail that led up into the forest. It seemed like the birds were louder than usual and I took it as a sign that it was time to let go of the past and let a little happiness and beauty come into my life. I glanced over at Seth just as he glanced at me. His face held a look of pure contentment, the same contentment that I was feelin'. . . it was gonna be a good day.

We wandered the trails for an hour or more and finally stopped at a small spring-fed creek and let the horses have a drink.

"Do ya wanna eat here or go on a little further?" Seth asked.
"It's still early . . . why don't we go a little further and see if we can find a little better spot."

We got back on the horses and started out when Seth suddenly pulled up short.

"Look at that Lilah. Now that's a strange, but beautiful sight."

I looked where he pointed and was very surprised to see what lay far below. There in the distance was a small pond that the creek kept full. One complete side and all the way to a small group of trees was brilliant with bright red roses. My breath caught in my throat as the significance of that spot hit home. That was the place that me and Chad had first made love. He'd had someone cover it with rose bushes to keep anyone from ever lyin' there again. I felt my face flush with the memory of that day.

"Why do ya think somebody would plant all those bushes in such a odd spot?" Seth asked as he removed his hat and wiped his forehead with his arm.

"I guess it was a old homestead or somethin'. How would I know?" I answered a little shortly as I turned Pride in the opposite direction. That was the last thing I needed to be reminded of.

"Well, whatever. It sure is pretty." Seth mumbled as he followed.

We rode in silence for some time as my head was spinnin' with memories that I didn't want to have. Seth seemed content to just admire the beauty of the mountains we explored.

It was a little after noon when we come to a nice little clearin' with lots of soft grass shaded by tall trees. It was a perfect spot for our dinner. Seth spread the blanket and I unpacked the food. We ate and talked for a good long while. He was so easy to be with and our conversation was as comfortable as if we'd been friends for years. Seth was a lot like Toby . . . just a sweet, soft-spoken country boy. As I sat and listened to him talk about his and Toby's childhood and the things they'd gotten into, I found myself starin' at his beautiful lips. I couldn't help but wonder what it would be like to kiss 'em. It was about that time that I become aware that he was no longer talkin', but was starin' at me like he'd heard my very thoughts.

"What?" I asked.

"I asked if you were in any hurry to get back to the cabin. Are you okay?"

"No . . . I mean, yes. I mean no, I'm not in a hurry to get back, and yes . . . I'm fine."

He laughed softly as he lay back on the blanket. When he looked up at the sky, his turquoise shirt reflected beautifully in his eyes. Now I can tell ya this . . . with that black hair, dark complexion, and turquoise-tinted eyes, he ran Chad a close second on looks. I couldn't help but stare.

"Are ya sure you're okay? Lie down here and look up at that beautiful sky with me. The Lord sure knew what He was doin' when He put this place together, didn't He? Toby told me the name of your ranch, but for the life of me, I can't remember."

"Terra de Gracia," I told him. "The boys' Daddy named it. It means 'Land of Grace'."

"Oh, yeah! I remember ya tellin' me that. It's a perfect name for it."

"Yes," I answered as I lay down on the blanket and gazed up through the trees.

I wasn't comfortable lyin' there beside Seth. I found myself wantin' to snuggle into his arms and lay my head on his broad shoulder. Suddenly he raised up on one elbow and was right beside me.

"Lilah?" he asked softly. "Would ya be terribly offended if I was to kiss ya right now?"

I shook my head *no* as his face neared and I felt his soft warm lips cover mine. Ever so slowly, he slipped his arm around me and his tongue slid softly between my lips. My heart pounded in my chest as I put my arms around his neck and pulled him even closer. I hadn't felt like that in forever and I couldn't believe how my body was respondin' to his touch. Our kiss deepened as I felt him pull me closer to his body. I wanted to make love with him . . . I wanted to feel his skin next to mine. At that minute I would have surrendered totally, but that was when Seth suddenly rolled away and sat up. I lay there tryin' to catch my breath while strugglin' to figure out what'd just happened. He sat there with his arm propped on his knee and his head down.

"Seth? Did I do somethin' wrong?" I whispered.

He took a deep breath and let out a long sigh. "No honey. You didn't do nothin' wrong. It's just that . . . I . . . I just can't do this. I can't let this happen."

"But Seth, it's just happenin' on its own. Some things ya just can't control."

He stood up and ran his long tan fingers through his dark hair and walked away. I just sat there and wondered what in the world was the matter. I got to my feet, walked to him, and put my arms around his neck. Seth stared at me with serious blue-gray eyes as he moved his hands up the length of my arms and took my fingers into his. He pulled 'em to his chest and kissed the back of each hand then took a step away.

"No, Lilah. This can't happen. I shouldn't have let it get this far. I'm sorry . . . but . . . no."

"Why? Just tell me why?" I asked him.

"There's no *why,* it's just the way it is . . . the way it has to be. Come on, let's go back," he said as he let out another deep sigh and started to pick up the picnic basket and blanket.

I was still in a state of shock. I had no idea what was goin' on with him. I felt foolish and embarrassed and was sure that Seth was thinkin' that I was too willin' to let it go all the way. Maybe I was, but I was so drawn to him that I'd just lost all sense of reason. Very little was said on the way back to the cabin.

When we got there, Seth helped me put the basket away and he started to take Pride to the stable.

"No. I can get that. I want to brush him down anyway," I said as I looked away from him.

He started to walk away and then suddenly turned. "Lilah, don't feel like this has anything to do with you personally. It's . . . it's somethin' I can't explain right now, but trust me . . . it's for your own good. I'm sorry that I let it go to the point that I feel like I hurt ya." He gracefully slid up into the saddle, sat there a moment, then shook his head.

"I'm sorry," he half whispered, then turned, and rode away at a fast pace.

****

I felt like a fool and even more than that, I was just down right mad. It was like a replay of a past moment, not a good moment, but just the same, I'd been there before and I was just down-right pissed. Once again, there was no explanation, just a mysterious *I'm sorry*. I found myself realizin' that I was glad it happened before it did go any further. I would never have dreamed that Seth would be like that, but then, I never thought Chad would be the way he was either. Damn 'em both!

Chapter 4

For the hundredth time, I searched through my room, even the bed! I'd looked everywhere, in the bathroom, and the kids' room. The livin' room had been taken apart a dozen times, as well as the kitchen. I decided that the only place left was the barn, so I headed out the door toward it. Somehow I'd lost one of my most precious treasures, the necklace Chad had give me on the only Christmas we was together. It was so tiny and so delicate and I knew that it could be just about anywhere.

I got down on my hands and knees and started to scratch through the straw, hay, and even manure that was on the floor. My head pounded as I searched frantically for that precious little piece of jewelry. I stood up and walked outside. I'd searched the car and every step I could recall for the last couple of weeks. In my gut, I felt like it was just barely out of reach, but for the life of me I couldn't find it!

Dee rung the dinner bell and I started toward the cabin. It'd become a habit to stare at the ground with every step I took. I kept hopin' that it would just appear out of nowhere.

"I've searched everywhere, Lilah. I looked in the laundry room and even in the washer. I still need to wash a few clothes and that blanket you and Seth took on the picnic a couple of weeks ago, but it's just nowhere to be found," Dee told me.

"Maybe it's just not supposed to be found. I wish I could just let it go, but I can't." I told her as I finished dinner and went in the livin' room and sat down.

I laid back on the couch as I watched Dee take the boys up the stairs for their nap. I was exhausted from searchin' and frettin' and I closed my eyes for just a short nap myself.

Birds fluttered among the tall trees as I lay there lookin' up at the crystal blue sky. It was so peaceful, so beautiful, and I felt like I could sleep there forever. Somethin' fell on the blanket beside me. When I turned my head to look, a large crow sat there with my gold necklace in its mouth.

"No!" I screamed. "That's mine!"

As I reached frantically for it, I tumbled from the couch and woke up with a start.

Oh God . . . I know where it is! I thought to myself as I rushed out the back door and down to the barn. I saddled Pride as quickly as I could and climbed in the saddle. We took off at break neck speed across the pasture.

It was early afternoon and I was sure that I could get there and back before Dee even knew that I was gone. I started up the mountain trail and before too long, I passed the place where I could easily see the little pond with the unusual field of red roses. That was where I'd turned and went higher and deeper into the forest. I had to slow my pace a lot 'cause it was a lot steeper than the ground we'd been on and I didn't want to take any chances of Pride losin' his footin'. We picked our way carefully for what seemed like forever. Suddenly I rode into the clearin' where Seth and me had our picnic. I hadn't even allowed myself to think about that day since. Now here I was, down on my knees crawlin' around on the very spot where I'd made such a fool of myself. I carefully combed the dense grass with my fingers until I was sure that I'd searched every inch of that clearin'. Nothin'! I couldn't find a single thing and I'd been so sure that it would be there. The bird had showed it to me. *Oh Lord* I thought, *what if the bird was right! What if that damn bird had taken it away?* I laid down in the grass and cried like a baby. I was alone, nobody in sight, and I let myself scream, cry, and curse to high heaven. I completely exhausted myself, but I felt so much calmer after my little temper tantrum. I wasn't sure, but I think I might have even kicked my feet like a child. The next thing I knew, I woke up and found myself a little confused as to where I was. It was dark and only the tiny sliver of a moon was out to give me a little light. The sky suddenly brightened and a huge roll of thunder seemed to shake the ground where I lay.

Damn, I thought, I need to get back home. I've been here and done this in the past and I ain't doin' it again. My hands shook as I reached for Pride's reins. Another flash of lightnin' and a bigger boom of thunder and Pride took off into the dark and left me standin' alone in the pourin' down rain. My mind spun as I realized that I was in a very bad way. As the black clouds covered the sky and the moon disappeared, I stood in complete darkness except for when the lightnin' lit the sky. I started down what I thought was the path that we'd come up, but it was hard to tell in the dark. Rocks rolled from under my feet and I tripped several times over roots and limbs. I was sure that I was still on the path until I walked straight into a large limb. I turned only to walk into another limb or maybe it was a small tree. No matter which way I turned, I found somethin' that blocked my way. Panic started to set in as I admitted to myself that I was completely lost and didn't have no idea where I was. I stood still hopin' to hear Pride nearby, but that didn't happen. I heard nothin' but constant thunder and pourin' rain.

I had to think! I felt my way to what seemed like a large tree and found a spot beside it that was at least a little sheltered. The more I thought, the more I panicked. I didn't have nothin' to protect myself with . . . I didn't have no food or water . . . and I was soaked to the bone and startin' to chill. I had to find my way down and sittin' there feelin' sorry for myself wasn't gonna find it. I rose on my shaky legs and waited until another flash of lightnin' gave me the chance to pick some sort of direction.

It felt like hours had passed as I stumbled, fell, crawled, and searched for the trail. I was most likely just gettin' deeper and deeper into the forest instead of findin' my way down. It was impossible to tell the difference. Then it got even worse as the downpour continued, the sky remained black, and the lightnin' stopped. I began to search my way just one step at a time. I would explore my next step with my foot before I took it. Progress was little to none. I finally come to what felt like a good size rock and I sat down on it for a minute. I wondered what time it was. Where did Dee and my babies think I'd gone? For the love of heaven, once again, no one had no idea where I was. How had I let this happen?

I sat and tried to catch my breath for a few minutes before I decided that I needed to keep movin'. I sure wasn't goin' to find my way home by sittin' on a rock in the rain.

As I stood up and took a step in whatever direction fate had in store for me, I felt the ground give way under my foot and as I flailed in every direction to grab somethin' to hold on to, I felt myself fallin' through the air and I landed hard on my back as my head hit solid on a rock. I looked up into the fallin' rain . . . saw nothin' . . . then felt nothin'.

****

The strong smell of smoke burned my nose and I had a really bad taste in my mouth. I could feel every beat of my heart in my poundin' head. Slowly I opened my eyes and looked around. This was no place I'd ever been before. There was only light from a low fire in a fire place and the shadows of some furniture. I knew I was dreamin' again and I closed my eyes to wait for it to end.

I don't know how much time'd passed, but I heard someone moan in the distance and I was surprised to open my eyes and find that it was me. My head still pounded and I felt nauseous. I turned my head to learn that it hurt even worse in that direction. As I started to wake up, I realized that every inch of my body hurt. I looked around the dimly-lit room. The log walls told me it was some sort of lean-to or hut. The ceilin' was low and sloped to one side. I couldn't make out anything in the room, but I could tell that there wasn't much. My eyes were tired so I closed 'em for only a second.

When I woke up again, I knew it'd been longer than a second. It was a little lighter in the room and I started to wonder how I'd got there. I heard the door quietly openin'. I closed my eyes out of instinct. Footsteps softly come across the floor and stopped beside the bed where I found myself layin'. I felt a strong hand as it carefully touched my forehead then lifted and the footsteps moved away. I fought against the urge to open my eyes and see who this person was, but for some reason I was terrified. I could hear the sounds of someone pokin' around in the fireplace. It wasn't long before I could smell meat fryin' and the strong pungent smell of some very strong coffee. My stomach rolled in protest at the thought of eatin'. I felt the weight of somebody takin' a seat on the side of my bed.

"Miss?" I heard the soft deep sound of a man's voice. "Ya awake, ma'am?" he asked in little more'n a whisper.

I opened my eyes very slowly so as to let 'em adjust to the semi dark room.

"I made ya some tea, here. It'll make ya feel better." The soft gruff voice whispered again.

As I began to focus, I saw two hands right in front of my face, holdin' an old tin cup. They was rough hands, rugged, manly hands. I let my eyes flow from those hands, up the muscular arms, to the chest, and finally the neck and face. I was confused by what I saw. It looked more like an animal than a man. I heard of the creatures they called Big Foot, but I never took it serious. Now, I wasn't so sure. The face was covered with a long, reddish-blonde beard and mustache. Very blonde, sun-bleached hair hung past the shoulders and the eyes was covered by the brim of what looked to me like an African safari hat.

"Can ya sit up a little?" he asked in that deep whisper.

He sat the cup down and picked up a couple of extra pillows as I tried to sit up on the bed. My head pounded even harder and my neck and back caused unbelievable amounts of pain.

"Wait." He ordered as he slid his hand under the pillow that supported my head and lifted me in one move. Once he stacked more pillows under me and lay me back down, I was almost in a sittin' position and in a tolerable amount of pain.

"Drink." He whispered as he handed me the very warm cup.

I could smell the distinct scent of wintergreen. I took a sip and was pleased that he'd sweetened it with some honey. The warmth, as it made its way down my throat and into my stomach, was soothin' to say the least. I nodded my head to let him know that it was good and that I was thankful for it. For the life of me I just couldn't figure out where in blazes I was and I didn't have no idea who this person was neither.

"Feel better?" he asked in the soft whisper.

"I guess. My head hurts like the devil though. Where am I? What happened?" I had a million questions and I needed answers.

"You're with me. You're at our home. Close your eyes and rest now." He said as he took the empty cup and walked away.

He had to be kiddin' me. I was wide awake now and felt like I'd been asleep for years. He went out the door and shut it. As I laid there and scanned the room once more, I recalled that he'd said that I was at *our* home. There wasn't nothin' that I recognized in that place. I wondered if this was where I lived? Did I live here with him? It was then that I realized that I didn't even remember what my own name was. Panic started to set in and I tried to get up. The room spun and I quickly lay down and shut my eyes. No way was this really happenin'. No way!

The next time I opened my eyes, there was a lantern lit and I could smell the coal oil it was burnin'. The man kneeled at the fire place with a bowl.

"Good. I bet you're hungry." He whispered as he brought the bowl to me. Try this, I think it'll make ya feel better."

I took the bowl and started to take the spoon, but my hands shook so much I could barely hold on to it.

"Here, give me that." He said as he took the spoon, put a napkin under my chin, and started to feed me.

"I can do it." I protested.

"Yeah, I could see that," he said as he slipped the spoon of soup into my mouth. It had an unusual flavor, but it was good. It didn't take long and I was full.

"Done?

I nodded my head and he took the bowl away. I still had a headache, but not anywhere as bad as it'd been. My stomach felt soothed and I relaxed somewhat.

"What happened?" I asked him.

He went about what he was doin' without even lookin' at me. I thought maybe he didn't hear any better than he talked.

"Sir? What happened to me?" I asked again, only louder.

He still didn't respond.

"Did ya hear me?" I spoke even louder.

"I heard ya the first time," he whispered in a agitated tone.

"Then why didn't ya answer me?"

He paused what he was doin' for a minute. "I want to finish these dishes before we get into it."

It kinda surprised me that he couldn't carry on a simple conversation while he done the dishes. We was in the same room and only a few feet apart.

Okay. Maybe it's just him bein' a man, I thought to myself. I waited patiently while he finished what he was doin' and dried his hands and set down.

"Needed to finish them dishes while the water was hot. Now . . . ask away."

"Well . . . what happened to me?" I asked again.

He paused and stared at me. "Ya really don't remember, do ya?"

"If I did, do ya think I would be askin'?"

Just as I noticed what vivid green eyes he had, he looked down at his hands.

"Ya was out pickin' berries for a pie and didn't come home, so I went lookin' for ya. I reckon ya slipped on them rocks and fell. I found ya down on a ledge on the side of the mountain. Looked like ya hit your head on a rock and knocked yourself out. It took me and the mule awhile to haul ya up outta there."

I was a little speechless. There was just nothin' about this place that felt like home.

"So you're sayin' that I live here . . . with you?" I asked cautiously.

"Well, yeah. Several years now. Don't ya remember nothin' . . . about us?"

"I don't even remember your name . . . or mine." I started to cry outta pure frustration.

"Don't cry. I'm right here and I'll help ya all I can. My name's Bridger. Remember? Does that ring a bell at all?" He asked in that soft whispery voice.

I thought as hard as I could, but nothin' about it seemed at all familiar.

"Bridger. Just Bridger? Can ya tell me what my name is Bridger?" I stammered.

"It's . . . Shelly. We been livin' together for several years, Shelly. Can't ya remember anything?" he explained as he put his hand over mine.

I pulled away and lay back down on the bed. "No." I whispered.

I curled up and faced the wall. I couldn't believe this was happenin'. How in the world could I not remember a man I'd been livin' with for years? I tried very hard to remember family, friends, or places. My mind was like a blank wall, I couldn't remember anything before openin' my eyes in this room. I don't know how long I had laid there tryin' to think of anyone or anything that might sound familiar. Eventually, I realized that the room was becomin' light. The sun must be comin' up.

I heard Bridger workin' at the fireplace again. It was plenty warm, almost hot in the room, but I supposed it was his only way of cookin'. I rolled over carefully. The front door was open and I could hear the birds singin' outside. Before long, Bridger had breakfast ready, helped me sit up, and we ate. By that time, the sun was shinin' across the dusty floor.

We sat in silence and glanced at each other ever' now and then. He didn't have his hat on and for the first time, I could see his face. His features were rugged, but very handsome. He had beautiful full lips and for a second, I thought I felt a twinge of a memory. His green eyes seemed to be touched with a few specks of blue and rimmed with extremely long blonde eyelashes; his eyes were almost hypnotic. I couldn't help but notice a long scar that went from the top of his forehead, down almost to the top of his left eyebrow and curved to his left temple. He had a deep furrow between his brows that made me think he was worried or maybe angry. I thought his beautiful long blonde hair suited him perfectly. Bridger. Sadly, I just couldn't remember anything about him.

"Do ya need anything else, Shelly?" he whispered.

I shook my head no then had a second thought. "Yeah, could ya tell me where the bathroom is please?"

"Sure," he said as he held out his hand.

I stood on shaky legs and he helped me toward the open door.

"No," I said. "Not the outdoors . . . the bathroom."

"It's outside, Shelly."

We walked very slowly toward the thicker forest and just as we entered, we come to a small shed-like hut. I looked at Bridger hopin' he wasn't gonna say that this was it. He pulled the make shift door open and showed me the hole in the seat and the toilet paper supply, which was a variety of papers, magazine pages, and what-have-you.

"You gotta be kiddin' me," I said.

"Nope. It's all we got. We'll probably have to move it again here in a few months." He smiled and shut the door. "Holler when you're done and I'll help ya back inside."

I cautiously, but very quickly, finished and stepped out the door. Bridger was standin' several feet away, leanin' against a tree. When he heard me come out, he turned, and started toward me.

"How in heaven's name could I forget somethin' so disgustin'? Surely I would remember that horrible place!" He took me by the arm as he chuckled quietly and led me back into the cabin. I found myself so tired from such a small amount of exercise that I could hardly lay down fast enough. Shortly, Bridger handed me another cup of that wonderful wintergreen tea that he'd given me last night.

"I added a few herbs and spices to help with the soreness and help you to relax. Just go with it and take a nap," he whispered as he walked out and shut the door. I sipped on my tea as I tried to think. Bridger... B-R-I-D-G-E-R... Brid... ger... Bridger. I repeated the name over and over in my head. Shelly... S-H-E-L-L-Y... Shelly. The name held nothin' for me. None of this did! How could I be somebody that I never even heard of? It wasn't long before I felt myself relax and start to yawn.

****

After several days of soup, tea, and rest, I was finally able to move without so much pain. I'd been shocked when Bridger told me that I'd been hurt almost a month ago. I guess I'd been unconscious for the most of it. As far as care went, he was very carin' and very gentle. However, he wasn't much in the talk department. I felt like there was so much I needed to know and he simply had no answers for me, or maybe he just didn't want to answer my questions. Bridger was busy all day, every day. He came and went like the wind. Always, he brought in food and water, but when night come, we would eat and he would clean everything, then go to the little area where he'd stacked some blankets and a pillow. Sometimes, he'd go straight to sleep and other times he would light a lamp and read.

One night, I noticed out of the corner of my eye, that he was just starin' at me. I felt a little uncomfortable and couldn't help wonderin' what he was thinkin'.

"Bridger? Is this what we do? I mean, is this all that we do?" I asked him.

He put the book, that he was not readin', down and looked me straight in the eye.

"What do ya mean?" he whispered. "Is there somethin' else ya wanna do?"

"I don't know? It just seems that all we do is eat and sleep . . . and you're gone all the time."

"Well, it's simple. If I don't hunt and gather . . . then we don't eat. If ya feel good enough, then ya could go with me when I gather vegetables and fruit." His piercin' green eyes held mine.

"I think I'd like that. It would give me somethin' to do besides just sit here all day. Did I usually help ya with those things?"

"Well, yeah. You used to like to cook too. You'd clean, cook, and sew sometimes," he whispered.

"Bridger? Why do you more or less whisper all the time?" I asked.

I was stunned when he glared at me as he put his hand to his throat, turned out the lamp, and turned over and covered up with his blanket.

I wasn't sure how, but I seemed to have offended him in some way. I didn't mean to, but I'd been wonderin' about it for quite a while. As I sat quietly in the darkness and waited, I realized that I wasn't sure exactly what it was that I was waitin' for. Bridger gave a big sigh as his breathin' became regular and I was sure he was asleep. My life was insane and I felt like there was just so much more that I didn't know. I didn't have no idea who my parents was or if they was even still alive. Did I have brothers and sisters or any family? I felt as if I'd just dropped down the chimney and into this bed. The few clothes that I'd found in the closet was a little big and pretty worn. I had one pair of shoes and a pair of boots, but the shoes seemed a little big. Most likely I'd lost weight since the accident. Bridger'd told me that I used to sew, yet I hadn't saw no materials for sewin'. Maybe we'd lived somewhere else when I used to do that. I had no idea! Flustered and aggravated, I laid down and finally fell asleep.

Sometime in the late night, I woke up to the sounds of somethin' rustlin' in the room. I stayed very still for a few minutes and listened. It was silent and I'd just closed my eyes when I heard it again. Without warnin', a hand clasped over my mouth and I heard Bridger whisper very softly in my ear.
"Shhhh, be still. Don't move and be very quiet. Stay here . . . I'll be back for ya." He gently removed his hand and in the dark, I saw him crawl on his belly very carefully across the floor. When he crawled under the old wooden table, he stopped and propped his chin on the back of his crossed hands. He stayed there a very long time while I watched, listened, and

tried to control the panic I felt inside. Maybe he'd heard somethin' outside and it'd scared him.

I was terrified as I slipped the covers up to my nose and continued to wait. After what seemed to be forever, I glanced over at Bridger again. He hadn't moved at all. It was about that time that I heard him snore softly. What in hell was goin' on? He wakes me up, scares the blazes out of me, and then falls asleep. I laid there and watched him for a long time before I decided that he'd most likely had a dream . . . or maybe a nightmare. Coverin' my head with the blanket, I finally fell back to sleep.

Chapter 5

Bridger left before daylight. He said he was goin' into town to get supplies and it would probably be the next mornin' before he got back. It was the first time I could remember bein' there by myself. I was a little nervous, but I figgered I'd probably done this many times in the past. He'd told me that there was a little town down the other side of the mountain where he went to get supplies every few months. I wondered why he didn't live a little closer to the town and he wouldn't have to walk so darn far when he needed things. I'd never mentioned to him about the nightmare he'd had and I certainly never mentioned his voice again. It'd upset him so bad that I just left well enough alone.

I busied myself with some cleanin' and went out and boiled some water to do a little laundry which was probably the hardest job on the place. We had to go carry water from the little spring up to the tub that set over a fire where the water was heated. By the time I washed, rinsed, and hung everything . . . it'd become a full day's job.

I stopped to eat at noon and made myself a glass of wintergreen tea from the cold spring water. With a little honey, it was a rare, but delicious, treat. Afterward, I went out to the lean-to where we used the bathroom. There was little to no light inside, but I could see fairly well. Just as I finished and was about to leave, I felt somethin' brush against my foot. Naturally I nearly jumped out of my skin and opened the door as fast as I could so I could get out of there. I was almost sure it was a rat, but ya just never knew. I stood with the door wide open so whatever it was could get out and go away. Instead of a scary old rat, I saw the tiniest little furball I could ever have imagined. Not at all sure what it was, I was hesitant to touch it. In the half-dark, it could've been a skunk or anything. I could see that its eyes were not even open yet and it could hardly move. This was a barely-borned little somethin' that'd apparently been abandoned in the outhouse. My nature over took me and I bent to pick it up. When I lifted its little face so I could get a better look, I found the tiniest little black masked animal I believed I'd ever seen. The itty bitty raccoon didn't even fill the palm of my hand. I looked around for its mama, but there was nothin' in sight. I didn't have no idea how it got where it was, but I knew I couldn't leave it out there by itself. I gently picked it up, discovered that it was a little girl and put her in the pocket of my shirt and went back to the house.

As I took the raccoon out and placed her in my lap, I wondered what I'd do with her now. She had to be fed and kept warm. I knew that I could keep her warm, but what in the world do baby raccoons eat? After awhile, I searched out a can of condensed milk and from somewhere in my head, I just knew how to make a formula for baby kittens. I picked up the little critter and decided that she looked enough like a kitten to try it. I looked around for somethin' to feed her with and finally located an eyedropper. Once the little critter figured out how it worked, she went after it like there was no tomorrow. Her tiny hand-like feet tried to hold the dropper like a bottle, but it was too slippery. Without realizin' what I'd done, I put my finger on the little glass tube and the baby raccoon latched on to it. It would barely let me move enough to refill the dropper. After several tubes full, she turned away and curled up in my lap.

"I guess now your tummy's full, ya need a little nap." She curled up in a tighter ball and I thought that maybe she was chilly, so I scooped her up and put her back in my shirt pocket. Even in the summer heat, a tiny baby anything needed extra warmth. Little did I know that my pocket would then become that baby's safe little warm world.

I spent most of that afternoon and night feedin' my little critter and when I felt a warm wetness in my pocket, I decided I had to figger out when potty time was. This was quite a job, takin' care of this little baby.

She seemed to eat all the time and go potty about as often. After findin' some old rags, I stuffed a couple in my pocket and since the baby didn't go very much, it worked fine. That is, until she pooped! The smell was more than unpleasant. I soon noticed that after about every third time she ate, she would poop and she ate about every hour or less. I spread out an old newspaper and when I thought it was about time, I'd set her on the paper until she went.

By mornin', I was exhausted, and by mid-mornin', I heard Bridger scrapin' off his boots on the edge of the porch. Somehow, I'd all but forgot about bein' alone and that he was gone. I was stretched out on the bed when he come in the door.

"You're still in bed. Are ya alright, Shelly?" He looked concerned.

"Yeah, I'm just tired. I didn't get no sleep last night."

"Why? Was ya worried about bein' alone?" he whispered.

I kinda giggled. "No, I had company all night."

Bridger looked both surprised and worried at the same time.

"Who?" he asked a little shortly.

I couldn't help but notice how tense he'd gotten the minute I'd said that.

"What's wrong? Are ya upset that somebody might come to see me?"

"No! It's just that . . . nobody . . . I don't like . . . I don't like nobody bein' around when you're by yourself. That's all." He sat two loads of supplies on the counter, turned, and went back out the door. When he come back in, he had two more big bags of stuff.

"How did ya carry all that up the mountain?"

"I got a wagon to put it in and pulled it back up. Who was here?" he asked.

"Oh, just Eesa." I told him as I reached inside my pocket and pulled out my little friend.

"What the hell? Where did ya get that little coon?"

"I found her abandoned in the outhouse. Look how tiny she is," I answered excitedly.

"So ya stayed up all night takin' care of that little nuisance? You're just askin' for trouble." He smiled as he started to put up the supplies.

I felt like I should be able to help, but for the life of me, I didn't remember where a darn thing was supposed to go. It was times like this that I almost panicked at the idea that I just couldn't remember anything. Bridger turned and looked at me.

"You keepin' that in your shirt pocket?" he asked as he looked at the bulge in my pocket.

"Yeah, why?"

"It'll have ya smellin' like a mama raccoon. We need to figure out somethin' else."

"But she loves to sleep with me. She gets so cold," I explained.

He thought for a minute, then opened a cabinet door. I've had this a long time. Let's see how it works." Takin' some more old rags, he put some in a small sized bag with a long strap on it.

"Now, try this."

"What is it?" I was hesitant.

"It's an old canteen cover. It's water proof and I've cut the top off so your little critter will get plenty of air" he said as he slipped the strap over my head and told me to put Eesa in it. At first she seemed a little upset, but soon curled up and went back to sleep. This was a great idea. I could do whatever I needed to while she rested safely at my side.

"Where'd ya come up with the name Eesa?" Bridger asked.
"I have no idea. It just come to my head. I think it fits her fine, don't you?"

He shook his head. "If you like it, I reckon it's as good a name as any for a raccoon."

For a while, Eesa took my mind off of all the things I couldn't remember. Bridger was a man of little to no words and went about his huntin' and gatherin'. I couldn't remember ever cookin', but it seemed to be somethin' I just knew how to do. Apparently, I was pretty good at it 'cause Bridger ate everything I put in front of him.

My body seemed to be healed, but my mind was still a fog. I finally quit worryin' and just went about the things I knew how to do. Eesa was gettin' bigger and stronger everyday. I was so excited when her eyes were finally open and she looked at me for the first time. I'd spent so much time rockin' her while she slept and hummin' to her that everytime I hummed, she hurried across the floor to me on her tiny, unsteady legs. She was such a blessin' to me.

One night after supper, I sat in the floor feedin' Eesa when Bridger walked in the door. He'd been gone all day and come in with a basket full of wild plums. However, the plums wasn't the first thing I noticed. I wasn't quite sure that the man who come through the door was really Bridger. It was obvious that he'd took a bath down at the creek and washed his beautiful blonde hair. The shock come when he looked up at me and my jaw dropped open. Although he'd been very handsome from the beginnin', he was just beautiful as he stood there before me clean-shaved. His hair was pulled back and tied with a string into a loose ponytail, he had no shirt on, just his jeans and he had a towel around his neck. This was the first time I'd really seen what he looked like. His rugged, handsome good looks were not the slightest bit marred by the scar on his forehead. Those sensuous, green eyes, his full lips, and the dimple in his chin could easily be seen now. I looked back at his lips and felt a twinge in my heart. It almost seemed familiar. Maybe I was startin' to remember him.

"I found some wild plums on the way back from huntin'. I thought we might make some jelly. I got some jars and lids in the storage and I picked up the other stuff in town. I got a rabbit and two squirrels for supper." He chatted on like it would keep me from noticin' his beautiful face.

I smiled. "Sure. If ya clean 'em . . . I'll cook 'em."

As he turned to go, I noticed a couple of tattoos on his arm and back left shoulder. I couldn't tell what they was at that distance, but they didn't seem any more familiar than he did. I couldn't understand how I could possibly foget this man. This man with the perfect face, body, and what I'd come to feel was his very sexy whispery voice.

When he went outside, I started to cook somethin' to go with the two squirrels I'd fry for supper and then I'd put the rabbit in a stew for the next day. I'd gathered some day-lillies that Bridger had taught me how to boil like spinach and I put on some oyster mushrooms with wild onions and garlic with a little sage and pepper to bake. I enjoyed the fresh meat and vegetables that we had every day, but the thought of winter in these mountains led us to a frenzy of cannin', dryin', and curin' to make sure we'd have plenty to eat durin' the cold months. Bridger told me that it got really cold and snowy up that high, but for the life of me I couldn't remember a day of it.

Later that evenin' after we'd finished eatin', I sat on the bed with Eesa and fed her. As soon as she finished, I took her to the paper that she'd gotten used to goin' to the bathroom on and waited 'til she was done.

"Ya got that thing rotten ya know?" Bridger whispered.

"I know, but ain't she just the cutest little thing?"

He stared at me for a minute or two before he answered me.

"Yeah . . . you're both pretty durn cute."

I looked at him and was surprised when he gave me the most gorgeous smile, bit his bottom lip, and winked at me. My heart skipped a beat as I realized that I remembered that!

"What?" he whispered.

"Bridger, I think I remember ya doin' that! You bitin' your lip and winkin' at me like that! I do . . . I do remember that!" I was so excited I could hardly breathe. I was really startin' to remember him.

The smile left his face and he looked back at the book he was readin'.

"Did ya hear me? I remember that!"

"I heard ya. That's a good thing. Maybe it'll all come back to ya."

I didn't understand why he didn't seem happier than he did. I would've thought that he'd be as excited as I was. Maybe he thought I might be gettin' my hopes too high and he just didn't want me to be disappointed. He was probably right.

"I'm sorry." I told him. "I'm probably makin' a mountain outta a mole hill."

"No, I'm the one that's sorry. Sorry I didn't get a little more excited about it. It's a big step, but I just don't want ya to be upset if that's all ya ever recall."

"Yeah," I said under my breath. "I shouldn't get so excited."

Bridger turned over on his make-shift bed and pulled his blanket over his shoulder.

". . . but I still think you're awfully cute," he whispered to the wall.

I giggled as I put Eesa back in my pocket for the night. She'd wake me up when she was hungry and wanted to eat and play for awhile, but for the most part we slept very well.

The moon was full and bright as it lit up the inside of our cabin, but it didn't take me long to fall peacefully asleep.

I was startled awake when Bridger suddenly put his hand roughly over my mouth and shook my shoulder.

"There's too much movement Ben," he whispered almost frantically. "We gotta back 'em out. Now! Follow me . . . I'll get ya outta here."

He released my mouth and started to slither soundlessly across the floor. This was what he'd done before, only he hadn't seemed this upset. I didn't know who Ben was and I didn't know what he'd seen or heard. Maybe it was another nightmare or did he really hear somethin'? I didn't know whether to be scared or just stay put until he settled down. I listened for a minute, but I couldn't hear nothin'. Bridger was still on the floor, but had stopped and held his hand up to warn whoever was behind him. I waited.

"Ben?" he called softly. "Ben? No! Oh God, no. Beni, wake up, Beni. I'm sorry . . . so sorry." He sobbed and put his head down on his arm.

By that time, I was sure that it was another bad dream so I lay quietly while he sobbed for a little while before relaxin' and eventually beginnin' to snore softly.

I had no idea what his dreams were about or what'd happened to him in the past, but my heart hurt so much for the tortured man who lay sleepin' near the front door. I wondered if I should talk to him about it and maybe get him to talk to me. Somethin' in my gut told me to just leave it alone. Since I'd been with him all those years, I probably knew all about it and it might be even more painful for him to drag it all up again. I felt sure that somethin' horrible had happened in his past.

****

It was still dark, but I woke up early 'cause of Eesa rootin' around in my pocket. She liked the canteen cover in daytime, but still preferred my pocket at night. Rootin' was her way of tellin' me that she was ready to eat and potty. I got up to go heat her milk and noticed that at some time in the night, Bridger had made his way back to his blankets. His silky blonde hair was spread out across his pillow and he seemed to be sleepin' peacefully. I felt a great desire to kneel down and kiss those pouty lips, but Eesa gave me a strong reminder of what my mission had been.

I finished feedin' her and took her to her area to potty. When she finished, I was so surprised to see her stand on her hind legs and hold her tiny hand-like feet up for me to pick her up. I was very happy to do that. I'd found myself fallin' in love with that tiny critter as I watched her grow and learn. She immediately crawled back into my pocket and curled up to sleep. I was noticin' that more and more, she wanted to sleep all day and was gettin' a habit of wantin' to be awake more at night. As I gave it some thought, I recalled that I never saw raccoons out in the daytime, but they was very active at night. Yep, she was a nocturnal animal and I'd better get used to it.

I took the dirty paper outside to the trash pile and quietly come back in the door so as not to wake Bridger. He'd had a rough night. I put on a pot of chicory and was slicin' a couple of strips of the left over squirrel when I heard a movement behind me. When I turned around, I saw Bridger gettin' up and foldin' his blankets.

"Mornin'," I said.

"Mornin'," he answered. "What ya doin' up so early?"

"Eesa wanted to eat, so I figgered I'd just make us breakfast too."

He stood there and stared at me for a minute. "Thank ya Shelly. You're a good woman." He smiled as he turned, went out the door, and toward the outhouse.

So many questions . . . his voice . . . his nightmares. Why did we live so far up in the mountains with nobody around? And who was Ben?

Several weeks later, Bridger left for supplies. I asked if I could go with him, but he said it was too far and too dangerous with all the steep trails and a large creek to cross that usually flooded about that time of year. I decided he was right and I'd rather stay at home with Eesa. I was sure I could've made it, but it would've been hard on her.

After he left, I went about cleanin' the place. It was so small that it didn't take very long. By this time, Eesa was no longer dependent on me to always fix her somethin' to eat. She slept all day and wanted to prowl all night. We'd finally built her a cage to keep her curious little self under control. I always stayed up late with her so that she had plenty of time to play. I sometimes hid food so that she would have to hunt for it. She seemed to enjoy that. However, when she was ready to rest, she still tried to crawl into my pocket. Sadly, she was gettin' too big for that, so I'd sewed a blanket into a bag with some supplies that Bridger had brought from town. She was happy to crawl inside and sleep through the day.

The next day, I got an early bath, washed my hair, and put on the best thing I had to wear. I didn't know exactly why but I wanted to look my best when Bridger got home. My dark hair'd gotten really long and I wanted somethin' to tie it back. There was nothin' in the place to use. I dug deep into the storage area and had about decided to cut up one of my few blouses when I found a large bag in the far corner. It'd been covered with everything I could've imagined. I started to pull it out when I saw that Bridger had his name on it. It must've held his personal stuff . . . stuff that he'd stored for whatever reason. I felt like it wasn't none of my business as to what was in there, but as I pushed it back, I noticed there was a black scarf tied to the long cloth handle on it. That would work great for my hair. I untied it and went to the only tiny mirror in the place and tied my hair back with it. That was much better and not nearly as hot. I went into the kitchen area and put on some water for a cup of hot wintergreen tea. Even though it was hot outside, I still enjoyed my cup of tea.

An hour or so later, I heard Bridger as he stepped up on the porch, wiped his feet, and come inside.

"I'm back," he whispered as loud as he could.

I'd been in the storage room just off the kitchen and hurried into the livin' area. He'd just set the first load of supplies on the table as I rushed toward him. I stopped short when I saw the look on his face. If I'd ever seen anger in anyone's eyes, it was Bridger's. His face was pale, then turned a deep red as his eyes flashed with somethin' akin to pure fury! I didn't know what to think. He took one huge step and was in my face. With one swipe of his hand, he snatched the scarf that held my hair back and clutched it in his fist.

"What the hell? Where did ya get this? Was ya goin' through my stuff. My personal stuff?"

He was firin' so many questions that I didn't have no time to even think about answerin' the first one.

"I . . . I . . . it was tied to a bag in the corner and I needed somethin' to tie my hair back and . . . ."

He stood tall and stiff and his handsome face was twisted with so much anger and pain that I backed away and crawled onto my bed. Eesa must have sensed somethin' was wrong, 'cause even though it was her sleep time, she crawled out of her sewed-up blanket bed and pulled herself to my shoulder.

Bridger crammed the scarf into his pants pocket and went straight out the door. I didn't remember bein' so scared. All I wanted to do was pull my blanket over my head and hide in the dark. Eesa and I lay like that for a couple of hours or more before I heard footsteps comin' across the front porch. I froze and my stomach churned with panic.

RAT !! RATS !! The words screamed through my head as I began to shake and sweat with a deep fear. It was a fear I didn't remember ever feelin' before. I felt a hand touch my shoulder and I jumped against the wall.

"Shelly?" I heard Bridger whisper. "I . . . I'm sorry. I . . . I, I . . . ."

I heard him walk away toward the other side of the room. There was a lot of shufflin' of stuff before I heard him walk out the front door and off the porch. On edge, I listened for hours on end to every sound as if it was a matter of life and death. I suppose at sometime, I drifted off to sleep and only woke up when Eesa started to fuss and get upset 'cause she couldn't find her way out of the cover. It was her time to eat, drink, play, and potty. We'd spent several hours of every night of her life bein' active. Bridger'd gotten used to it and most time slept right through it. I tried to be quiet, but Eesa made such a production of washin' every bite she took and tryin' to climb everything in the room. About 4:00, I could usually get her to settle down and go back to sleep. Tonight was not a time that I really wanted to uncover my head or get out of bed. She was insistent, so I finally gave in and got up. The cabin was dark and quiet and there didn't seem to be any moonlight at all. Carryin' Eesa, I tip-toed to the food pantry and lit a candle so we could find her food. That was when I noticed Bridger was not on his bed. As I lit a lantern and the room brightened, I could tell that he was nowhere inside. I was sure that once I had Eesa in her home made harness and leash and we went outside, that we would find him asleep on the porch swing. He was nowhere to be seen. I was a little concerned but I went through our usual routine and when Eesa come back to me, we went back inside and into our bed.

****

The sound of thunder and the crack of lightnin' brought me straight out of bed that mornin'. Before I could get my head straight and my eyes fully opened, I heard rain come pourin' down yet again. It'd been rainin' for several days now and still I hadn't seen or heard from Bridger. I was past bein' concerned now, I was downright worried. Where in the world could he have took off to? He'd brought home plenty of supplies when he'd come home and I just couldn't imagine what he was doin' for food and shelter. I knew he was mad when he'd left, but enough was enough. It was past time to get over it and come back home.

I made myself some hot wintergreen tea and walked to the window. It was rainin' so hard I could barely see the trail to the outhouse. I needed to go, but there was no way I was wadin' out through all that mud. *Yeah, I thought to myself, I can wait awhile.*

Eesa was asleep in her make shift bed, which was in the middle of mine, but I made the bed in spite of her. After I fixed my breakfast and sat down at the crude little table, I started to think about things. What if Bridger was gone for good? I didn't have no idea where I was or how to get anywhere else. I hadn't seen nobody else since I'd fell. Okay, I had plenty of smoked and dried meat and stored and canned vegetables and fruits. The fact was that it wouldn't last forever and I had no idea how I was gonna replace 'em after they was all gone. I felt a great fear come over me.

"Dammit Bridger . . . get your ass home and act like a man!!" I yelled out loud. Eesa chattered a little in response to bein' disturbed.

I set about cleanin'. Nothin' made a woman feel better than a clean house. Somebody used to tell me that, but for the life of me I couldn't recall who it was. I dusted, scrubbed, swept, and straightened up till I reached the point that I just couldn't find another thing to do. It'd rained all day except for a few little breaks now and then. I made a small stew for supper and after I ate, I crawled in bed with Eesa. Before I knew it, I was sound asleep.

A beautiful golden Palomino stood before me. I ran my fingers through the thick, silky mane. It was silver-blonde and his bangs fell casually over his eyes. When he looked up at me, I could hardly breathe. I looked into the most unforgettable crystal blue eyes I'd ever seen. As we locked eyes, I realized that I knew this . . . this. And before I could even finish the thought, he turned and walked out of sight. "Wait!" I screamed. "Wait!" I could hear my boots on the hard dirt road as I ran after him. He started to run and the sound of my boots became louder as I tried with everything in me to catch up! Thud . . . thud . . . thud! Thud . . . thud . . . thud.

I opened my heavy eyelids as I listened. Thud . . . thud. There it was again. I'd thought it was part of my dream until I sat up and heard it yet again. It sounded like somebody was stompin' on the porch. I got Bridger's other rifle from the kitchen and stepped to the door.

"Hello? Is somebody out there?" I yelled over the poundin' rain. I heard nothin' for a minute and then the poundin' again. I got the lantern and eased the door open as I shook from head to toe. It took a couple of minutes for my eyes to adjust and then I saw him. Bridger lay half on the porch and half out in the rain. He raised his hand and pounded on the porch again.

"Bridger!" I screamed as I set the lantern down and rushed out to him.

The thought'd never crossed my mind that he could be hurt somewhere out there. I knew that somehow, I had to get him inside and dried off. Bein' as he was a very large man in height, I didn't think I had it in me to pull him across the porch and into the room. Somehow, I found the strength and after a long stressfull 10 or so minutes, I finally rolled him inside. He was soaked to the bone and he shook so hard I could hear his teeth chatter.

"Bridger?" I said as I removed his hat and started for his boots. "Where are ya hurt?"

He didn't respond at all.

"Bridger?" I raised my voice and lifted his head.

He opened his eyes slightly, but didn't look at me. His beautiful green eyes were glazed and fixed on somethin' on the ceilin'. I looked up, but there was nothin' any different there than had been all along. I got a towel and struggled to remove his shirt and dry him off. As I shifted him into a half-sittin' position and pulled the soaked shirt from his body, I noticed for the first time that he had more than a few scars on his back and chest. I didn't have time to think about that right now. I needed to get him dry and warm. I pulled his boots from his feet and took off his wet socks. His dark green pants were heavy and awkward to remove, but I finally got it done and started to dry his lower half. Pullin' a blanket from my bed, I covered his top half and continued to wipe the dampness from his legs. In the bright lamplight, it was impossible not to notice the dark purple scars in each thigh. As I came to his ankles and feet, I found the deep scars around his ankles, like chains or bracelets might make. A sudden fear raced through my head as I sat starin' at his healed wounds. Maybe he was a convict . . . an escaped convict and that was why we lived hidden in these mountains . . . but there was no time to think about any of that now.

 I finished dryin' him and covered him in several blankets and then I wiped his face with a damp cloth. He was burnin' up with fever, his face was very pale, and he seemed to be strugglin' to breathe. After I put a pillow under his head and made sure he had plenty of blankets, I rushed to the shelf where we kept the medicines. Bridger had showed me and gone over all these things so I would know what to do if anything happened while he was gone in for supplies. He had bottle after bottle of dried leaves, roots, and flowers that were labeled so it wasn't hard to know what each one was, how to use it, and what it was used for. I hurriedly looked from bottle to bottle tryin' to decide what was best to try. I'd looked him over from head to toe and found no injury or bite of any kind. It had to be some type of flu or cold, and I knew that I had to get that fever down as quick as I could. I chose the dried root from American Holly. Takin' water and bringin' it almost to a boil, I dropped some of the root into the pan. After it come to a good boil, I turned it down, and let it set for a few minutes. I waited and then added a little cool water and took a small cup of it in to Bridger. I had no idea how much to give him, but I knew he had to have enough to get rid of his fever.

 I knelt on the floor beside him and placed a clean cloth around his neck. His mouth was slightly open and I trickled a little of the tea from the teaspoon between his lips. I started to get a little worried as he laid there and neither swallowed or moved. After several seconds he finally swallowed. I gave him a couple of more seconds and then delivered another half teaspoon full. He shivered and made a terrible face. It took some time, but I finally managed to get almost all the tea down his throat and leaned back against my bed to watch. He was such a beautiful man and I was beginin' to be so drawn to him. I was almost sure that at one time I'd been very much in love with him. Even now, I wanted to kiss those beautiful lips. How I wished I could remember him . . . him and our life together. He groaned and continued with the violent chills. Finally I decided to crawl under the blankets and hold him and maybe my body heat would help to warm him. I snuggled beneath his arm and wrapped my arm and leg over him and cuddled as close as I could get. It didn't take long before I felt like I was wrapped in one of those heated blankets. I felt the sweat start to roll down my face and neck, but Bridger still shook with chills. They seemed to have lessened somewhat, but was none-the less, still there.

As his chills seemed to ease up, I relaxed and finally fell asleep beside him on the floor. Sometime in the night I woke up drenched in sweat. Bridger's fever had broken and he was sleepin' peacefully. I thought about gettin' up and changin' my clothes, but I didn't want to disturb him. I curled back up beside him and went back to sleep. I think I'd barely closed my eyes when Eesa decided it was her prowlin' time. For the first time, I was really irritated with her. I finally got up and staggered through our usual routine. About daylight, she went back to bed for the day. I was so tired I could hardly think.

When I went to check on Bridger, his fever was back up but not as high as it had been. He was strugglin' to breathe and seemed to have developed a cough. When I rested my head on his chest, right off I recognized the deep rattle that I'd heard somewhere in the past. I set there for a minute and tried to remember where I'd heard it. Somethin' in my head was so close to finishin' that thought that it almost hurt.

I'd have to think about that later as I needed to do what I could for Bridger. I went back to the medicine shelf and started to search for what I needed. He had so many home remedies that it took me some time to find just the right one. Finally I found it. I was familiar with this one. One ounce of dried boneset leaves in a pint of boilin' water left on low heat for 1 hour . . . one half to one ounce of this tea as needed. It was an old mountain cure for pneumonia or flu. It would have to do since it was the only thing I had to give him. I set to work right away and made a batch of the elixir. While it brewed, I worked to get some of the fever remedy down him. His chills were back, so I built up the cookin' fire to make it a little warmer inside the lean-to. When he finally started to sweat again, I wiped his beautiful face with a damp cloth and moistened his lips. I noticed that he'd taken the black scarf and tied it around his neck. Not seein' that it was necessary, I undid it and as I removed it, for the first time, I noticed the deep scar across his throat. Dear Lord, what had happened to this gentle, kind man? It was almost as if he'd been tortured to no end.

He was pretty much unconscious as he started to mumble and push the blankets away.

"Beni . . . no . . . no . . . ," he sobbed. ". . . leave her alone, you bastards." He growled between gritted teeth.

"Shhhh" I tried to settle him down. "It's okay Bridger. It's okay."

But somehow, I sensed that it was not okay and most likely never would be.

Chapter 6

Two days had passed and I was really gettin' scared. Bridger's fever would break from time to time, but would come right back. He coughed a lot, but I could tell the congestion was startin' to break up in his chest. How I wished I knew where to find a doctor.

I continued with regular doses of the elixirs and pushed a lot of water, hot tea, and soup down him. Sometimes he slept peaceful and other times he was restless and tormented.

I'd managed to get him on his bed, and some times I'd sleep beside him to keep him warm and try and comfort him when he had the nightmares. On the third night, after I'd got Eesa settled in, I crawled under the blanket next to him. His fever was down a little at the moment. He wrapped his arm around me and pulled me close up against him. I was a little unnerved by the heat of his all but naked body against mine. His face was next to the back of my neck and I could feel his hot breath on my ear. His breathin' was slow and steady, but I sure couldn't say the same for mine. I wondered if he'd always made me feel that way. My mind wondered further and I found myself tryin' to imagine what it must've been like to make love with him. Why the hell couldn't I remember?

I lay there for as long as I could and then decided that I had to move away. I carefully and slowly lifted his arm and had started to slide out of his embrace when he raised up and pulled me directly under him. I looked up in the dim light and could see that his beautiful green eyes were open, but glazed again with fever. His full beautiful lips come down on mine. The fevered heat of 'em and the passion of his kiss stirred somethin' inside of me that I didn't recall ever feelin' before. Within a minute's time, I had my arms around his neck and was clinging to his burnin' body. Before I realized what'd happened, my night shirt was gone and Bridger's fevered kisses covered my body. His hands roamed freely as they touched places that drove me to the brink of insanity. Those lips found mine again and as I gazed into his eyes, his beautiful golden blonde hair fell like a curtain around our faces. At that moment, we became one. His lovemakin' was passionate, yet desperate, and we soared to the top before I knew it. I couldn't believe the intensity and complete satisfaction that I felt. That was when my heart sank as Bridger snuggled into my neck and whispered, "Awww . . . Beni . . . Beni, I needed you so bad, baby. I love you." Then he rolled to his side and fell back to sleep.

I lay there a little stunned and a lot hurt. He hadn't even realized who he'd just made love to. My mind whirled. If we'd been together all this time, then who in the hell was Beni? I assumed from what he'd said earlier that Beni was a girl. If he loved her so much . . . then who was I? I got up quietly and grabbed a fresh night gown and towel and went out the door. The moon was bright as I made my way carefully down to the spring-fed creek. Slippin' into the cold water, all I could think of was to wash him off my body . . . him and her. Tears of frustration began to flow from my eyes as I scrubbed from head to toe. After a few minutes, I calmed down and let myself float on my back in the cold water. I opened my eyes and looked up at the full moon. My heart jumped in my chest as a simple thought shook my entire bein' . . . *Mr. Moon, watch over him 'til he finds his way back home.*

Where in the world did that come from? I studied the moon as if it would blurt out an answer at any second. It was as if the answer to everything was only a heartbeat away. I could feel it so close I could almost taste it. A breath later and it faded into thin air. Frustrated, I was climbin' out of the water and reachin' for my towel when my foot slipped on the wet rocks. My towel flew through the air, as did my feet and arms, and I landed back in the water and rocks. Other than a good solid thud on the back of my neck and head, I was okay. As I bent to pick up my towel again, my head began to spin and I had to sit down for a minute. I sat and rubbed the back of my neck and dried off with the towel as I waited for the dizziness to go away. It was about that time that I thought about Bridger and how ill he was and got myself up and went back to the lean-to. He was lying spread-eagle on his bed with a blanket barely coverin' his midsection. I stood there for a second and couldn't help but admire the beauty of the muscular, yet scar-covered, man with the silky golden blonde hair that rested on the floor before me. I shook my head and once again, I wondered what in the world he'd been through. It had to have been horrible, yet he'd survived it all. My head began to spin again and I was gettin' a bit of a headache, so I laid down beside Eesa and soon fell asleep.

I was so exhausted and was in a very deep, dreamless sleep when I was jerked back into reality without warnin'. The first thing I heard was a blood curdlin' scream that shook the walls. I sat up so fast I almost fell off my bed. Bridger lay with his face crammed against the wall, his blankets were bound tightly around him, and somehow he'd managed to tip a chair on top of him. He screamed again.

"Leave her alone . . . don't touch her you son-of-a-bitch! Don't . . . don't touch her." Then he cried with such heartbreakin' sobs and so much pain that I felt my throat tighten as tears began to flow from my own eyes. I hurried to him and moved the chair. "Bridger?" I talked as soothin' and calm as I could 'cause I knew he was still asleep and havin' another nightmare. "Bridger." He continued to cry and I could tell that the pain reached into the depths of his soul.

"Bridger?" I said a little louder and more forcefully. "It's just a bad dream." I tried to assure him. By this time, my heart was just breakin' for him. I rolled him over on his back and he began to struggle frantically to get free. I wasn't sure what might happen if he got loose. I felt like he was somewhere else in his mind and it certainly wasn't there with me. Out of pure fear and instinct I did somethin' I was pretty sure I'd never done in my life. I slapped the tar out of him. He gasped, then slowly opened his eyes. I watched him as he glanced around the room with bewildered, glassy eyes. He finally looked directly at me, blinked, and tried again to focus.

"Sh . . . Shelly?" he whispered.

"Yes, it's me."

"What . . . what's . . . I don't understand."

"You've been sick, Bridger. Really sick for several days."

"Here? Not . . . not back . . . not back there?"

I wasn't sure where *back there* was, but I nodded and answered him.

"Right here. Right here with me and Eesa."

He tried to move, but was too tightly bound in blankets.

"Let me help ya. I don't know how ya got so tangled up," I told him as I started to unroll him from the mess he was caught up in with his covers.

Once I got him straightened up and restin' comfortably, I heated up some soup and hot tea. It was the first time he'd been able to help with eatin' and drinkin' in a long time. His fever was down and I prayed it would stay that way. He still had a nasty cough, but it needed to be a little more productive. Later I went through the medicines again and found some blood root that was really good for helpin' to break up that congestion. I stopped the American Holly tea and stayed with just the boneset and bloodroot. I hoped and prayed that would be all he'd need. After he ate and took his elixirs, he slept very peacefull and feverless for several hours. I have to admit that even with all the unanswered questions that whirled inside my achin' head, I took the opportunity to go back to bed and sleep with the rest of the household.

****

Several hours later I woke up. Eesa was still in her daytime hibernation state and Bridger was still out like a light. I got up and walked around the place for a little while and straightened up a few things. I was bein' very quiet as I didn't want to awaken him. I wanted him to sleep for as long as he could. I'd found myself very uncomfortable when he'd looked straight into my eyes earlier. Even though I was sure that he didn't have no idea of what had happened, I did . . . and I was very embarrassed about the whole thing. I'd been stupid enough to think that Bridger and I . . . we were . . . but I was wrong.

I found myself in back of the lean-to where his stuff was stored. I'd tied the black scarf back on the strap of the pack against the wall. A sudden strong, irresistible urge to look inside that bag come over me. It wasn't that I wanted to be nosey, it was that I wanted to know more about this man with whom I lived.

I sat down on a stool near the bag and unzipped it very quietly. There wasn't a lot, but what there was told me volumes. There was a pair of pants a lot like the ones he wore all the time. I also found a pair of dress slacks and an Army coat. It was covered with medals. I don't know all the names of them, but there was several purple hearts, a bronze star, more medals and ribbons than I could count. There was some kind of patch that said 1st battalion, 2nd infantry on it, and another sayin' he'd served in Viet Nam. I also found some plaques, some citations of valor, and beneath it all was a flat wool hat that I knew was a green beret. I picked it up and held it to my heart. This explained so very much to me. As I put the cap back, somethin' fell out into my lap. It was a piece of green silk, tied into a bow that'd been tucked inside the cap. I put it back as it was and picked up a folded paper to return to the bag when I saw what it said. It told of how heroic Captain R.W. Bridger had been and the many heroic acts he'd performed while a prisoner of war in Hanoi.

I'd had no idea about any of it. I could't recall a single thing about readin' or hearin' any of it. I replaced all the stuff with great care and put the bag where it belonged. Goin' back to my bed, I sat for some time just studyin' Bridger's beautiful face. How had he got the scar on his forehead? What about the one on his neck? My mind reeled with the thoughts of the ones on his thighs, wrists, ankles, and every other part of his body. Dear Lord in heaven . . . what horrible cruelties had this sweet, beautiful man suffered?

****

Two days later, I started to see some improvement in Bridger. He had a little fever occasionally, but his cough was more productive, and he sounded and looked a whole lot better. He slept a lot, but he was eatin' better. This had been the hardest job I could ever remember. I had the most difficulty gettin' him to the outhouse and back. He was very weak and still a little unsure on his feet, but between us, we managed.

That night, Bridger sat up in bed and leaned against the wall starin' at me. He hadn't been able to shave and his hair was a blonde mess. The only bath he'd been able to get was when I washed him with a wet cloth and soapy water. He was a bit of a mess. I handed him a cup of wintergreen tea and took mine and sat on the edge of my bed beside him.

"How do ya feel today?" I asked him.

"A little like I got the worst hangover I ever had," he whispered as he sipped his tea.

We sat there in silence for several minutes. I thought about the night we'd had sex. I couldn't call it makin' love, 'cause I knew that I was just a stand-in for someone else. I had to wonder if it'd always been that way. For all the time we'd been here, and all the times I was sure that we'd been together, had I always been a substitute for this Beni?

"Ya look awful serious, Shelly?" he said. "Ya been really good to me while I was sick and I just want ya to know how much that means to me."

I sat there for a minute before I said anything. "Ya done the same for me when I was hurt. Now I guess we're even."

"What, are we keepin' score?"

"I didn't mean it that way. I just mean that . . . well, it's just somethin' ya do for each other. My Nanny always said that ya should do for others just like you'd want 'em to do for you."

Bridger looked at me with a startled expression, then just nodded his head.

"You're right, but I still want to thank ya, especially after the way I acted before I took off and left. That was really dumb and I didn't mean to be so hateful to ya."

"What upset ya so bad?" I asked.

He sat starin' into his tea and I could tell that he was havin' a hard time decidin' just how to answer my question.

"It . . . it was . . . it was the scarf, Shelly. Ya had no way of knowin' what it was and I overreacted when I saw it so casually wrapped around your hair. That black scarf is somethin' that carries a lot of importance and a lot of memories with it. You see, I was with the 1st Battalion, 2nd Infantry and we were well-known for our black scarves." He paused for a few minutes as if to organize his thoughts a little.

Suddenly he seemed to open up more than he ever had and his story rolled out like a flood that'd been dammed up for way too long.

"Back in the sixties, I volunteered to go to Nam. I joined the Army as soon as I could. I didn't wait for no draft letter. I wanted to go help the people of South Viet Nam. I didn't have no idea of what I was gettin' involved with. I was young, stupid, and thought I could be their hero." He paused and took another drink of tea.

All the medals and ribbons and letters I'd seen in his bag flashed through my mind. He sure sounded like a hero to me.

"There was a bunch of us from Tennessee that really believed in the nickname, The Volunteer State, so we took right off and joined. When we got there, it was nothin' like what we thought and nothin' like what basic trainin' led us to believe. Yeah they told us about all the confusion and we should expect arm-to-arm combat, booby traps, and all that stuff. But they never told us about the beautiful people that would give up everything to help us to help them. They didn't explain how these people would sacrifice their own lives for ours, and just to see so many of 'em butchered like cattle . . . we never saw it comin'. It didn't take long to realize that it was almost impossible to tell the good guys from the bad guys. I spent nine months in the mud, the blood, the rain, and playin' hide and seek in the jungle. That was about the time I met . . . I . . ." he stopped and stared out the window as if he'd gone to another time and place. I sat there for a few minutes waitin' for him to say it. I knew what he wanted to say and I could only guess how hard it was to say her name.

"Bridger . . . ya don't have to talk about this if ya don't want to."

"No," he whispered, and I noticed tears that rolled down his cheek. "I need to tell ya, just you. I've never told anyone before."

"There was a . . . a girl I met . . . in one of the villages. Tiny little thing with long black hair and the sweetest smile I'd ever seen. She had a small shop where she sold baskets and woven hats. She seemed really shy at first, until I stopped by her shop for about the third time.

"You want basket? Take home to girlfriend. I have many for you. I have much for you, Captain Bidger." The girl said the last part under her breath.

"I couldn't believe she knew who I was. I took a basket from her and looked it over carefully as I spoke under my breath. I asked how she knew me. She smiled and giggled a little and told me that she'd asked around the streets. We continued to talk softly as we inspected the baskets.

"I work for South Viet Nam government. I watch market place to see who go and who come in to village. They tell me tell you that much is happening . . . you keep eyes very open, Captain sir."

"I asked her name, but I never could understand exactly what it was. It sounded like . . . like, Beni. That's what I called her from there on out. We met often, sometimes in secret and many times in public at the market. She openly giggled and acted like so many of the young girls in the town, but she whispered under her breath as she pointed out strangers and several she was sure were Viet Cong. We became very . . . very close.

After weeks and weeks of gettin' information that I took back to HQ, she told me she wanted me to meet her outside the village. She wanted to show me where she'd heard that somethin' big was buildin'. I got it cleared with my commander for my platoon to do recon on the information. That night we met up with Beni at the designated site. We was a good mile into the jungle and we was as silent as the grave when we was on missions like this. After around another three fourths of a mile, Beni stopped and motioned for us to take cover. We silently slipped behind trees and plants and disappeared into the dark. We had night vision binoculars and we could easily see that there was the beginnin' of a large build up of troops and weapons that was very cleverly hidden beneath a carefully woven canopy. It would have covered at least two football fields, but if ya wasn't lookin' for it . . . you'd have never seen it. We couldn't see how many there was, but we knew it was an extraordinary amount. While we watched, I started to see an awful lot of movement, like maybe they knew we was there. I signaled the men to move back and out as quick as they could." Bridger stopped for a minute.

"Why don't we talk about this later. Ya need your rest now." I suggested.

"No!" he insisted. "I gotta tell ya now. Right now."

"It can wait. Ya need some rest!" I insisted.

"I have to tell ya now, while I can."

I got up and brought him a cup of tea, got one for myself, and sat back down.

"We . . . we woulda made it if it wasn't for Grear. He panicked and didn't watch where he was goin'. He knew how to spot those traps. He was a damn expert at it. Not that time! That time he stumbled right into it, a pit lined with punji sticks. It was the scream that Grear let out when one went through his chest." He paused for a minute. "Ya coulda heard him for miles. Then we heard Charlie comin' after us."

"Who's Charlie?" I interrupted.

He sat there with his head down for several minutes.

"It's a nickname we picked up for the Viet Cong. We all freaked I guess. My men were runnin' in ever' direction. Beni took off after 'em and before I could stop her, she tripped a wire that released a limb covered in punji sticks." He choked up and it took a long time before he could speak again. My heart ached for him. I couldn't even begin to imagine what had happened in that jungle. I felt my own tears trickle down my cheeks.

"She . . . she, she was so tiny and short that . . . it caught her right in the chest. She never made a sound, she just stood there stuck all the way through on those sticks." He stopped again as he was overwhelmed with the pain of the memories. He sobbed openly and I wanted to go to him, but I was afraid that if I moved he would stop talkin' and I knew the best thing for him was to just get it all told. In a while, he continued.

"I . . . I got to her as quick as I could, but she was already gone. I didn't even get to tell her that . . . that I loved her. I turned away for just a second and that was when I felt the trip wire on my boot. Before I could think, I heard the swish of the limb and felt the piercin' pain that stabbed through my thighs. Up until that moment, I'd never felt anything like it. There's no describin' the amount of pain I felt. It wasn't just in my legs, but in my heart as well. I couldn't move and just hung there on the spikes as Charlie surrounded us all. Half of my command was already dead and the others was no better off than I was. I lost it when their commander stomped up to Beni, jerked her tiny, limp body loose, and held her before him. He grabbed her beautiful long black hair and pulled her head up so he could see her. Then he spit his contempt for her right into her face. I screamed and cursed the bastard for all I was worth. He turned toward me as if he hadn't even seen me. Still holdin' Beni by her hair, he dragged her right in front of me, pulled her head up, and . . . (he choked and sobbed again) . . . he slit her throat from ear to ear while he laughed. He laughed and all his men laughed while all I wanted to do was to kill him with my bare hands." Bridger stopped and took a long drink of his now cold tea.

A cold chill ran up my spine and the hair raised on my arms as I pictured the horrible scene inside my head. How had this adorable man lived with this nightmare? He'd said he never told nobody before and I had to wonder if that included me. I didn't recall hearin' anything about it, but then, I didn't recall anything in our life together. He started to talk again.

"They was anything but gentle when they ripped them sticks out of my legs. I guess I passed out 'cause I don't remember anything after that but wakin' up in time to see the little bastard take his knife and cut part of Beni's green blouse off and stuff it in my mouth. Again I heard that evil laugh and I promised myself and Beni that one day I would kill him. It wasn't long before I realized that the metallic taste in my mouth was Beni's . . . blood . . . her blood that'd soaked the blouse. I reached to get it out just as I saw the butt end of a rifle comin' at my face. I suppose I took the coward's way out and let myself slip into unconsciousness. Just before I went into that black, empty world, I heard one of 'em mention Hanoi. That was one place I knew we didn't want to end up."

Bridger laid back on his bed and covered his eyes with his forearm. I sat quietly and waited. Several more minutes passed and then I heard him sigh. I looked closer and realized that he had quietly fallen asleep. He'd put hisself through a very hard time by bringin' all those horrible memories back to mind. I knew he needed to rest and sleep, hopefully for the rest of the night.

Eesa stirred beside me, so I took her out for her play time and sat on the porch thinkin' about all that Bridger had told me. It was hard for me to imagine bein' captured and held like that, yet somewhere deep inside, I felt I could almost feel his fear and pain.

****

I woke up suddenly with the feelin' that I'd over slept. I sat straight up in the bed before I realized that it was barely light. Bridger sat on the other side of the room starin' at me. I went straight over and sat down beside him.

"Mornin' honey. How do ya feel today?"

He shook his head and just sat there.

"I'll make us some coffee and we'll have breakfast in a little while, okay?" I said.

As soon as I had the coffee done, I brought Bridger a cup and sat down on my bed.

"Thank ya," he mumbled. "Sh . . . Shelly. I need to finish my story. I need to tell ya all of it . . . before it's too late."

"What do ya mean . . . before it's too late?"

He stood up on shakey legs and walked to the front door and opened it.

"Let's set on the porch, okay," he whispered in his soft voice.

I sat there on the porch waitin' while the early mornin' breeze brought with it the sweet smells of the forest and the mountains that surrounded us.

"When I come to, I found myself in a make shift hospital of sorts. I was tied to a cot that was in the hall. I could feel blood tricklin' down my face and in to my eye and I could still taste the blood on the cloth that was still crammed in my mouth. I guess my legs and my head hurt almost as much as my heart. I opened my one eye just enough that I saw the little bastard who had killed my Beni and I worked to memorize that ugly, grinnin' face. Plannin' his death was the one thing that I swore would keep me alive." He took a long drink of the black coffee and sat there starin' into the distance.

"At some point, I felt a needle go in my arm and that was it until I woke up sometime later. When I opened the only eye I could see out of, I found myself in a concrete box with barely enough room to sit. Somebody had tied bandages around my legs and head. It was done sloppy and I thought they'd probably just done enough to keep me from dyin'. I found that I had chains on my ankles, as well as my wrists, but I could still move my arms. I was groggy, but I could feel the gag that was still in my mouth. I carefully removed it 'cause it was dried to my tongue. When I spread it out on my knee, I almost choked tryin' not to let nobody hear me cryin'. I knew I couldn't let 'em think I was weak. The green silk piece of cloth was caked with blood as I held it to my chest and did my very best to cry without sound." Suddenly Bridger stood up and walked slowly to the outhouse. I didn't know if he needed to go to the bathroom or throw up. I could sure understand, although I wasn't really sure how I was able to feel it so strongly. It was so real I could almost smell the stench of blood. Somethin' flashed in my head and I saw the body of a man roll out of a piece of cloth and across a rocky floor. I shook my head and leaned back against a post that was behind my back.

Bridger suddenly appeared, standin' only a couple of feet away from me.

"Are ya okay, Shelly?" he asked.

"Yeah . . . I guess. There was a flash of a man in my head . . . like a memory or somethin'. I don't know what or maybe who, but it was really weird."

"Maybe I should stop tellin' ya all this. I think I'm upsettin' ya," he whispered.

"No. Tell me the rest, please."

"Are ya sure? It might be better just forgotten."

"Tell me, Bridger. Go on," I encouraged.

"Well . . . I took the piece of cloth and wrapped it as tight as I could and put it in my pocket, at least until I found out where I was gonna be permanently. Every day, we was tortured and questioned and tortured some more. They beat us, starved us, then fed us crap with worms in it. There were times they hooked electricity to our . . . I'm not gonna go into all that. Let's just leave that with tortures that I could never have imagined I could live through, but every time I glimpsed that little bastard, I felt a new strength. I was bidin' my time 'til I could get my hands on him.

There was a man, Stockdale, and him and some other officers had developed a code for communication with other POWs. Somehow, just knowin' that others were there gave me courage.

One day, they opened the door and I braced myself for the usual round of questions and beatings. Only this time, they took me and a bunch of men, some were a few of my troops that'd survived, and put us in a truck. We was all shackled and chained together by our wrists. We rode for an hour or more and I figured they was takin' us out to be shot. Instead, we pulled into another camp. It was much smaller and deeper in the jungle. When we got down from the truck, we was marched across the grounds to a buildin'. The camp commander come out of the hut-like buildin'. When I looked up at him, I almost grinned. It was that little bastard whose blood I wanted on my hands. He looked us over, but he made no indication that he recognized me. After barkin' a lot of warnings and threats, he turned and went back inside. We was taken to cages that was set up on a hill. There was huge leaves that covered the tops and the floors was just dirt. We was put about eight to ten in each cage. We had water in troughs, the kind ya would put water in for the pigs. Then they throwed slop in the cell about twice a day. It was a scramble every time to see who got the best crap. I still couldn't hardly get around 'cause of my legs, but there was one guy, Ronnie, who would always scrounge a little extra and give it to me. About the time I got to where I could fend for myself, they come and took Ronnie away. I don't know where or why, but we never saw him again. They replaced him with a new guy, but not new to me, he was Sherll, one of my platoon. He'd been there when they'd killed Beni." Bridger paused.

I didn't know what to say to Bridger or what to do. My heart hurt so bad for him. Somehow I was sure that if I'd heard any of this before that it would ring a bell somewhere in my mind.

"The three men that'd brought him started to walk away when one turned back and stared at us. His arrogance was nauseatin' and it was even worse when he spit on the ground in contempt. My blood boiled as I recognized the little bastard. I vowed not to die or leave until I'd settled the score with him. Shelly, it took months of questionin', beatings and stuff I won't even tell ya about, but eventually Sherll helped me make a plan. I didn't care what they done to me as long as I got my hands on that animal. Once the others understood what'd happened, they was more than willin' to help out. They only took us out one at a time, so the rest of us had plenty of time to work on the plan. We dug at night and sometimes in the early dawn. We would dig as much as we could and then put the loose soil back in the hole. It was easy to dig out once we loosened it. Every night we would dig deeper until we had about four foot of loose dirt in the back of the cage. Then we waited. On rare occasions, the little bastard would stroll through the camp, most times with one or two others, but sometimes he would be alone. That was what we had to wait for and then lure him on up to our cell. One of the prisoners spoke very good Vietnamese and had learned that the target was very nervous about being charged as a war criminal and had been advised that he shouldn't lose another prisoner in his care. When the chance finally come, we had it down. I leaned against the door like I was unconscious and the other men started to call out to him. The one who spoke Vietnamese told him that he thought I was dead. Hell Shelly, they was so convincin' that they had me wonderin' for a minute. The little jerk kicked at the wire door, then kicked again only harder. I fell over against the wall. He pulled out his gun and told the others to get back in the corner and he grabbed me by the neck of my shirt and started to pull me out. That was when I grabbed the arm with the gun in it and Sherll knocked him out with his fist. We dragged him inside as quietly as we could. Now, we knew that there was no way we could escape 'cause the camp was very heavily guarded, but my friends knew what this chance for revenge meant to me. They quickly dug the loose dirt from the hole and we rolled him into it. Then we waited. It took awhile for him to wake up and I took great pleasure in seein' his eyes widen when he realized what'd happened. That night I found in myself a very vile animal that wanted nothin' more in life than to see him suffer . . . to see him pay for what he'd done. He opened his mouth to yell, but I filled it with the very dirt that would cover what was left of him when we was done. I tied his own scarf around his mouth to make sure he couldn't spit it out. I told the interpreter to tell him who I was and remind him of the beautiful young girl he'd mutilated. Then I saw true terror on the face of the animal I hated so much. The men sat all around keepin' watch on the camp as I took the bastard's own knife and put it to his throat, just as he'd done to Beni. Very slowly I sliced from ear to ear and watched his eyes as the life slipped out of his body. When it was done, I felt like the life had drained out of my own body. I'd lived on hate and revenge for so long that there was nothin' inside anymore." Bridger started to sob openly. "That . . . that wasn't me, Shelly! I'd never hurt anybody in my life. In war yes, but that was kill or be killed, not just outright kill just to see somebody die." He paused for a long time and I thought that maybe he was finished.

"Sherll . . . Sherll and some of the others finished our plan. The hogs was just below where we were held so we tossed . . . parts of . . . we got rid of him piece by piece, then we buried his clothes and weapons in the ditch. We packed the ground down as good as we could and then, to discourage anybody from searchin' there, we dumped the toilet bucket on the area and tossed it down into the pig sludge below. We watched that disgustin' bucket sink as we rubbed the blood from us with sand and gravel. It was done! Our little bit of revenge gave me a feelin' of happiness at fulfillin' a promise, but it gave me even greater doubts about my real self.

Oh they searched, they cussed and yelled, and beat every one of us in the camp for weeks. It was durin' one of these times that one of the soldiers was adamant I knew somethin' about the disappearance. He put his knife to my throat, I guess just to scare me, but it upset the new commander more than it did me. He reached to knock the knife away, but jammed it in my throat instead. The result was the voice I have now. They never learned or found a thing and after awhile the matter just disappeared.

Several months later we were moved back to Hanoi and after a few more years we finally got to come home. I never expected to see America again. Most times it was all like a friggin' nightmare. When I got home, nothin' felt the same. I couldn't handle crowds at all and I hated towns and cities. I just wanted to be alone." He stopped again and picked up a stick and started to doodle in the dirt. "Ya know, I still have that little piece of material. I held on to it the whole time. I don't know how I ever thought I could replace her . . . but I come damn close, Shelly. I owe ya so much and I'll make it up to ya. I promise and I will." With that, Bridger got up and walked into the woods and disappeared.

I had no idea what he meant by that last part. My head was spinnin' with all he'd told me and I couldn't help but wonder where we'd go from here.

Chapter 7

Eesa was gettin' big, but she still thought she was my baby. She was into everything! I really enjoyed the late night when she wanted to play outside. She never wandered very far from me and her pan of water that I kept outside for her to wash her food and everything else she thought needed washin'. Sometimes she even washed rocks and I so loved to watch her little hands as she handled each item so carefully. I always put some food out for her to find, but she done pretty good at findin' some stuff on her own. It was late, or early, however ya looked at it.

"C'mon Boots, let's go inside." Eesa just looked at me and made no move toward the door. Then it dawned on me, why did I call her Boots? Who was Boots? It sounded familiar, but then again . . . it didn't.

"Let's go Eesa, I'm tired."

We slipped in quiet-like so we didn't wake up Bridger. He seemed much more relaxed and at peace with hisself since he'd opened up and told me his story. It was hard for me 'cause every time I looked at his beautiful face and saw that scar on his forehead or heard his sweet whispery voice, I remembered how it'd happened and my heart would hurt for him. It was easy to see why I was attracted to him, yet he'd never said how we met or anything about our relationship.

****

I woke up the next mornin' to the smell of coffee and food. I'd always cooked for us and I was surprised to find Bridger at the stove.

"Good mornin'," I said as I crawled out of bed. "Here, let me do that."

"No, sugar, you've done enough for me. Today I'm makin' it all up to ya."

He handed me a plate and a cup of coffee and I sat down on my bed to eat. Bridger took his and come and sat beside me.

"You're a good cook, but why so much?" I teased.

He smiled at me, "I gotta keep ya full and happy."

We finished eatin' and sat quietly drinkin' our coffee.

"I am happy, but I'll be a lot happier when I can remember everything about our life."

Bridger looked down at the floor and his silky blonde hair fell around his face. My heart skipped a beat as I took in the beauty of the man beside me.

"I . . . I . . . I think you're startin' to. That's why I have to tell ya that, I wish we'd met in another time and place."

I started to speak, but he put his finger over my lips.

"Let me finish, while there's time. I do love you, very much, but this just ain't right and I have to fix it. I don't want to, but I know it's the right thing to do." Then he took me into his arms and kissed me with true love and passion. I kissed him back in the way I'd wanted to for so long. I felt a warmth cover my body and my head started to spin. Wow! What a kiss! I pulled back and looked into his eyes and I heard him say, "I'll always love you Shelly."

****

I stretched as the sunlight began to shine brightly on my face. I needed a drink, my mouth was so dry I could hardly swallow and my eyes were so heavy I couldn't seem to open 'em. I reached for my covers and pulled 'em over my head and immediately fell back asleep.

"Hey! Hey!" I heard someone say as a foot nudged my backside.

"Are you okay? Ya can't be sleepin' out here. Sit up." The voice commanded.

I tried to ignore it and curled up tighter.

"Did ya hear me? You're not aloud to sleep on the sidewalk." The voice spoke louder.

It started to get through to me that somethin' was goin' on. Why would Bridger be talkin' to me that way?

"Get up, now," I heard as somebody pulled my blanket away.

I opened my eyes and was stunned to find myself starin' up at a very tall man that I didn't recognize at all. I quickly pulled my wits about me and sat up straight. Where in the hell was I at? A car went past and I heard a dog bark nearby. I pushed the hair out of my face and looked around for a minute. Then I heard the voice almost yell.

"Lilah? Lilah Parker, is that you? Oh my dear Lord, where have ya been?" The man squatted down beside me and brushed the rest of my hair back and looked at me like he'd just seen a ghost.

"C'mon, let's get ya inside. Where the hell have ya been girl? We been searchin' all over for ya!" he said as he helped me to stand. I didn't know what to say. I didn't know the man and I had no idea where I was. He wrapped the blanket around my shoulders and led me into the door of the buildin'.

"Stan!" he yelled. "Stan! Look who I found sleepin' just outside the door."

It was only a minute and another man come into the room. He stopped dead in his tracks. "Lilah?" he almost whispered. "Oh hell, Lilah girl! You're back! Where have ya been honey? We was just about to give up the search and . . . and now . . . now you're here."

I just sat quietly and stared at the two strangers like they was mad or somethin'. I didn"t have no idea what they was talkin' about.

"Lilah? Talk to me. What's wrong? Don't ya know who I am? It's me, Stan." He said.

I looked him over and tried with all my strength to recall if I knew him, but there was nothin' there.

"Where . . . who are ya?" I managed to ask.

"It's me, Stanley, the sheriff. We known each other all our lives. What's happened to ya, honey?"

"Where am I? Where's Bridger? I don't understand what's goin' on here." I felt tears roll down my face. I was so confused and just down right scared.

"It's okay sugar. Just relax for a minute," Stanley said. Then I heard him say to the other man, "Hoyt, go get Doc Garren. Hurry, quick as ya can." The other man didn't waste no time runnin' out the door and slammin' it behind him.

"C'mon Lilah, lay down over here and rest for a minute. Everything is gonna be just fine."

I wasn't at all sure about lyin' down, so I just pulled my legs under me on the couch and wrapped my blanket around me. This man seemed to be sure that he knew me. But why oh why could I not recall him at all.

"Do ya have any idea where ya been for the last few months?" he asked.

I sat there not sure what I should say. Of course, I knew where I'd been. I'd been with Bridger up on the mountain where we lived. I wasn't sure if that was any of his business, but I was even more confused about how I'd got on the sidewalk where they'd found me. The door opened and the man Stan had called "Hoyt" and another man that I guessed was the doctor hurried inside the room.

Stan got up and took the doctor just outside the door. They was gone only a couple a minutes.

The man I thought was the doctor pulled up a chair and sat down in front of me.

"Lilah, Stan tells me that you don't seem to recognize him. Is that true?"

Somehow I felt comforted by this man's quiet voice and gentle manner.

"I . . . I don't know any of ya'll. I don't know where I am or how I got here. I just wanna go home."

"Okay, well, let's get ya over to the clinic and check ya out and then we'll see about gettin' ya back home. Okay?"

"Then I can go home?" I asked. "Do ya promise?"

"Yes, honey." He answered as he helped me off the couch and we walked toward the door. He turned to Stan, "See if ya can find Floy and Toby and . . . yeah, Dee too."

****

I sat in the doctor's office on a bed and we talked for quite awhile. He was real easy to talk with and I was pretty comfortable with him.

"Do ya remember where you've been?" he asked quietly.

"Yeah."

"Would you tell me where?"

"Sure. I was at home."

"What do you mean, 'home'?" he asked.

"I was at my home on the mountain. Why?"

"Lilah, was you at Terra de Gracia?"

"My name's Shelly and I have no idea what you're talkin' about."

He looked at me strange like and just sat there.

"Me and Bridger live up on the mountain in our lean-to. I don't know how I got down here. I think I'm lost." I told him. "Can ya help me get back home?"

About that time, the door to the office opened and two people come in the room. The man was tall with blonde hair like Bridger's only short and the woman was short with long dark hair and big dark eyes. They started towards me, but the doctor put his hand up and stopped 'em.

"Shelly . . . did you say? Shelly, this is some friends of mine. Do they look at all familiar to you?"

I looked at the man for several minutes, but after awhile I couldn't find nothin' about him that I recognized. Then I turned to the woman who was with him. I studied her face carefully 'cause I felt like I should know her. It was like a thought or a memory was just a blink away. I wondered why she had tears in her eyes. I thought that she was very pretty. I looked back at the doctor and shook my head no.

"Lilah!" I heard the woman cry out. "It's me, Floy. I've been your best friend all our lives!" I looked more closely and suddenly I had a flash of someone who looked a lot like her standin' in a doorway with a little girl.

"No . . . no my name is Shelly. How could I know you?"
The man stepped toward me and gently took my hand.

"Don't ya remember me, honey? How could ya forget somebody so big and ugly. I'm Toby, Floy's husband. You and Chad was in our weddin'."

There was another flash in my head of a man with silver-blonde hair and sparklin' blue eyes and he was cryin'. I grabbed my head and jumped from the table to run to the door. I just wanted to go home. These people was confusin' me, and scarin' me to the point that I thought I was losin' my mind. I barely hit the floor when I caught my foot on somethin' and fell head first into a desk that was sittin' there. I faded into the thick dark that surrounded me.

****

The first thing I realized was that I could hear people talkin' in soft tones. I tried to open my eyes, but somebody had put a wet cloth over my forehead and eyes. I reached up and pushed it away and looked around the little room . I was layin' on a bed in a room and for a minute I thought I was in a hospital room; that was when I recognized that it was one of Dr. Garren's exam rooms.

"She's startin' to come around," I heard somebody say. "She'll be okay. She just knocked herself out when she fell. I'll check to make sure she doesn't have a concussion, but I think she'll be fine."

"Are ya gonna put her in the hospital or keep her here?" someone else asked.

"I'm not real sure at this point exactly what to do."

"Well, I'd like to go home if I can find my car." I mumbled.

There was dead silence.

I finally managed to sit up to find several faces that was all starin' at me. I had a heck of a headache, but it was clear to me that I recognized all those faces. I wasn't sure about the names or how I knew 'em . . . but I was aware that I knew 'em well. "Dr. . . Garren? Is that right?" I asked.

"Yes" he answered slowly. "Can you tell me your name?"

I thought for a minute. It was like a fog was liftin' and things started to roll inside my head. Memories, names, and places were almost new to me, yet I was rememberin'.

I looked at him and started to grin like an idiot! "Yeah, I can. My name's Lilah Parker and I live on the ranch with my boys and my friend Dee. I remember! I do! I really remember!"

Floy started towards me, but Dr. Garren stopped her.

"Who's this lady?" he asked.

I started to cry as it all flooded back like a river. "That lady's my very best friend in the world, Floy Ellis!"

Her and Toby come to me and we hugged 'til I thought I'd never breathe again. I could remember everything.

Dr. Garren sat there and smiled as he scratched his chin. "I've heard of this happening, but it's the first time I've ever seen it. It's a documented fact that sometimes amnesia patients can receive a knock on the head and the memory will start to open up, so to speak. Lilah, your memory not only opened up, it streamed right through whatever was causin' the amnesia in the first place. Are you dizzy or nauseated?"

"No, but I do have a awful bad headache," I said.

He took my blood pressure and looked into my eyes with a flashlight.

"I don't see any sign of a concussion, honey. I'll give you somethin' for your headache, but I want you to stay awhile and let me observe you for a few hours, okay?"

"Then I can go home?"

He looked at Floy and Toby. "What do you think? I'm wondering how to handle this with the babies. This has really been hard on them." He questioned.

I stayed for several hours while the doctor kept watch on my blood pressure and Floy went out to the ranch.

We'd decided it was best to just tell the boys that I'd been on a trip and I'd had to leave unexpectedly. Toby, Floy, and Dr. Garren had been full of questions about where I'd been for so long and how I'd survived. They said that Pride had come in after two or three days, but there was no clue as to where he'd been. I thought for a long time about all that'd happened up on that mountain. I finally told 'em that I wasn't ready to talk about any of it yet. There was a lot I had to come to grips with before I shared it with anyone.

Chapter 8

I'd been home about two weeks and I'd put up with a million questions from Stanley, the sheriff, as well as Floy, Toby, Dee, and even my little boys. I'd answered as honest as I could, but I never told any of 'em Bridger's name. I only said I'd been rescued by a man who lived alone in the mountains. I said he'd saved my life and that was pretty much the truth. One of my deepest hurts besides Bridger, was Eesa. I missed that little girl so much and I prayed that he was takin' good care of her. I felt sure he would 'cause he knew how much I loved her and I hoped against hope that she would bring him some comfort.

It seemed like life'd picked up pretty much where it'd been left. It didn't take long for me to fall back into our regular routine. Dee'd kept everything close to normal for the boys, but I could tell that she'd been under a lot of stress.

****

Dee and the boys was already up when I managed to force myself out of my bed. I couldn't remember the last time I'd slept-in like that. I laid there for a few minutes and thought about how I would have been up already with Eesa and it still seemed strange that my old rooster hadn't woke me up in the mornings. I missed that old pain in the butt! I went downstairs and found 'em finishin' up their breakfast.

"Mommy!" squealed Jonny as he bailed from his chair. "You're alive!"

I had to laugh. "Well, of course I am. What did ya think I was?"

"Well, Dee says ya was sleepin' like the dead," he answered very seriously.

"Yeah, dat's what she say, Mama," chimed in Eli.

"That just means that I was sleepin' really good. Not that I was dead!" I shook my head and Dee and I tried to control our need to laugh out loud.

Among the nonstop chatter and giggles, I finished my breakfast and went upstairs to dress. I felt a great need to go into town to the nursin' home where I'd been volunteerin' for several years. It'd been a long time since I'd been in to see 'em all. I'd developed a very close relationship with several of the residents there. Lamar was one of my favorites. He was an elderly, blind man that I'd fell in love with on day one. When I first started to work there, I met a precious little lady that everybody just called Miss Mae. She had passed away just a few months before I found out that I was expectin' the twins. I named my Jonny after her son, Jon Barron. He'd died in the war and I don't think she ever quit grievin' for him. She put up a brave face, but somehow I just knew.

****

"Lamar?" I asked as I peaked my head in the door.

"Yes, sweet girl?" He answered. "Come on in."

"I was hopin' ya was awake. I haven't got to see ya in a very long time. How ya doin'?"

He laughed and wagged his finger at me. "Now you know darn good and well that I don't sleep in the daytime. I might up and miss somethin'."

"Oh really . . . is that why Mr. Gresham next door teases ya about your snorin'?" I asked him.

"Well, he must've confused me with somebody else. I know I don't snore 'cause I listened to find out!" He broke out in a big belly laugh. "Oh, I'm so glad to see ya. We was all just worried to death about ya. It seems to me that if there is a mess anywhere to fall into . . . you have a way of findin' it! Ya workin' today?"

"I guess, if ya want to call this workin'. I call it just visitin' with the people I love."

"When ya gonna bring them little 'uns up here so we can see 'em? It's been a long time. I bet they growed a foot by now."

"Yeah, they sure have and they're gettin' as ornery as a pair of wolf cubs. They're curious about everything and into most of it!"

"Honey, I don't mean to bring up ill memories, but . . . do ya ever hear from their Daddy? Does he call or come see 'em?" He asked uneasily.

I thought for a moment before I answered. I could never lie to Lamar. Even though he was blind, he could tell more from your voice than ya would think.

"He calls sometimes around Christmas, but he's never seen 'em. It's not 'cause he don't want to . . . I think that for whatever reason, he can't."

Lamar set there for a couple of minutes with his head down and rubbed his wrinkled old hands together. "Lilah, I don't share this with many, well, actually none." He motioned for me to sit down in the chair beside him. "Ya see, before I lost my sight, back when I was a kid, I realized somethin' that I knew nobody would understand. I realized I had a gift. Some might call it a curse. In some ways I guess it might be, but I can see things that other people don't. Yeah, I know I'm blind . . . but before that, I could see things."

"What do ya mean Lamar? See things like what?" I asked a little nervously.

"Hmmm . . . I . . . I could see people. People that'd already passed. I saw my grandpa many times, but he died before I was born. I recognized him from pictures I seen of him. He was usually down at the fishin' pond where I often went by myself. It was really hard sometimes 'cause I could hardly tell who was real and who wasn't."

I guess I had a shocked look on my face 'cause he stopped short.

"I can sense the look that must be on your face, honey. I don't want to spook ya. I'm just tellin' ya the way it is. When I lost my sight, I already knew it was gonna happen 'cause grandpa had told me. It was a big change for me, but even though I couldn't see life . . . I could still see the people and events from the past, the present, and the future. For instance, there's a little woman that comes here with you most times. She's a tough lookin' old bird but she has a heart of gold and she loves you more'n anything in the world. She told me I should just call her Nanny. She likes comin' here and seein' ya with older folks. She says you have a way with older people that makes them love you very much. I can vouch for that. I saw it from the beginin'." He paused for a minute. "I was just informed that ya spent many years takin' care of her up on the mountain. The love and appreciation she has for ya is limitless."

I could hardly believe what he was tellin' me. I'd never told anyone at the home much about my private life. My job was to listen and tend to them.

He raised his head and held out his hand to me. "I have to tell ya somethin' sweet girl."

"What is it, Lamar? You look a little upset." I said.

"It's about your friend, Chad. He, well, he . . . he's not who ya think he is. That's not a bad thing. He's a good man, in fact, he's one of the most descent people I ever met. I feel honored to have met him. You're right, he wants more than anything to come back. His situation in life just won't allow it."

"Lamar? Where is he? What's his real name?" I asked as tears began to roll down my cheeks.

The door suddenly swung open and Junie from the front desk rushed in the room. "Lilah!" She said breathlessly. "There's a call from your friend, Dee. There's been an accident. She needs to talk to ya real quick."

I forgot about everything as I ran down the hall to the phone.

"Hello?" I almost shouted.

"Lilah . . . it's me. Eli took a tumble off the fence and split his chin. I'm on my way to Bigby with 'em. Meet me at the hospital."

"Okay, I'm on my way." I told her as I hung up the phone.

I rushed to the car and headed toward the hospital.

Chapter 9

I hurried into the emergency room to find Eli on a table with a bloody cloth pressed to his chin.

"Are ya okay baby? What did the doctor say?" I asked as I turned to Dee.

She was wide-eyed and pale as she hurried to me.

"I'm so sorry Lilah. I should've been out there watchin' 'em. I went in to get a drink when Jonny came screamin' through the front door. He said Eli was dead! I went flyin' out in the yard and found him lyin' on his back on the other side of the fence." She paused for a breath.

"Dee . . . what did the doctor say?" I begged.

"Oh, yeah. He said he has to have some stitches and . . . well, he lost a tooth." She answered.

It was then that the doctor walked in the room.
I held out my hand to him. "I'm Eli's mama. I just got here."

"It's a pleasure to meet you. We need to put a few stitches in this young mans chin and then he'll be ready to go home."

"You ready big guy?" He asked Eli.

"Me can do dis." Eli answered with a shaky little voice that held a lot of determination. "Can't me Mama? I can do it!"

The way he looked at me with those wide, crystal blue eyes, pulled my heart strings. His little top tooth was gone and his little chin, neck, and shirt was covered in blood. The doctor explained about deadenin' his chin and then doin' the stitches. Eli was okay until there was talk about a needle.

"No, me goin' home now. It be fine. Mama can puts a banage on it and a kissy and it be just fine," he stated as he began to try to climb down from the table.

"No baby. We have to do this. If we don't, it will look ugly and we don't want that on your beautiful little face," I tried to explain.

He thought a minute before he declared that he liked ugly and again, decided it was time to go home.

"Lay down and let the doctor do his job and I'll tell ya the story of how I got all those scars on my foot," I told him.

"Let me see." He demanded.

I slipped my foot out of my shoe and held it up for him to examine. He studied my foot for some time while he traced the scars with his little finger.

"Does dat hurt Mommy?" He asked as he frowned.

"No, it just tickles a little." I smiled.

"Will mine tickle too?"

"Probably, after it gets well. Will you let the doctor fix it now?"

He nodded his little blonde head and laid back on the table.

"Here, let me hold your hand." I told him as I tried to take his cold little hand.

"No fank ya. Me can do dis. 'Member, Uncle Toby says me and Jonny is the man of your house," he stated firmly.

"You're right. Ya sure are the men of my house and I am so proud of how brave ya are."

It was tense for a few minutes as the doctor deadened the wound, but true to his word, Eli stared straight ahead as a few little tears rolled down his cheeks. He never said a word. I couldn't believe the determination on his little face.

"I think this might require a trip by the ice cream store. What do ya think Eli?" I asked him.

"Yes ma'am. I sure 'nuff do." He turned and smiled at me with a few tears still glistenin' in his Daddy's beautiful blue eyes.

By the time Dee, Jonny, Eli, and me had finished ice cream and visited the Toy Barn, we were more than ready to find our way home. We just got to the car when an almost familiar voice called out.

"Miss Parker? I mean . . . Lilah. How are you doin'? I've tried to get in touch with you several times."

I turned to see Ross Tyler comin' toward us.

"Hi. We're doin' pretty good, Ross. One of my boys here tried to ride the fence and it got the best of him. Cost him five stitches in his little chin and a tooth." I told him.

"Oh, no. That's too bad." He answered as he knelt down to Eli. "When I was about your age, I tried to fly off my granddaddy's barn. It cost me a broke arm, six stitches, and a red butt."

Eli looked puzzled. "What's a red butt?"

"It's what I got from my daddy after I got well . . . for jumpin' off that barn!"

"What did ya do wif it?" Eli innocently asked.

"With what?" Ross looked surprised.

"Wif the red butt."

"Well, I sat very carefully on it for awhile. Have you never gotten a red butt?" Ross teased.

"Do I got one of 'em, Mama?" Eli asked.

"No. But ya have had a couple of pink ones." I laughed. "Ross means that he got a spankin'."

"Oh, no. I sorry, Mr. Ross." Eli answered sincerely.

"Thank ya, but it's okay. I lived to talk about it." Ross smiled as he turned to me. "Are ya about ready to bring that colt in? We had agreed to a date, but then you didn't show up. That's why I'd tried to call you."

"Well, somethin' come up and I had to go out of town for awhile. I'm really sorry. Do ya think we could do it this Saturday? Say five o'clock?"

"Yep . . . I'll be lookin' forward to it. I knew something must have happened. Did you have a good trip?" He asked.

"Yeah, it was interestin' to say the least. Sooo . . . I'll see ya then."

Before I could turn around twice, it was Saturday. Toby's cousin, Seth, was back for a short visit, and he brought his truck over so him and

Toby could help me load Promise into the trailer. It was his first time in a trailer since he was just a little colt. For a moment, I was afraid to let myself recall that day. It was just before Christmas that Mr. Colonel had his men deliver him to my house. He was gonna be Chad's surprise for Christmas. That was the night . . . the night I dared not let myself remember. I shook my head to clear it. Promise let out a very loud neigh and tried to kick the doors. I climbed up with a couple of cubes of sugar for him. Once I gave him the little treat and stroked his head gently, he calmed down.

After he was settled, I climbed in the truck with Toby and Seth. I still was very uncomfortable with Seth. I well remembered what had happened and the way he'd simply said he was sorry and rode away. He acted like nothin' had ever happened. I wouldn't be forgettin' it any time soon. We headed out to Bigby and The Split T Farriers. It was a rough ride down the old mountain road, but we finally hit pavement and I knew that my little horse probably appreciated it as much as I did. We arrived, still in one piece. Mr. Tyler was outside when we arrived and come straight to the truck. "Five o'clock sharp. I like that." He grinned as he opened my door and held out his hand. I stepped out of the truck and walked around to the back of the trailer.

"I need to help get him out. He is really only used to bein' handled by me." I told him as I opened the back gate.

I stepped inside and went to the front to reassure Promise that everything would be okay. I rubbed his neck and nose and talked softly to him like I always did. It was no time and he settled right down. Once we got him out on solid ground, he was much more at ease.

Ross walked around him and stroked his neck and flanks. "This is one beautiful horse, Lilah. He looks like he comes from excellent stock. I'm surprised he hasn't already been broken."

"Well, I just kept thinkin' that . . . well, I just kept puttin' if off. He's kinda like a baby to me. You'll be sure that he's well taken care of? I'd like to meet the guys who are gonna be trainin' him, if that's okay."

"Sure, come on and we'll take Promise around to his stall and I'll introduce ya to the fellas." Ross answered as he took the reins and started around the buildin'.

There was several guys around the stable. They all stopped and stared at Promise and immediately come over to him.

"Is that a gift for me, Ross?" One of 'em called out over the others.

"In your best dreams!" Ross answered. "He's just here for a little fine tunin'."

One of the men come right up and began to pet my horse. He wasn't as tall as Ross and had the dark skin of an Hispanic. His black hair glistened in the sunlight as he walked all the way around the horse.

"He's very beautiful, Señorita." He smiled and flashed a set of beautiful white teeth.

Ross stepped up and said, "This is Lilah Parker, Mike. Lilah, this is Miguel De La Cruz. He prefers to be called Mike. He will be in charge of trainin' Promise.

I held out my hand, "It's nice to meet ya, Mike. I hope you'll take good care of my baby here. He's very, very important to me."

Mike wiped his hand on his pants, then took mine, "Yes ma'am. You can be sure he'll be my most important project. Now come with me Promise, and I'll get ya settled in your temporary home."

As he led my horse away, I turned to Ross. "I hope you'll keep an eye on him."

"Of course I will. Mike's my best handler. He's only been here a little over a month, but he has a way with horses like I've never seen before. He came in with a horse he had and wanted shoes on him. By the time we were done, I hired him. Best thing I've ever done!"

I felt very comfortable by the time I left and headed back up the mountain. Seth and Toby chatted endlessly on the way home about the different horses and how the trainers seemed so close to all of 'em.

When I got home and back in my house, I was relieved to be out of the truck and away from Seth even though I was tryin' not to be resentful. Mostly, I felt a little sad 'cause I knew that Pride was down at the barn all alone. I was sure that he didn't have no idea what was goin' on in his life. First Patton had left and now Promise was gone. I gave my babies a quick hug and went back out and down to the barn. Pride had just come up from the pasture and was waitin' at the corral gate. I could almost see the questions in his big brown eyes. I offered him a cube of sugar and rubbed his neck. "It's okay, sweet boy. He'll be home before ya know it." I felt a twinge in my gut when I said that. I thought about Patton . . . and Chad. They would never be home. No matter how often I told myself that, I always seemed to have a little thread of hope buried up in there somewhere.

I'd just walked in the door when the phone rang. "Hello?" I answered.

"Lilah? This is Ross. Were ya busy?"

"No, I just come in from the barn. Is somethin' wrong?" I asked nervously.

"No. There's nothing wrong, I just wanted to know if you would be interested in going to dinner with me tonight. I meant to ask you while you were here, but we were so busy and you left before I realized it. So how about it? Would you like to go get a bite to eat?"

"Well, yeah. Sure. Do ya want me to meet ya in town?" I asked him.

"No. Just tell me how to get to your place and I'll pick you up there. No self-respecting man would ask a girl out and then make her drive half way." He laughed.

I hadn't had a real date in so long. I hardly knew where to start. I made sure that Dee was okay with watchin' the boys and then I went upstairs to figger out what to wear. As I dug through my closet, I come across the powder blue shirt I'd wore when Chad and I'd gone out years ago. He'd worn a shirt to match, the same one the babies still slept with at night. An uneasy feelin' crept into my stomach as I stood there. I felt guilty, but I wasn't sure why. I'd been willin' to get involved with Seth and hadn't give it more than a passin' thought and I didn't even want to think about what'd happened with Bridger. Still I found myself starin' at that shirt like an idiot! For the first time, I really felt like I was cheatin' on Chad or somethin'. I knew I wasn't and hadn't done nothin' wrong.

Chad was gone and I hadn't seen him in over 3 years. Yeah, we talked for a few seconds once a year, but that was nothin' I could call a committed relationship. I loved him with all my heart and soul and I knew he loved me too, but I didn't feel I could live my entire life on just a few seconds a year.

I sat down on the bed for a minute. After a couple of deep breaths, I stood up and continued my search.

I took my bath, fixed my hair, and got dressed. Before I knew it, there was a knockin' on the door.

"Hi. Come on in." I said as I opened the door.

Ross stepped inside. "Hi. Wow, you look gorgeous."

"Thank ya. I wasn't sure what to wear. I hope we ain't goin' nowhere too fancy."

"No, there's a little café over in Dover that I thought we would try and then maybe a movie, if you'd like. He smiled handsomely.

****

The drive was nice enough and I enjoyed the conversation. Ross was a real pleasant person. We talked about horses and how he'd got in the business of providin' services for horse owners. He sure seemed to know a lot about horses and their care.

It wasn't long before he pulled into the parkin' lot of the café. I was surprised when I realized that it was the same one that Toby, Floy, Chad, and I'd come to several times. It didn't feel at all right bein' there with somebody else. I suddenly wished I'd just stayed home, but it was way too late now. Ross was already openin' the car door for me.

"Is this okay, Lilah? I've been intending to try this place. I hope the food is good."

"Yeah," I answered, "It'll be fine." I felt sick to my stomach.

When we walked up to the door, it felt like that dej . . . de . . ., like when you've been there before, but ya know ya haven't. However, I knew I'd been there; it was just that everything in my life had changed. I'd had two babies with the love of my life who'd vanished for reasons known only to himself.

I took a deep breath and walked through the door that Ross held open. It seemed like the same people doin' the same old thing they was the last time I was there. The last time I'd been with Chad. I'd never planned on goin' there again, yet there I was.

We'd just sat down when I looked up to find my friend, Stanley, the Sheriff, standin' beside my table.

"Hey girl, how ya been? I ain't seen ya in a while. Are ya feelin' better? We sure was worried about ya for a while there." He said as he leaned over and gave me a hug.

I hugged him back. "I'm doin' lots better now. I pretty much got all my memory back and I'm sure glad to be back with my family. How 'bout you, how you doin'?"

"Yeah, I bet them boys was glad to see ya. I heard that they're cute as can be." He laughed. "I bet they do keep ya busy. Not much new with me. Same old same old, chasin' speeders and breakin' up fights. Not a lot of serious stuff in these small towns. Sometimes I wish we could get a really big case, like old Scott . . . aw . . . I'm sorry! I didn't mean to come out and say that. Runnin' my mouth without thinkin'! Forgive me?"

I was a little shook by his reminder of Scott O'Grady and all the terror he'd brung to my life. "It's okay, Stan. I know ya didn't mean nothin' by it."

He gave me another hug and after apologizin' again, he returned to his table.

"Are you okay, Lilah?" Ross seemed concerned.

"Yeah, I am. Just caught me off guard. I'm sorry I didn't introduce ya to Stanley. He's the county sheriff. I guess I've known him all my life. He's a really good friend."

Ross seemed as unnerved as me about the whole thing. "It's okay. Nothing to concern yourself about."

We ate our supper and, as always, it was very good.

Ross was set on goin' to a movie and I was pleasantly surprised to discover that I really did enjoy it. It took my mind off everything else and I relaxed for a good hour and a half. I thought Ross was a little quiet on the ride back.

"Is there somethin' wrong, Ross?" I asked.

"No. Not a thing. Why?"

"You just seem a little withdrawn and distracted." I told him. "Did I say or do somethin' wrong?"

"No. No, I was just thinkin' about the movie we just saw. I'm sorry. I didn't mean to ignore you." He smiled as he reached and took my hand.

I couldn't decide if I liked him holdin' my hand or not. In one way it felt very nice. He had big, warm, strong hands. However, I began to feel guilty again. Chad was a memory that I hadn't been at all prepared to deal with at the moment.

Now that I thought about it, that time I'd spent with Bridger was kind of a relief. I hadn't even remembered Chad, and I hadn't felt the pain in my heart that was growin' stronger ever day. I began to wonder about Chad. Had he gone out with anybody else? To be honest, I couldn't begin to imagine him not bein' somewhat involved with a woman. I knew him well enough to know that he was a normal, hot blooded male. The thought made me start to boil with jealousy. It's the first time I'd dared to let my thoughts go in that direction.

****

We pulled up in front of the cabin and Ross stopped the car.

"I had a really nice time tonight," he said as he turned in his seat.

"I did too. It . . . I . . ." that was as far as I got. Ross leaned in to kiss me, or so I thought. Instead, he just hugged me, kissed the tip of his finger, and placed it gently on my lips.

He got out of the car and come to the passenger side and opened the door. I stepped out and he put his arm around my waist and walked me to the door.

"Good night, beautiful." He said as he turned and walked away.

He didn't have no idea what he'd just done. I stepped quickly inside and shut and locked the door. As I leaned back against it, my head continued to spin. *Good night, beautiful!!!!* If I'd never heard them words again, it would've been too soon. Memories of Scott O'Grady come rushin' back like a rollin' flood.

That's what he always called me, "beautiful." It was the trashy way he had of sayin' it. The last time I'd heard it was before he brutally raped me in that damn cave where he'd held me captive for weeks. To add to the humiliation, Chad was just across from us and had to witness the whole horrible event. He'd been chained to the other wall after Scott had knocked him in the head and drug him into the same situation that I was in. I think Scott simply wanted him to witness my humiliation.

A light flicked on.

"Lilah? Is that you?" Dee called softly.

"Yeah. It's me. I didn't mean to wake ya."

"I was already awake. Eli had a bad dream that led to a trip to the potty and then a drink of water. He's back asleep, but I heard a car pull up and I figured it was you. I heard ya come in, but I got worried when ya didn't come on up the stairs."

"I was just about to. I'm really tired." I slid by the subject and started for the stairs.

"Are ya sure? Do ya need to talk?" She knew me only too well.

"No, I'm just tired and ready for bed. Good night." And with that, I made my way past her and up the stairs.

I went in to check on my babies. They was fast asleep and cuddled together with the powder blue shirt they so loved. I bent over and kissed their little sleepin' cheeks, and the collar of the blue shirt, turned, and went into my room.

As I changed and crawled into bed, an unbelievable sadness come over me. I missed my love! My heart ached to the point I thought I was havin' a heart attack. I started to cry. Cry like I hadn't allowed myself to cry for years. I eventually cried myself to sleep.

****

Just after sunrise, I got up, dressed, and headed to Floy's house. I needed to talk to someone who knew more about me and what I'd been through than anyone else. Toby had just left for work and Floy was clearin' the breakfast table when I stuck my head in the door.

"What ya doin' sis?" I called softly so I didn't wake little Laurel.

"OOhh . . . ya scared the pee out of me! What ya doin' up and about so early?" She asked as she struggled to catch the cup she'd almost dropped.

"Ya got any coffee? Maybe a little time to go with it?"

"Sure honey. What's the matter?"

"I don't know . . . nothin' probably . . . I . . . I just need to talk I guess." I tried to sound calm, but the truth was that I was about to come apart.

Floy poured the coffee and sat down. She slid a cup, along with some cream and sugar, toward me.

"Okay, what happened." It's real obvious that ya been cryin' again. Did that Ross guy do somethin'? Does Toby need to pay him a little call?"

"No. No not really . . . it's just that . . . well, I was feelin' kinda guilty from the git go. But we had a nice supper and saw a fairly good movie. But . . ."

"But what? What did he do?" She demanded.

"It's what he said, Floy. It scared the hell outta me."

"Well, what did he say? Come on Lilah, spit it out!"

I thought about it for a minute, and for a second had about decided to let it go. After all, it was probably what a lot of people say. I shook my head.

"Oh no you don't. Ya cry most of the night, come up here at daybreak, and then start shakin' your head like that . . . I don't think so!"

"Okay, you're right. Well, when Ross walked me to the door, he smiled and said . . . 'good night, beautiful.' I almost got sick to my stomach."

Floy looked at me for a moment and took a sip of her coffee.

"And that's what you're so upset about? Any girl in the world would love to be told that. What the heck is wrong with you?"

I sat there a minute and stared into my cup. "That's what Scott used to call me all the time. He said it in such a way that it almost sounded nasty. I can still hear him sayin' it just before he . . . before he raped me in front of Chad."

Without warnin', the tears started up again.

Floy sat there and stared at me. "I didn't know honey, I didn't know that! I'd heard Scott say that a few times at the hospital, but I didn't know the rest. I'm sorry."

"Now that I think about it, I guess it's somethin' a lot of guys say to women. It was the last thing I expected to hear and I panicked." I told her.

"I'm sure he didn't mean nothin' but a compliment when he said it. He seems like a really nice guy. Give him a chance, sweetie. He might be just what ya need. Ya know, me and Toby was real disappointed when you and Seth didn't work out."

"Floy, the only thing I really need is Chad. When I went to bed last night, I realized how desperately alone I am. I needed him to be there, and hold me, and make me feel safe again."

"I understand that, I really do. But honey, he made his choice. I don't understand it anymore than you do, whatever his reason . . . he made his choice and he's stood by it. I knew that was why it didn't work out for you and Seth. Ya got to let it go. Ya got to let him go. I don't think he's ever comin' back. I think you know that too. I so wish I was wrong." She paused a long minute. "Honey, when ya gonna open up and tell me where ya was for those months?"

I just looked at her over the rim of my coffee cup and shook my head "no." We sat there in silence and sipped our coffee.

****

On the ride back home, I gave a good deal of thought to what Floy'd said. I was bein' ridiculous, and I was tryin' desperately to hang on to the past. Maybe she was right, maybe I needed to try and live again, but for the life of me I didn't see how that was gonna happen when every time I looked at Chad's sons, I could so clearly see their Daddy lookin' back at me.

I finally got back to the cabin and went straight to the barn to let the horse, cows, and chickens out. Pride was ready to go. He loved so much to run in the early mornin'. The cows headed for the pasture and the chickens followed me to their feed barrel. I caught myself lookin' among 'em for that stupid old rooster, my feathered alarm clock. He was nowhere to be seen and the memory of both him and Eesa still hurt my heart.

I heard Boots and Roz, my ever faithful dogs, come barkin' from under the cabin porch. I guessed I must've sneaked up on 'em when I drove up to the cabin. I fed and watered 'em and then we played some fetch with a couple of sticks they'd dragged up from somewhere in the pasture. It felt good to be outside where everything was startin' a new day.

The dogs soon tired of the game and took off barkin' up towards the little cabin. Most likely a rabbit got their attention. I was almost to the house when Eli and Jonny come racin' out the door.

"Mama? Did ya sleeped in the barn?" Jonny asked with wide blue eyes.

I picked him up and swung him around a time or two. "Well, no. Why would ya think that?" I asked him.

"'Cause ya not in you room. We looked and then we finded ya out here. What ya lookin' for?" Eli questioned. He was always askin' about everything in the world. Jonny was a little more reserved; however, there were times when they switched roles. "I was lettin' the animals out and feedin' some of 'em, then I saw that Dee let my other two animals out, so I guess, I better go feed them too." I teased.

"We not aminals, Mama. We you chidrens, 'member? We the mens of you house!" Scolded Eli.

"Unca Toby said." Added Jonny as he stared at me with those unforgettable blue eyes.

"I know. Now, let's go feed these hungry men." I said as we began to race across the yard.

Chapter 10

Several weeks had passed and I'd talked to Ross on the phone several times, but I'd avoided anymore dates with him. I didn't really know why, but I just didn't feel like I was ready just yet. Floy nagged at me a lot and Toby kept hintin' that Seth was comin' back to town before long, and I kept tryin' to ignore 'em both. There was no way I would ever even attempt to make that work!

Dee had taken the boys into town on some errands and I was just comin' downstairs with a basket full of little kids' laundry. The phone rang.

"Hello?" I answered.

"Lilah? This is Ross. I was wonderin' if you wanted to come out to the stables and see where we are with Promise. I think you'll be pleasantly surprised."

"That'd be great. What time would be good?" I could hardly contain my excitement.

"How about we go have some lunch and then we'll go to the stables?"

"Well, I do have some errands to run, but I can meet ya somewhere." I lied.

"There's a little place in Bigby that serves really good barbecue. It's called Quimpers. Would you like to try it?" He asked.

"I know where that's at. Sure, I can meet ya there about 11:00, if that's okay?"

"See you then." He said as he hung up the phone.

I only had a couple of hours and it would take a good 45 minutes to get there. I got my shower and dressed. I left Dee a note on the table and hurried to my old Jeep.

By the time I got to Mason and turned toward Bigby, I was beside myself with excitement. It'd been awhile and I'd missed my Promise more than I'd thought I would. I hoped he hadn't changed too much.

I pulled up at Quimpers at the same time Ross did. I was glad. I didn't like to be the first one there. We went inside and sat down at a table near the back. When the waitress come to the table, Ross ordered for us. I couldn't help but notice how she cleverly tried to flirt with him. I guess she thought it would bother me. No. It did not! Well, maybe just a little. I thought it was awfully rude of her seein' as how I was sittin' right there and for all she knew I might have been his wife. I could see where she was tempted, after all, he was a very good-lookin' man. Not as gorgeous as Chad . . . or Bridger, but still extremely nice to look at.

Our conversation was light and friendly. We ate and then left for the stables.

****

When I walked around the corner and into the stable where Promise was bein' kept, I stopped dead in my tracks. Standin' in the center between the rows of stables was Miguel De La Cruz. He was brushin' a horse. It was not just any horse but, a very beautiful Arabian.

"Mike?" I little more than whispered.

He looked up over the horse, "Si Señorita?"

"Where . . . how? Who's horse is this?" I asked in disbelief.

"Oh, he is mine, I guess. I found him several months ago in the forest behind my home. He was injured and very frightened. I have been caring for him and trying to get him back in good health. I have no idea how he come to be there." He explained.

"I think I might be able to answer that for ya." As I spoke, the horse suddenly turned and looked at me. He gave a loud snort and a whinny and began to run to me.

"Whoa!" yelled Mike. "Look out Señorita, I have never seen him act like this!"

Patton raced up to me and laid his beautiful head on my shoulder. I wrapped my arms around his neck and began to cry like a baby.

"Patton! You're alive my sweet boy! You're alive!" I cried out loud.

"You know this horse, Señorita? You know his name?" Mike asked excitedly.

I explained about the tornado and what I'd thought was the tragic loss of my wonderful horse. He looked at me in both shock and excitement.

"I love this horse very much." He said. "But I can see your love for him is as great, and his love for you is very great also. I will be very sad to give him up, but he is not mine to keep. I am only very happy to have been able to help him when he needed me." He smiled a sorta sad smile and handed me the reins that'd fallen to the ground.

I stood in silence. I ldidn't have no idea what to say.

"Lilah?" questioned Ross. "Is this the horse you told me about?"

"I still can't believe it." I almost whispered. "I was sure I'd never see him again. I have all my horses again."

I looked at him with tears still rollin' down my face.

"Mike, how can I ever thank ya? I'll gladly pay ya for any cost or trouble. I've been mournin' this horse for months."

"No ma'am, I am only too happy to see you two together again. But, I would like to come and visit him from time to time, if that's okay?"

"Of course, anytime ya want to, you're more than welcome."

****

As thrilled as I was with Promise and his wonderful progress, I hated to admit that it was overshadowed by havin' found Patton. Ross told me that Promise would be ready to go home by the next weekend and he would be glad to deliver both horses for me. I could hardly contain myself on the drive back home.

As I started up the mountain, I passed by Floy and Toby's place. I parked my Jeep and rushed to the door.

"Floy?" I called as I knocked frantically on the door. "Floy?"

The door swung open.

"What in the world is wrong, Lilah?" She looked frightened.

"I found him. He's alive and well! Can ya believe it? After all this time, he's comin' home!" I rambled like a maniac.

Floy just stood there with a stunned look on her face. Then a huge grin appeared as she grabbed me and gave me a big hug.

"Ya mean he's comin' home? Oh Lilah . . . I can't believe it. After all this time. Oh my sweet God . . . the boys will be completely beside theirselves. They finally get to meet their Daddy!" She was thrilled.

It suddenly dawned on me what she'd just said. "Floy . . . no . . ." I could hardly get a word in edgewise! "Floy, I'm not talkin' about Chad."

She froze and stared at me. "Not Chad? What do ya mean, not Chad?"

I hated to ruin her excitement, but I had to tell her. Somehow the joy of my news had dimmed a little.

"I wasn't talkin' about Chad, I was talkin' about Patton. I found Patton. A man at the Split T found him after the storm and nursed him back to health!

I told her the whole story and she was really surprised and happy for me, but the reality of what she'd said at first, still weighed heavy on my heart.

We sat on the porch and had iced tea and talked about what the odds of ever seein' Patton again would've been. We talked about our trip to Lexington when we'd bought Pride and Patton and how excited I was. Floy carefully avoided mentionin' that the sale we went to was the first time we'd ever laid eyes on Chad Barrett. She didn't have to, how could I ever forget? We talked about shoppin' and our stop in Memphis and our visit to Graceland. We agreed that it'd been a life changin' trip. After a while, I decided it was time to make my way back home and I left.

Chapter 11

The week passed so quick I couldn't believe it. I'd cleaned the stalls and put fresh hay and some feed in the bins and made sure everything was ready for the horses. Toby and Seth had done a great job on repairin' the end that'd been tore off by the storm. It looked better than new.

By the time Saturday got there, I was so excited I could hardly control myself. Dee had taken the boys to her mom and dad's for the weekend and I seemed to just be rattlin' around in the empty house. About noon, I heard the truck pullin' up the drive and I raced out the door. The big black truck and trailer sittin' in front of my cabin made me stop in my tracks. For just a second, I recalled Chad's black truck and trailer parked in the exact same place. I felt a twinge of pain in my chest. But when I heard one of my horses nicker loudly, I snapped out of it and ran to help Ross unload 'em.

By the time we got 'em to the barn, I could hardly wait for Pride to see 'em. I knew he would be excited. We'd hardly got to the fence when Pride come gallopin' across the pasture. Patton and Promise rushed up to him. They nuzzled each other and ya could just tell that they was so happy to be back together. Ross opened the gate and the two couldn't get inside quick enough. Of course they had to sniff and carry on for a while before they galloped away.

"I think they must have missed each other." Ross commented.

"Oh, I know they did. It's a really happy day for us all." I smiled and answered. "Do you have time for a glass of tea or maybe a cup of coffee?"

"Sure I do . . . that sounds good," answered Ross.

We drove back up to the cabin and I made us a couple of glasses of tea. We sat on the front porch while we visited.

"I really love your ranch here, Lilah. It's nice and private . . . secluded." Ross said.

"Yeah, I've lived here on and off most all of my life. It's been in the family for over a hundred years. I named it Terra de Gracia . . . or maybe I should say, the babies' Daddy named it."

"Hmm . . . Land of Grace. That's a perfect name for it . . . sounds like he was happy here. May I ask why he left?"

"That's a really hard question to answer, Ross. I think he had a lot of problems in his life and he just didn't have no choice. The only thing I know for sure is that he loved me and he didn't want to go."

"It's none of my business, but that just makes no sense. Why didn't he take you with him? What in the world could be so important that any man would leave a woman like you behind?"

I just shrugged my shoulders and shook my head. It wasn't the first time I'd asked myself that question and I doubted it would be the last. I didn't have no answer for him.

"Can we just drop the subject. I'd just as soon not talk about it." I told him as I looked out across the road.

"That's no problem. Let's talk about dinner tonight. Where would you like to go? We'll celebrate the homecoming of two beautiful thoroughbreds."

"I . . . uh . . ."

"I just won't take no for an answer." He smiled.

It was too hard to resist. He had a certain charm about him that I could hardly ignore.

"Okay. That sounds real nice."

****

Ross waited while I changed my clothes and we headed for town.

"Where do you think you would like to eat?" He asked.

"It don't matter to me. Just about anything'd be good. What sounds good to you?"

"I'll surprise you." He teased.

We drove a ways past Bigby and before long we turned up a little paved driveway. Ross parked in front of a beautiful big home and come around and opened the door and took my hand.

"Where are we?" I asked him.

"This is my home." He answered as he opened the front door. "Welcome."

I'd never seen such a beautiful place in my life. Of course the plantations in Lexington had took my breath, but I'd never thought of anyone really livin' in 'em. This was somethin' I'd only seen in magazines.

"Ross, this is so nice. I never seen nothin' like it." I must've sounded like a for real hillbilly.

"Well, I have to tell you. I'm just leasing the place. It was all I could find when I first moved here. I'm hoping to buy it one day. Sit down for a little while and I'll have dinner ready in just a few minutes." He said as he turned on the TV and went into another room.

"Ross?" I called after him. "Can I help you? I don't feel right just sittin' here."

He poked his handsome face around the door. "I got this, Princess. You just sit there and do what you do best. Look beautiful!"

It seemed like no time and he come and took me into the dinin' room. I couldn't believe what I saw. There was a white tablecloth with lit candles and a place set for each of us. Ross pulled my chair out for me and I sat down. He poured us each a glass of wine and began to serve up our meal. I'd never in my life been treated so . . . well, like royalty. We had real nice grilled steaks, steamed broccoli, some kind of cheesy potatoes, and dinner rolls. We each had a small salad beside our plates and a dessert, one of my favorites, strawberry shortcake with fresh strawberries. I couldn't a done better myself. We talked a little while we ate, but mostly just about everyday things.

"I know it sounds strange, but I feel like I've known you forever. I really enjoy your company." Ross smiled across the table.

I felt kinda, I guess, warmer toward him. A lot about him reminded me of Chad, his gentleness and kindness said a lot for him.

"I enjoy bein' with you too, Ross. This sure was a good meal and my very favorite dessert." I smiled back.

He came around to my chair. "Let's go in the living room."

I stood up and we went into the fanciest livin' room that I could ever imagine. Ross went over to a cabinet and began to pour a couple of drinks.

"How about a little after dinner sherry?" he asked as he handed me a little glass of whatever the heck sherry was.

I really didn't want it, but he simply put it in my hand and I didn't really know what to say.

"It's supposed to be very good for the digestion." He said casually as he sipped the drink in his hand.

I put the glass to my lips and took a small drink. Well, I have to say that the name sherry sure sounded better than it tasted. I barely controlled my need to gag. Maybe it would be better with the second sip. I tried, but it was just as bad that time as it'd been the first. I just couldn't bring myself to be rude, so I slowly choked down the rest. I got to admit that it got a little better toward the end.

"Would you care for another?" he offered.

"Oh, I don't really think I ought to . . ." I stammered as he poured more into my glass.

We sat on the couch and talked and sipped on our drinks. A nice warm tingle started crawlin' around my body and up my neck. My lips started to feel a little fuzzy and I was becomin' very relaxed. By this time, we'd had yet another glass.

"Where's your bathroom, Ross?" I heard myself kinda slur.

"It's right down that hall and to your left. Are you alright, Lilah?" He asked.

I stood up and the room seemed to tilt just a little bit. "Yeah . . . I'm . . . fine. Just fine." I heard my voice slur again as I caught hold of the chair beside me.

When I come out of the bathroom, I found the room dark with a few candles burnin' and there was music playin' from somewhere.

"Ross?" I called. "Where are ya?"

"I'm right here." He said softly as he stepped in front of me.

He put his arm around me and we started dancin'. *This is ever so nice.* I thought as he held me and we moved across the floor. When the song ended, he pulled me in very close as his lips covered mine. His kiss was soft and very sexy. I hadn't been kissed like that since Chad. Neither Seth nor Bridger could even compare. I felt myself drawn to him and I didn't want him to stop. My senses reeled and I started to feel that deep need that only Chad had ever been able to satisfy. For an instant, a flash of shame raced through my mind as a little guilt, once again, come over me.

Ross stopped dancin' as if he knew what was goin' on in my head. I looked up at him.

"What's wrong?" I whispered.

He stood lookin' into my eyes and I couldn't help but think what beautiful blue-green eyes he had. I'd never been there, but I was sure the Caribbean Sea would be that same stunnin' color. As he pulled me closer and his lips touched mine, I felt myself melt into his strong arms.

Without a second thought, I let him gently lead me to the couch, where he laid me down and kneeled down beside me. His kisses were gentle, but passionate. I felt myself return 'em with equal passion. He kissed my neck as his hand slipped to my breast and I felt myself shudder with pleasure. I sat up and unbuttoned his shirt and ran my hands across his dark muscular chest. I could feel the chill that went through his body as I pushed his shirt off his broad shoulders. I was amazed at the very muscular body that I'd never really noticed before. His dark auburn hair shined in the candle light as I ran my fingers through it. He reached for the buttons on my blouse, then looked at me and hesitated.

"Lila, are you sure about this? I don't want you to feel obligated."

I paused for a second, "Yes . . . I'm sure." I whispered as I leaned forward and nuzzled his neck.

My blouse and bra removed, I should've felt embarrassed, but all I felt was an intense need to be with him. Ross removed my skirt and slip as I slipped out of my shoes.

"You are so unbelievably gorgeous, Lilah. You take my breath." He whispered as we slid onto the carpet. The recent rejection of Seth and the still very hard to accept loss of Bridger, had left my emotions more confused than ever.

My head spinnin', I soon found myself caught up in the passion that I'd not known for a very long time. Ross's hands caressed my body and his kisses deepened as did mine. I wanted him so badly and I knew there was no turnin' back at that point. When he moved over me, I didn't hesitate to accept him completely. Our lovemakin' was so intense that I could hardly breathe. As we joined with each other in total satisfaction, my heart pounded in my chest. The one time with Bridger, couldn't even compete. Ross lay there for a minute, then rolled to my side.

"My God, girl! You take my breath. It hasn't been that way for me in . . . I can't even begin to guess." He smiled at me then leaned over and kissed me softly. "I hope it was as good for you as it was for me."

I looked into his passion-filled eyes. "It was wonderful, Ross, absolutely wonderful." I didn't lie. I couldn't believe the satisfied warmth that covered me like a blanket.

We laid there for some time and listened to the music. Ross rolled over and began to nibble my neck. I couldn't believe the affect it had on me. I put my arms around him and held him close, very close. Kisses became instantly passionate and before I knew it, we were once again climbin' that sensuous hill to complete bliss! It wouldn't be the last time that night.

****

"Chad, I've missed ya so much." I looked into his crystal blue eyes. "I can't believe you're back, you're home at last."

He stood there. There was no smile, no embrace, only a deep sadness and disappointment in those unforgettable blues.

"Chad? Say something. Don't just stand there like that. What's wrong?" I begged.

He simply shook his beautiful silver blonde head, looked down, and walked away.

"Chad!" I cried. "Chad, wait! I'm sorry honey! I'm so sorry! Wait!"

I jumped up in the bed and with a whirlin', spinnin' head, I realized I'd only had a dream! No . . . a nightmare. I looked around, confused. I didn't have no idea where in the world I was. The door opened.

"Good, you're awake." Ross said as he come in with a tray of food. "I fixed us a light breakfast. I hope you're hungry." He smiled that very handsome smile.

I had to sit there a few minutes to try and get my poundin' head straight. I began to blush as a ton of recollections flooded my mind. Oh, Lord. I'd spent the night in Ross's house. In Ross's bed!

"Lilah? Are you okay? I brought you some aspirin. I thought you might need it." He said as he handed me three pills and a glass of water. "Don't drink but a little water. I made you a concoction that is guaranteed to make you feel better in a very short while." He sat down on the side of the bed.

I took the pills, then downed the mix of heaven knows what, and laid back on the pillows. "Thank ya, Ross." I said very meekly.

"Lilah? I don't want to think that you have any regrets about last night. I sure don't. I haven't felt like that in years. Please tell me you aren't sorry."

I sat there so embarrassed I could hardly breathe. He most likely thought that I was some over sexed bimbo. I hadn't known him long enough to let things go that far. I'd only known my ex-husband and Chad in that way. Well. I guess I needed to include Bridger in that. Although I couldn't have called it anything but what it was, just somethin' that happened and never should have. Now there was four! What was I turnin' in to. I was no better than Danna. She had pursued Chad with no shame. I dropped my head and stared at my hands.

"Princess, don't do this. Please. It was a wonderful night. It meant the world to me. If it wasn't what you wanted, then I'm sorry. I'm so sorry. I never meant to push you into anything you didn't want to do."

I looked up at him as he sat with real hurt in his eyes. "No, Ross. Ya didn't push me into anything. I . . . I, uh . . . I wanted it as much as you did. I just feel shameful to let it get to that point when I ain't known ya that long. I'm really not that kind of a girl. I guess it was just the drinks. I'm so ashamed of myself."

"Don't be. I know you're not . . . what they call, easy. I could tell that right off. You're a very decent, kind, respectable young woman. I look forward to spending a lot more time with you . . . a lot more time." He leaned over and kissed my cheek very sweetly.

Chapter 12

I sat on my front porch with a cup of coffee and watched the deer as they grazed in the pasture. Dee and the boys was still asleep and I'd had another sleepless night. It was the same thing every night. Chad had haunted me every time I closed my eyes. I remembered him sayin' once, "Ya better never let me hear of ya bein' with another man. I couldn't handle it. I just couldn't." Even though I knew there was no way he could know, I knew . . . and no one knew about Bridger but me. I tried to reassure myself that there was no way Chad had been without a woman for all these years. Women were drawn to him like a magnet. The very thought of him in someone else's bed made me sick to my stomach. So why did I feel so terribly guilty? Hell, we weren't married. We weren't never even engaged. Yes, I loved him with my heart and soul, but did he really expect me to live without any kind of relationship for the rest of my life?

The screen door opened. "What ya doin' up this early, Lilah? Did you not sleep again last night?"

"Mornin' Dee." I answered. "No, I didn't get much sleep again."

"I wish you'd tell me what's botherin' ya. I know somethin' is eatin' at ya. Does it have anything to do with the time you were gone? Ya know ya can trust me."

"I know. It's nothin', just a little depressed is all. Are the boys up yet?" I asked as I tried to change the subject.

"No, not yet. Do ya want some breakfast?"

"I don't think so. I'm goin' into town. I won't be gone long." I answered as I stood and went into the house.

I dressed and was drivin' down the road in no time. My thoughts seemed to be wrapped around my neck like a scarf that I couldn't get rid of. No matter what I was doin' or where I was, there they was.

I pulled into Floy's drive. Toby was just walkin' out the door. He paused and walked toward the car.

"Mornin', sweetheart. What ya doin' up and out this early?" he asked.

"I come to have a cup of coffee with ya but looks like you're leavin' already."

"I know it'll be disappointin', but I reckon you'll just have to settle for coffee with Floy." He grinned as he gave me a big hug.

"It will, but I guess I can suffer through it. Have a good day, Toby."

"I will." He said as he headed across the yard whistlin' and climbed into his truck and drove away.

I knocked on the door and walked inside. Floy was sittin' at the table drinkin' coffee.

"Hey, come on in. What ya doin' out so early?" She asked.

"Stopped to see if ya had any coffee made."

"I sure do. I have some breakfast ready too. Toby ate his and left and I was just fixin' to have mine. I got plenty. Sit down and enjoy your coffee.

We had a really pleasant breakfast and chatted as we finished our coffee.

"Now, what's the matter? I can tell when ya get here this early that there's somethin' ya need to get off your chest. So, let's have it." She poured us another cup of coffee and sat down.

I sat there starin' into my cup and tried to think how I wanted to say it. It seemed that anything I thought of just didn't sound right. I shook my head and wondered what she might say.

"Come on Lilah . . . somethin' is weighin' on ya and ya might as well go ahead and say it. Ya know ya will sooner or later."

She was right. I always spilled my guts to her.

"I . . . I . . . I don't know where to start. I might've done a very stupid thing, Floy. I'm pretty good at that sometimes, ya know?" I said as I watched a couple of coffee grounds float around in the bottom of my cup.

"Okay. I'll agree so far. If it helps, I can tell ya this much . . . Toby saw ya comin' home the other mornin' . . . with your date."

I was humiliated. There was no tellin' who all had seen us. It was probably the talk of the town by now.

"I know it was a stupid thing to do. I really only knowed him a few weeks. I don't know what I was thinkin'. Floy I feel so ashamed and yet . . . I don't know why. I think I feel as much guilty as I do ashamed."

"Guilty of what, Lilah? I'm sure Dee was with the boys and ya know she takes great care of 'em."

"I feel . . . like I . . . I cheated on Chad. It's like he knows. I can feel it. I dream about him every night and every night he looks at me with those beautiful, hurt blue eyes and I just wanna die!!" I confessed as tears rolled down my cheeks. "I can't eat. I can't sleep. But still I . . . I."

"You what, honey?" she asked.

I thought for a moment. How could I say it without her thinkin' worse of me than she probably already did?

"Floy, I feel so guilty, but . . . but I'm not sorry. Does that make any sense or have I lost my mind?" I sobbed.

She looked at me for a minute before she answered. "No, ya haven't lost your mind. I think ya like Ross Tyler more than ya feel ya have a right to. He seems like a really nice man, and he is very, very nice lookin'. I can understand why you're drawed to him. Besides, you're lonely sweetie. Ya haven't even given a man the time of day since Chad left. I was surprised ya agreed to go out with me and Toby and Seth. Ya have stayed hid up on that mountain with Dee and them young'uns for years now. Just waitin'!"

"I know." I whispered. "But that doesn't give me no right to act like some . . . sorry piece of . . . ."

"Hey!" Floy interrupted. "I'm not gonna sit here and listen to that crap. I know that Chad left ya for reasons unknown. But, Lilah . . . I think it's just silly for him to expect ya to live like some kinda . . . lady monk! I can bet ya a brand new dollar that he ain't livin' no life without . . . well, ya know what I mean."

True, that thought had visited my brain more'n once. I had the same reaction every time. I felt sick and wanted so bad to break somethin', anything at all! I just couldn't let myself imagine him in someone else's arms. Let alone someone else's bed. The jealousy boiled in my veins even thinkin' about it.

"Lilah? Ya know I'm right. I'm sure he ain't in love with nobody else. But . . . a man has needs and ya can bet he ain't been livin' like no monk either! I know ya didn't ask me, but I think it's time to let it go and move on with your life honey. Maybe Ross is the right man to make ya happy and help ya raise them boys. They need a full time man in their lives. At least give him a chance."

I knew she was right, it was past time. But how do ya let go of your heart? How do ya learn to breathe again? How do ya quiet the burnin' fire that even his very name starts inside ya? How in the name of all that's holy do ya learn to unlove and forget the daddy of your babies when every time ya look at 'em, he's lookin' back at ya? How?

Floy let me cry for some time. There were times I sobbed and times I just sat with tears soakin' my face and the front of my shirt. After a bit, she took my hand and we went into the livin' room.

"I wouldn't hurt ya for nothin' and ya know it, but it's been needin' to be said for a long time now. It's time to pack the memories and stash 'em in the barn and let it go. Please, for everyone's sake. Okay?"

"I have to tell ya somethin', Floy. Ya know you and Toby and even Stanley, never pushed me about my stay in the mountains. You know I told Stan in confidence, most of what I remembered. I just want to say this and nothin' more. I had no hurt, no pain, and no memories up there.

Bridger is a man I respect, admire, and I was startin' to fall in love with. You know . . . if I'd known that my memories would never come back, I would have stayed there and lived a wonderful, happy life. The only reason I woke up on that sidewalk was that somehow Bridger knew that my memory was comin' back and he gave me somethin' to make me sleep and then carried me down and left me where he thought I'd be safest. Ya have no idea what a remarkable man he is. But now, I'm back and so is my memory . . . every damn bit of it. With it come the hurt, the tears, and just as much heartache as there ever was. Now . . . I don't ever want to talk about it again."

I sat there with swollen' eyes and a runny nose and thought about all she'd said. "It's so hard to say it, but you're right. I need to break away from yesterday and move into tomorrow. It's just . . . I'm so . . . hurt. How do I turn that off?" I asked her.

"Ya don't Lilah. Ya just let it heal. Like any wound, it'll take time, but it will heal." She smiled sweetly at me.

I nodded my head and went into the kitchen for another cup of coffee. I filled me and Floy's cups and sat 'em on the table as she come to sit down. We sipped our coffee in thoughtful silence.

Chapter 13

"Hi, sweetheart. What are you making?" Ross asked as he came into the kitchen and wrapped his arms around me.

"Supper. Are ya hungry? I've been havin' to chase the boys outta here every five minutes. They think they're gonna starve. Their little appetites sure have picked up since ya been comin' over for supper." I teased.

"Good." He answered. "They need to put some meat on their little bones. They're growing boys." He added as he took his hat off and hung it on the coatrack.

Ross'd been comin' about ever other night for supper. Some nights just me and him went out to eat in town. I'd become very comfortable with havin' him there and the boys just loved him. He often took the boys out ridin' the horses. Then let 'em help brush the horses before he fed and put 'em back in their stalls. Them and Ross seemed to be gettin' pretty close. Sometimes I wondered if it was a good idea to let the boys get so involved in my personal life. If it didn't work out, I was afraid they would be hurt the most. Then, I wasn't sure exactly what it was I wanted to work out. I sure wasn't thinkin' about marriage. There was only one man that I wanted to . . . . Nope, I'd been makin' a huge effort to not let my mind go in that direction. Chad was a very hard habit to break.

Dee come down and we all ate a pleasant meal. I'd started cookin' again for the first time in a long, long time. I think Dee was enjoyin' the break in her routine. After we finished, Jonny wanted dessert.

"I'm sorry baby, but I didn't have time to make no dessert. We'll have one tomorrow night. As he tuned up to cry, Dee suggested she take 'em into Mason for a ice cream. Tears dried as shoes and socks were searched out.

"Thanks, Dee. Ya know ya don't have to do that. They can do without sweets for one night.

"I know, but I thought ya'll might want a little time alone." She said as she winked at me and picked up her purse. "Do ya'll want anything from town?"

"No. I don't think so." I couldn't help but smile as the boys rushed her out the door.

"Wow. That was subtle." Ross laughed as he stood up and started clearin' the table.

"No, just leave 'em. I can do that in the mornin'. There ain't that many anyway." I took his hand and led him into the livin' room.

We sat on the couch and relaxed. It was very quiet with Dee and the kids gone.

"Sugar, I've been wanting to talk to you about something." He wrapped his arm around my shoulders.

I looked up into his beautiful Caribbean Sea eyes and was held captive there for a moment. He had such a beautiful face and such an awesome, muscular body. I wasn't sure I'd realized before that moment how incredibly handsome Ross Tyler really was. I'd always been so blinded by memories. I felt a pleasant little shiver run thru my entire body.

"What is it, Ross?"

"Well, I've been thinking about something. I'm just not sure how you would feel about it." He sighed.

"How will I know how I'll feel until ya spit it out?" I teased.

"Well, I've been coming out here four or five times a week for a couple of months now."

"Yeah, I know, and I really enjoy ya bein' here." I smiled at him.

"I love spending time with you and the boys so much. I really love the animals and just this whole big, beautiful place." He hesitated.

"Ross . . . quit beatin' it to death and just come out with it." I encouraged him.

"What would you think about me just moving out here with you and the kids?" He asked in his deep, sexy voice.

I was startled. I'd never let that thought cross my mind. It'd never even been somethin' I'd considered.

"Well, I don't know Ross. It's kinda sudden. I would have to give it a lot of thought." I answered him truthfully.

"Is it that you don't want to live with me?" He asked with a disappointed tone in his voice.

"I didn't say that. I'll just need some time to think on it. Okay?"

"Sure. I didn't mean to upset you. I just seem to be lost when I'm not with you." He gently pulled me toward him. "You're all I can think about day and night. I want to be near you, touch you, kiss you . . . make love to you. Lilah, I'm very much in love with you." He whispered as his gorgeous lips covered anything I might've had to say. The kiss became deeper as his tongue gently slid between my lips. I felt my body shiver with anticipation. Ross picked me up and carried me up the stairs and to my room. He carefully put me on the bed and shut and locked the door. As he walked back to the bed, he unbuttoned his shirt and let it slide off his shoulders onto the floor. His eyes never left mine as he removed my clothes, slipped out of his jeans and lay down on the bed beside me. Everywhere his carressin' hands touched my body brought a gentle shiver. When he kissed my breasts and then my stomach, my body convulsed as if it had a mind of its own. His kisses were startin' a fire that was beginnin' to burn outta control. By the time he slid his knee between my thighs and we became one, I was barely able to breathe. Our passion became more intense with each movement until I thought I would scream. Then . . . at last, we were there, together on that final ride to complete satisfaction.

We laid there for a few minutes without movin'. Ross raised up on his elbow and looked deeply into my eyes. I was hopin' he would see the same satisfied contentment that I could see in his. His dark hair fell around his face and his beautiful blue-green eyes held me captive. I felt a new warmth in my heart. I never thought it possible to feel that again. It was different, but it was a start. Maybe there was hope after all.

****

It'd been two or three days since I'd heard from Ross. He'd left the night we'd discussed the idea of him movin' in and I hadn't talked to him since. It was unusual 'cause I almost always talked to him daily, sometimes a couple of times a day. I wasn't sure what to think and I hoped I hadn't upset him when I hesitated. I'd pondered it over and over in my mind. I definitely wanted to move on with my life, but it was still very hard. I hadn't slept well at all since the night we'd made love in my bed. I'd tried to ignore it, but afterward it was as if Chad was right there with us. That night I'd dreamed of him again. He was in my bedroom standin' right where he was the last time I'd seen him. He looked at me with tears in his crystal blue eyes.

"How could ya do that, Chica? Here . . . in our bed." He shook his head and looked down as he walked out the door. That sick guilty feelin' began to creep back into my heart. *No, how can ya dare to look at me with such disgust in your eyes? You're not here. Ya haven't been here. I'm livin' my life now and you're no longer a part of it, ya haven't been for a long time!*

I picked up the phone and dialed Ross's number.

"Split T Farriers." The woman's voice said.

"Hi, this is Lilah, is Ross in?" I asked.

There was a long pause before she answered. "Yes."

While I held for Ross, I couldn't help but think that his sister had sounded a little cold. Maybe she was just havin' a bad day.

"Hello?" his voice was soft and sexy.

"Hi, Ross. Are ya busy?" I asked him.

"Yeah, let me call you back later." He hung up the phone.

Well, okay then. It seemed like somethin' was definitely goin' on at the Split T. I put it out of my mind as I headed down to the barn to let the animals outside. Boots and Roz was at my heels. When the horses took off for the pasture, the dogs were right with 'em. It was a beautiful sight to see, all three horses together again, as they raced the dogs through the flowin' green grass. I turned and went through the barn to see what all needed to be done. I made a note in my head that the stalls needed to be cleaned and the saddles needed some attention too. I paused and looked at 'em. I'd put Chad's saddle back against the wall and had allowed Ross to use the spare one. I started toward Chad's saddle, but stopped short. This was no way to let go. I took a blanket, covered it, and walked away. I'd always rode Pride, but had taken to let'n Ross ride him while I rode Patton. There was one thing I couldn't handle and that was anyone else ridin' Chad's horse. I stepped back and walked quickly out of the barn.

It was my day for volunteer work at the senior home, so I went upstairs, cleaned up, and headed that way. It was a nice drive and I felt a new kind of freedom. Maybe I was goin' into that next level in my life. I felt good!

It'd been a long time since I'd been to the home and I felt that I'd been neglectin' my friends. I visited for a while with several of 'em, but I saved my favorite for last.

"Good mornin' Lamar." I spoke as I entered the open door. "Ya probably don't even remember who I am." I teased.

"Oh you can bet that'll never happen sweet girl. I heard ya comin' down the hall. Besides, I'd been informed early this mornin' that you'd be comin' by." His laugh was deep and rich.

"And how would anybody know that I was comin' in when I didn't even know?" I asked him.

"I'll just say . . . the one we call Nanny let the cat outta the bag." He grinned.

I was taken aback when he said that. I suddenly remembered that he'd told me about his unusual gift the last time we'd visited. That was the day we were interrupted by news of Eli's accident. He'd just started to tell me somethin' about Chad when Junie come in with the news.

"Yeah, ya was just startin' to explain all that when we got interrupted. Do ya want to pick up where we left off?" I asked him.

"No . . . not today. I have a couple of other things we should talk about. I ain't got it all figured out yet, but I think we should talk." He looked very serious.

"What is it Lamar? Are ya okay?"

"I'm 'bout as good as I can be at this age. That ain't what I need to talk with ya about."

"Then what is it? Ya look so serious."

"Lilah, I been gettin' some . . . messages. They're bits and pieces and very confusin'. There's somethin' comin' up, like a storm, but it ain't got nothin' to do with the weather. I can see it gatherin' like storm clouds brewin' on the horizon. Nanny's worried too, but she's not sure what it is either. She wants ya to be on your guard and so do I. I wish I knew more. Just keep a sharp eye on them babies and be alert to anything that seems out of place." He cautioned.

"I don't understand Lamar. My life's in a very good place right now. Things are better than they've been in years. For the first time since Chad walked out, I'm happy."

"I know sweetheart and ya deserve every happiness, but . . . I . . . I don't know yet. It'll come to me in time. Just keep your eyes open and I'll call ya when I come to know a little more about it."

"Don't ya worry none. I'll be extra careful and keep my eyes wide open. Ya just call when ya know and I'll be right here." I patted his withered little hand.

Lamar raised his head as if he was lookin' straight at me through those very dark sunshades. "We'll be lookin' out for ya sweetheart, me and Nanny . . . and a few others."

A chill ran the entire length of my body as I hugged his neck and left. As I stood in the hall for a few seconds, a small red rubber ball rolled across the floor and stopped at my feet. It was the kind people use to exercise their hands. I looked around, but the only open door was Lamar's and I knew it didn't come from there. I picked it up only to find that it was cold as ice. Once again, I had chills from head to toe. I tucked it in my purse and left for home. I was very uneasy as I drove toward the mountain. The day had taken a strange turn and I wasn't at all sure that I was likin' the feel of it.

I pulled up to the house to find Dee and the boys in the front yard weedin' my little flower bed. When I got out, both boys ran to the car. Jonny had a pretty red flower in his little hand.

"It for you Mama. Do ya like it?" he asked with pride beamin' in his bright blue eyes.

Before I could answer him, Eli spoke up. "Mama, it's red! It's red like the ball ya bringed us!"

I froze in my tracks. "How did ya know that I've got a red ball, Eli?"

"Somebody dis told me." He said as he shrugged his little shoulders and ran across the yard after the dogs.

I looked at Dee who was just standin' there lookin' back at me, "He does that a lot Lilah. It's like maybe he knows things nobody else seems to know."

"Yeah, I've noticed that a few times myself, but I thought maybe it was just coincidence. But, this is somethin' he had no way of knowin', Dee." I told her about what'd happened in the hallway.

"Maybe we should pay a little more attention and take notes of some of this," she suggested.

"I agree. We'll start doin' that from now on."

I went to my desk and pulled out a notebook and wrote down the latest things Eli had said. The more I thought about it . . . the more uneasy I felt. Most all my life I'd had feelin's about certain things that often come to pass. But Eli made me think a lot about the things that Lamar had been tellin' me. It concerned me, but not enough to talk to Floy or Ross about it. I decided to give it awhile and just see what happened.

The next couple of days went by quickly without a word from Ross. I thought I'd probably really hurt his feelings when I didn't jump on the idea of his movin' in with us. He didn't stop to think that I had a lot to consider, like Dee and the boys. In all honesty, I wasn't sure I was ready for nobody to step in where Chad and me had lived. Yeah, there was still a few things that I hadn't come to grips with just yet.

One of those things that hammered in the back of my brain was Bridger. I still couldn't accept why he just dumped me on the sidewalk and left me there. Why had he lied to me about my name and about our relationship? I felt a little like a stray puppy that'd been picked up on the side of the road, kept for a couple of months, and then hauled on down the road. I still needed some answers.

For whatever reasons, I went to the barn and saddled Pride and decided to take a little ride. Before long, I found myself in the forest, lookin' down at the field of red roses that I so cherished. I turned up the trail and continued to ride further into the woods. It took longer than I'd remembered to get to the clearin' where Seth and I'd picniced on that day so long ago. Somethin' in my heart just wouldn't let me believe anything, but that my necklace was lost in that clearin'. I was still determined to find it.

I slid out of the saddle and tied Pride to a nearby limb. I picked out a square area and swore to comb ever inch, one square at a time. After a couple of hours of searchin', I went to the rock that I'd sat on and leaned against it and rested my back. I closed my eyes, but I refused to let my mind wander back to anything at the ranch. With the rich smell of the forest and the sounds of the birds . . . I felt the serene calm of my days up there with Bridger. I relaxed and felt myself start to doze off.

"Oh no! I don't think so!" I yelled out loud. "This happened before and we ain't gonna do that again!"

When I turned to go to Pride, I suddenly noticed something on the edge of the tree across from him. As I got closer, I was sure that I was seein' things. There on a limb hung an old canteen cover with the top cut out. Inside was a glass jar. I reached in and took it with shakin' hands while memories washed through my mind.

I took the jar and sat down on the rock again. It was closed tight, I suppose so it wouldn't get water in it. I opened it and poured the contents into my hand. An envelope and a familiar medal fell into my palm. I picked up the medal and carefully studied it. It was one of the many purple hearts that Bridger had earned. I opened the envelope and pulled out a folded note. As I opened the note, a flash of gold slid gracefully out and into my lap. It was my precious necklace, the one I'd been searchin' for all this time. I took a deep breath and started to read.

My very dearest Shelly, I could spend a lifetime trying to explain all that happened, but I'll just get straight to the point. When I found you on that ledge and took you home, somethin' inside of me just needed to have you there with me. I have no idea what your real name is, but you will forever be my Shelly. You helped me more than you can ever know and I will forever be indebted to you. At first, I guess I just wanted the company but later, it was becomin' so very much more. When I watched your sweet gentle way with baby Eesa and then the way you cared for me when I was sick . . . I was falling in love with you, Shelly. As I realized that you were gradually regaining your memory, I knew in my heart that I could not bear to see the hurt and disappointment in your beautiful eyes. I lied to you out of my own selfishness and never thought about you or your family and friends. I hope you find this, I'm almost sure this is what you were looking for when you fell. I also want you to have this purple heart for the pain that I must surely have caused you.

Again, I'm sorry. I will remember our time together with much love and I pray that you will find it in your heart to forgive me. With all the love I have to give, Bridger.

On the bottom of the note he had added a post script.

P.S. Eesa is fine and keeps me company. I don't know what I would do without her. Thank you.

I sat for a long time and read and reread that message. I put my necklace back around my neck and held the medal close to my heart for the longest time. It was a while before I put it back in the jar with the note and closed it up tight. As I held the canteen cover, I found myself missin' Bridger and Eesa more than I'd ever dreamed I could. I hung it on the horn of my saddle as I climbed into it and started to leave. Somethin' deep inside led me to turn and look over the drop-off and scream at the top of my lungs, "I love you too, Bridger!!!"

It was true. I did love Bridger, but nothin' nor no one could compare with the insane passionate love I had for Chad. There were times I wanted to rip his head off and never hear his name again, but I knew I never could 'cause I heard his name with every beat of my heart.

Pride and I slowly and quietly rode back down to the ranch. My first stop was the little cabin where I slipped inside and put the canteen cover and its contents safely in one of the metal boxes in the cave behind the door. It'd been a long, drainin' day.

****

I woke up the next mornin' with an uneasy feelin' in the pit of my stomach. This was kinda like butterflies chasin' somethin' on the inside of ya. I recalled havin' that feelin' pretty often when Chad and me was together. Sure enough, somethin' always seemed to happen shortly after the feelin' would go away.

I went downstairs for some coffee and found the kitchen empty. There was a note on the table from Dee lettin' me know that she and the boys had gone into Mason for a few groceries. Just as I started to sit down, the phone rang.

"Hello?" I answered.

"Hi, Princess, are you busy?"

"Ross. No, I just come downstairs and was fixin' to have a cup of coffee." I suddenly didn't know what else to say.

"I'm sorry I took so long to get back with you. There were some problems here at work that I had to solve. It took a little longer than I expected. I wanted to call, but most nights were so late that I didn't want to wake you or the boys up. Forgive me?" He asked so sweetly that I found it impossible to be too upset with him.

"Of course I do. Believe me, I've learned how much time business can take up. I was hopin' ya wasn't mad 'cause I told ya that I'd have to think over what ya suggested. Ya know, about ya movin' in out here. I didn't mean to hurt your feelin's, but it is somethin' that will take a good deal of considerin'."

"I know and I shouldn't have pushed it like I did. I just really enjoy spendin' time with you and the boys. I can't help it . . . I love you Lilah." He almost whispered.

I paused for sometime before I finally managed a response. "Let's just give it some time, Ross. Okay?"

"Yeah, okay. But I wanted to let you know that I'm going be out of town for a week or two. I'll call you and I want to see you as soon as I get back. Can I look forward to that?" he asked.

"Yes, of course. Where do ya have to go?"

"Texas. I'll be back as soon as I can. Love you Princess." He sounded so sad.

"I'll be here. Take care now, ya hear?"

The line clicked and he was gone. This was a good thing, maybe. It would give me ample time to think things out without any interruption.

I finally went down to Floy and Toby's and got up enough gumption to tell her about it.

"He seems like a nice guy, Lilah, but what do ya really know about him?" Toby asked. "Where's he from? Is this the same line of business he's always done? I think ya should take your time, sweetheart."

Floy was in agreement and I felt like I had the reassurance I'd been needin' to not rush into anything. For some reason I felt like a huge load had just been lifted off my shoulders. Feelin' like I had my life a little more under control, I headed back up to my cabin.

The trees was full and the wildflowers was in full bloom. It'd been much cooler up in the mountains and I missed the thick forest and the breezes, yet I was thankful to be at home again.

I pulled up through the little grove at the beginnin' of the driveway and parked in front of the cabin. The dogs was down at the barn barkin' their fool heads off. Dee come out the door with a tray of snacks.

"Oh, good. You're home. The boys was lookin' everywhere for you. They think you're hidin' down at the barn. They have such imaginations." She laughed.

We sat down on the porch to drink some Kool-Aid and wait for the boys to figger out that I was hidin' on the porch. While we visited, I lost track of how long we'd been sittin' there until I heard Jonny yell from about halfway up from the barn.

"Mommy! Mommy! Look what we maked. See, it like Mr. Ross! Mommy! Eli can fly!! He pointed his little finger upward toward the roof of the very tall old barn. My breath caught in my throat as I jumped off the porch with Dee close behind.

"Eli!!" I screamed as I saw him spread his little arms while he held the corners of a ragged old blanket. "No! Stay right there! Don't move, Eli!!!" He was perched on the very top!

The world stopped and flickered like an old movie at the theater. Eli ran and jumped off the point. I could see his little arms flappin' for all he was worth as the ratty old blanket folded around him and for just a minute he seemed suspended in mid air. Then he crashed to the ground like a limp rag doll.

Dee and I both screamed as we flew across the yard. For a split second, we just stood there and stared at him.

"Don't move him!" yelled Dee as she knelt down beside him. It was all I could do not to grab him up into my arms. I kneeled with her while she felt for his pulse. Tears blinded my vision as I struggled to detect any rise and fall of his little chest.

"He's got a pulse, but it's weak! Listen to me . . ." she commanded. "Go to the house and call Dr. Garren. Tell him we may need to transport him by air to Louisville. Lilah, run for all you're worth."

She didn't have to tell me but once. Somehow I managed to keep control long enough to get to the phone and call Dr. Garren. I blurted out the story. He assured me he would have somebody on the way. Then I called Floy. All I could get out between sobs was for them to come now! Eli was dyin', and then I hung up and raced back to the barn.

Dee'd managed to get the dirt out of his little nose and mouth but there was fresh blood appearin'. He was so pale and still and I instantly flashed back to a time when I'd seen that same look on his Daddy's face while I sat in the kitchen floor and waited for help. This, this was different! This was my baby! I was so close to losin' control that it took everything in me to keep it together.

"Mommy?" sobbed Jonny. "Mommy is Eli dead? Hims bleedin'. Is him dead Mama?" He pulled away from me and went over to Eli. Lyin' down on the dirt, he put his little head right beside Eli's and spoke so softly and sweetly. "Eli? Eli? You wake up now. You open you eyes and wake up. You not dead Eli. I not let you be dead. Eli . . . you flied." He placed his little arm across his brother and cried.

What was only a few minutes, but seemed like weeks later, we heard the distinct sound of a helicopter. It landed in the near pasture as Dr. Garren and several others rushed over to us. They quickly took control of the situation and all we could do was stand back and watch. I held Jonny while the three of us sobbed and waited.

It seemed like forever before they loaded Eli and me on the helicopter and we took off. Dee and Jonny would ride with Floy and Toby to Louisville. I couldn't believe that this was happenin'. Things like this happened to other families, not mine. Please God, not mine. I'd been through so much in the last five years. Horrible things that I could hardly bear to remember, but this . . . this was by far the most horrifyin' thing I could ever have imagined.

****

The five of us sat in the emergency waitin' room in total silence. It'd only been a few minutes since they'd asked us to sit in there, but it seemed like hours.

"Lilah? Are ya okay?" Floy asked as she placed her arm around my shoulders.

I sat there a moment before I answered her. "I will be as soon as they tell me my baby's gonna be okay. He has to be okay, Floy. He just has to be."

"Mama, him be okay some day. It be long time . . . but him be okay. Me promise Mama." Jonny said as he took my face in his tiny hands. I looked into his vivid blue eyes and I saw Chad lookin' back at me with tear-filled honesty. My breath caught in my throat. For an instant, I truly saw his Daddy so worried, so afraid of disappointin' me.

"I know baby. I know the doctors and the Lord will see to him. I just know it."

The door opened and Dr. Garren come in and sat down beside me. "Honey, they just took Eli into surgery."

I gasped. "But he's just a baby! He's too little to have surgery!"

"He has some internal injuries that have to be addressed. I need you to sign this consent form for the operation. We don't have time to talk about it, Lilah. Please, trust me, and just sign." He handed me a paper.

I looked into his eyes and knew I could trust him. He'd brought me through so much, so many times. "Of course," was all I could whisper.

"I'm going to observe. I'll be out when it's over and I'll tell you everything." He paused and kissed me on the forehead. "Just pray honey!"

He walked back through the door and we all sat quietly and stared at it.

****

It felt like days had passed since Dr. Garren'd walked out the door. In fact, it'd only been a couple of hours. Even at that . . . a couple of hours was an eternity when it was my baby they was tryin' to save. I paced the floor, Toby paced the floor, and Floy sat with her hands folded and her head down. I knew she was in prayer. Somethin' bumped into me and I turned around to find Jonny right behind me. As Toby paced with his hands in his pockets and head down, Jonny did exactly the same. For a moment I was amused, but then I remembered what was goin' on and I just continued to pace.

Five hous later, we were all sittin' in a row when the door finally opened.

"Is he okay, Dr. Garren? Please tell me he'll be alright," I whispered in muffled sobs.

"Sit down, honey. Dr. Kline will be in when he changes. He'll go over everything he found and did."

"But, why can't you just tell me? You know what's goin' on! Just tell me! Is my baby dead?" I demanded.

Floy and Toby come to my side as if to support me.

"No! No! He's not dead Lilah. Just try and be patient. Dr. Kline is the expert in this area and I'm not a neurosurgeon." He tried to comfort me.

"What's a neurosurgeon? What does he do?" I questioned.

"Well, he's pretty much a brain surgeon."

"Why does he need a brain surgeon? What's wrong with his brain?" I begged.

The door opened and a small, black man with a pretty large Afro hair style came in the room.

"Lilah, this is Dr. Kline." Dr. Garren paused. "And this is the boy's mother."

Dr. Kline shook my hand and started to say somethin', when Jonny caught his eye. He stood there a little speechless and I could see that he was more than a little surprised.

"This has to be Eli's brother. They are perfect identical twins. I've seen a lot of sets of twins in my time, but these two are absolutely amazing. Beautiful . . . beautiful boys."

"It's nice to meet ya, but how's my baby? I want to know everything!" I said as I grabbed his arm. "Don't ya dare lie to me. I want to know and I want to know now." I felt like I was about to lose what little control I'd managed to hang on to.

"Okay, Mrs. Barrett . . . ."

"My name's Parker. Barrett's my boys' names." I interrupted.

"Okay. I'm sorry. Ms. Parker, let's sit down and discuss this situation."

We settled on the couch across from Toby and Floy. Jonny walked up to Dr. Kline and looked him straight in the eye. "Did my Bubba die? Is Eli in heaven? He can fly now . . . he can. I sawed him."

"Jonny, shhh. Eli's not dead. Now listen and be quiet." I sat him down beside me.

"Here's the details, your son has suffered a broken ankle and a broken rib. We put a splint on the foot, but we will wait a few days to do surgery. We found it was more critical to get right to the head injury. He suffered a brain bleed when his head hit the ground. That's a very serious injury. We had to go in and repair the bleed and and try to help limit the swelling. Ms. Parker, he is in a coma at this time and he may be for quite some time to come. Time and prayer is what it will take now. We are and will be doing everything we can, medically speaking, to see him through this. Do you have any questions?"

I thought for a moment, "I'm sure that I do. But right this minute . . . I'm just speechless. Do ya think he'll make a full recovery?"

"I can't tell you for certain, but I can tell you that the surgery was a complete success. I couldn't have asked for it to go any better. Now we wait."

Now we wait . . . that's what he'd said. One thing I wasn't good at was waitin' and I was really gettin' tired of sittin' there. The doctor'd said it'd be a little while before we could see Eli. It'd been more than a little while and my patience had run out. I stood up in frustration and headed toward the door. Just as I reached for it, it opened.

"Mrs. Barrett? You can come up to ICU now. We've gotten him settled."

I started to correct her, but at the moment I didn't care what she called me so long as I was gonna see my baby. I followed her up to the elevator that took us up to the fourth floor. At the end of the long hall was a double door. We had to ring a buzzer in order to get inside ICU area. There was several little glass rooms in a circle around the nurses' center. I looked into each room as we walked down the short hall. I saw a lot of children in those rooms that looked very sick. Finally we entered the room that was Eli's. I come to a sudden stop. I'd not been at all prepared for what I saw. I didn't recognize the tiny form that lay motionless in the big stainless steel crib that set in the middle of the room. He was on some kind of breathin' machine and he had tubes and needles all over and in him. His little head was wrapped in a ton of gauze and tape and his little face was so swollen that I wasn't sure that it really was Eli. I could barely see the ends of his eyelashes and his little cheeks were so pale. They had his foot elevated and his hands rested at his side. The machine at the head of his bed beeped with each little heartbeat. I was so thankful for that. I watched as his chest rose and fell with every breath. I covered my mouth as I burst into tears.

"Honey, it's not quite as bad as it looks. The swelling is good. It shows us that the swelling is outside and not inside the head. The breathing machine is because he's in a coma and we need to make sure he's getting plenty of oxygen. The wires are hooked up to monitors to let us know that everything is okay. They'll signal if anything changes. The IVs give him fluids and are convenient for any medications he might need. These type of injuries are nothing new to us. Dr. Kline is a great surgeon and knows exactly what he's doing. Now try to relax and just spend time with him. Many parents like to talk to them. They believe that they can still hear and that they need all the encouragement they can get. It seems to help a lot. Some even read books to them or sing songs. Please feel free to do whatever you think might help. I'll be right outside here. If you need anything, just let us know. My name's Bonnie, I'm the RN on duty for the rest of the night." The heavy set, older woman turned and left the room. I watched as she took a chart and went to the desk and sat down and started to write. I felt more alone than I'd ever felt in my life. I stood and stared at my baby as if he were a stranger. I was afraid to touch him, I was even afraid to go near him. I didn't know what to do and everything looked so complicated that I was afraid I would mess somethin' up. I finally got the courage to step a little closer. The constant beeps and the sound of the breathin' machine were overwhelmin' for me. I pulled the blue cushioned chair that sat against the wall, closer to the bed. I wanted to reach out and hold his little hand, but I was afraid to disturb him. How could this be happenin'? This mornin' he'd been fine. He was happily runnin' and playin' with Jonny and the dogs and now . . . this. Tears streamed down my face as I set there in deep thought. *Chad Barrett, this is a time I need ya more than ever. Ya should be here with me and these babies. If ya give a great big damn, ya would've been here three years ago. I don't know how ya found out that I was pregnant, but I almost wish ya hadn't. At least then, there would be a sane reasonin' behind it all. It wasn't so bad goin' through the nine* months without ya. It broke my heart that ya wasn't here when they was born, but if I ever needed ya . . . ever . . . it's right now!

The nurse walked in, "Mrs. Barrett, there are some people that want to talk to you in the waiting room just down the hall. When you get back, I'll have some papers for you to fill out and sign."

I turned and went down the hall like a sleep walker in a fog. When I got to the waitin' area I found Toby, Floy, Dee, and Jonny.

"How does he look honey?" Floy asked.

I burst into tears again. "Like the only thing in this world that's keepin' him alive is those machines . . . I . . . I just can't hardly bear to look at him."

"But honey, ya have to remember that he just had serious, major surgery. He's gonna look bad for a little while. Just give it some time. The doctor said everything went very well. Now try and have a little patience. What Eli needs right now is for you to give him your strength and encourage him."

I knew she was right, but would she do any better in my situation? We talked for a little bit and I held and comforted Jonny, tryin' to reassure him.

"Do ya want me to take Jonny home and keep him while you're here?" Dee asked.

"Yeah, I would appreciate that very much. I'll call and keep ya posted." I turned to Jonny and took his hands. "Baby, I want ya to go on home with Dee until Bubba gets better. I'll call ya ever' night before ya go to bed, okay?"

"But me wants to stay wif you and Eli. He needs me Mama." His eyes teared up to cry.

"Well, I need ya too. Remember what Uncle Toby said? You're the men of my house now and with Eli hurt, ya have a very big job ahead of ya. You'll have to help feed the dogs, horses, and all the animals. Can ya do all that?" I asked him.

He stood there for a minute and thought it over. "Yeah ma'am. Me and Dee can do dat. Me not a baby, me am a man!"

I hugged him and then the four of 'em left for home. I hadn't brought one thing with me, but the nurse took good care of me. I had to sleep in a chair in Eli's room or I could go to the waitin' room and lay down. She brought me pillows, sheets, and a blanket, along with a toothbrush and toothpaste. I chose for the most part to stay in the room with my baby. I wasn't worried about comfort.

I felt a little more relaxed with Eli and wasn't so afraid of him like I'd been in the beginnin'. I sat and watched as Miss Bonnie come and went with her charts and listened to the endless beeps, clicks, and noises the breathin' machine made. The lights was turned down very low and there was an errie quiet that seemed to have come over the whole place.

From time to time, I would hear a child whimper or cry and sometimes an adult would wander out into the hallway and go to the bathroom or maybe the snack area. I guess I dozed off at sometime in the very early mornin'. I don't know how long I slept, but the bright lights that flipped on woke me right up.

"Is ever' thing okay?" I asked.

"Yes, everything is good. I'm sorry I woke you." Bonnie answered.

"It's okay. I can't believe I dozed off like that."

"Mrs. Barrett, it's perfectly alright for you to take a little nap. These machines are here to let us know about any little change. Don't feel guilty, just try and get some rest." She said as she patted me on the shoulder and left.

I got up and went over to the crib where Eli slept. He didn't even look like my beautiful baby. I reached and took his hand. It was cool and limp, but I felt so much better just havin' the courage to touch him. I moved my chair closer and held his little hand while I rested my head on the crib bars.

Mornin' came early. How well I remembered all the weeks I'd been kept in the hospital after my accident. I didn't let myself remember anymore than that. It was only a couple of hours and Dr. Kline come back in the room. He picked up the charts and studied 'em very carefully, then walked over to Eli and checked some of the readings on the medical equipment and come back toward me.

"What do ya think Dr. Kline? Is he any better?" I asked with a very shaky voice.

"I'm sorry, Mrs. Barrett, it's just too soon to say. He's been stable through the night, but only time will tell."

That wasn't what I'd wanted to hear. I wanted, I needed to hear that there was at least some kind of improvement. "How much time?" I asked.

He looked at me very seriously, "That's entirely up to Eli."

He walked out the door and I sat and stared at my little boy. *He's only three. How can it be left up to him? He doesn't even know what happened. Please* dear God, help him. Bring him back to me. I need him so much. Only time will tell, he'd said.

Chapter 14

Every bone and muscle in my body ached. I had a splittin' headache that threatened to make me be sick to my stomach. I'd been settin' in that chair for three days as I watched and waited. I only left to go to the bathroom and to get somethin' quick to eat. Floy'd brought me clothes and what I needed for the stay and visited for a little while before she had to go. I talked to Jonny ever' night and I'd even started to put the phone to Eli's ear and lettin' Jonny talk to him. I didn't have no idea if he could hear him, but I felt like it would be good for him to hear his twin's voice. Accordin' to Chad, there was no stronger bond nowhere than the one between twins.

I sat by his bed for countless hours and read his favorite stories to him. Sometimes I sang little songs that he liked and often told him stories about my brothers and sisters. When I couldn't hold my eyes open no more, I went down to the waitin' area and slept. It'd been a long tiresome day and about 1:00 a.m., I went to lay down. I hardly remember puttin' my head on my pillow. I was the only one in the room and I was exhausted.

I could only sleep in short two-hour periods. It seemed impossible for me to stay asleep any longer than that. As usual, I opened my eyes and was wide awake. I sat up and stretched for a moment, then went down to the bathroom. When I come out and started down the hall, I noticed Miss Bonnie standin' in the door to Eli's room.

"Nice to meet you Father John." She said as she turned and walked down the other hallway. The lights were very dim and no one was at the desk for the moment. I slipped quietly into the room and I noticed someone standin' by Eli's bed.

"Is there somethin' wrong? Who are you?" I was a little unnerved.

He stood facin' the crib and said nothin'. I felt a sudden chill and my heart began to race. *Oh dear God!! What's happened to my baby?* I shoved the man out of my way as I leaned over the crib. The machine was still workin' and everything was as it'd been for the last three days. I whirled to face this stranger. He'd turned his back to me and appeared to be starin' out the door.

"Who are you? Why are you in my baby's room?" My voice rose.

With his back still to me, he answered softly, "Because . . . uh . . . he's my baby too." Then he turned. Even in a dark suit and a priest's collar with dark-rimmed glasses, a full beard, and his hair pulled smooth back and bound in a short ponytail, I knew that voice. I knew those incredible lips and those unforgettable blue eyes. I felt the blood drain from my face and suddenly found it very difficult to breathe. His arms wrapped around me just as my knees buckled and I started to sink to the floor. I heard the nurse ask what'd happened, and Chad gave her a short answer. He told her that I seemed exhausted and he needed a place where I could lie down comfortably. The next thing I knew, I was in a semi-dark room and layin' on a bed. I stared in complete disbelief. There was no doubt I was sound asleep and havin' another one of those dreams that always left me devastated when I woke up.

"Honey?" he little more than whispered. "Are ya okay? I . . . I didn't mean to scare ya. I'm sorry."

I reached out my hand and touched his face. I was half expectin' to touch nothin' more than air. I was wrong. I touched his soft satin skin, caressed the silky silver blonde beard, and eased my fingertips across those beautiful, pouty lips. He caught 'em with his hand and held 'em to his lips as he stared into my eyes.

"How can dreams be so real?" I whispered back.

"It's . . . it's . . . this ain't no dream, Chica." He looked up and I could see tears formin' in those incredible eyes. Eyes that I never expected to see again.

His fingers moved gently over my cheek, then the tip of his finger lifted my chin slightly as his lips touched mine ever so softly and ever so briefly that I wasn't sure it'd really happened. My heart pounded in my chest as the reality hit me. He was here! After all those years of waitin', prayin', and hopin', he was really back. My arms found their way around his neck as I come off the bed and into his. Somehow, I couldn't find the right words . . . hell, I couldn't find any words at all. I couldn't hold him close enough or tight enough and that was when the tears began. Once it started I couldn't stop. I cried so hard that I couldn't breathe and my legs barely supported me. Chad held me so tight and ever so close as he kissed my face and my neck. At last, his lips found mine again only this time, they were eager and demandin' and I melted against him like always. The scent of his cologne and the warmth of his body combined with the fire of his kisses sent my world spinnin' out of control.

A sudden light knockin' on the door brought us both back to reality. We stepped apart just as the nurse walked in the room.

"Mrs. Barrett, are you feeling any better?" she asked.

"Yeah, I . . . I'm sorry if I scared ya. I think I just need some rest and somethin' to eat." I stammered.

"I'll see what I can find for you. You do look a little pale. Father John, is there anything I can get you? Maybe a cup of coffee?"

". . . uh . . . uh, yeah. Thank ya." Chad answered.

She left the room and I turned to look at him. He had a very puzzled look on his face.

"Did . . . uh, did she call ya . . . Mrs. Barrett?" he asked softly.

"Yeah. She just assumed since that's Eli's last name that it's mine and I just never bothered to correct her. I'm sorry."

"Sorry for what? That's perfectly understandable. I'm the one that's sorry." He turned away. "I'm sorry that I couldn't be here with you and the boys these past years."

"Why are ya here now?" I asked him. "How did ya know?"

Chad walked over to the window and looked outside. I watched him as he leaned on the window sill and studied the rain drops that made their way down the pane. As he turned to face me, a bolt of lightnin' lit up the room and a chill raced over my entire body. For a minute he looked like a spirit in one of my dreams, the ones where he just stood in my bedroom and glared at me.

The door opened and Bonnie come in with a tray.

"I didn't find much, but maybe this will help. Here you go Father." She handed Chad the cup of coffee and set the tray down on the hospital table beside me. "Can I get you anything else?"

"No, no that's more than enough. Thank ya Bonnie." I answered.

"This room won't be needed tonight, so you can sleep in here if you want, Mrs. Barrett. I'll put a 'do not disturb' sign on the door and no one will be the wiser. Good night. Good night Father John, stay as long as you like." She answered as she left the room.

Chad sipped his coffee and I took a drink of the iced tea she'd brought. I sat down on the side of the bed and put my glass of tea on the tray.

"Ya didn't answer my question, Chad. How did ya know about Eli?" I pushed the subject.

"I . . . uh . . . uh, well I . . ." he looked around the room like a caged animal.

"Is it that hard to explain?"

"No . . . yes . . . I mean, I don't know what to tell ya."

"How 'bout the truth? It can't be that difficult." I stood up and walked toward him. Those unforgettable blues locked with my eyes and I couldn't quite decide if I saw love and passion or hate and disappointment. There seemed to be a lot of emotions reflectin' on his beautiful face. I stood squarely in front of him and asked him one more time.

"Did ya really think I wouldn't keep up with ya, and especially after I learned about the babies?" His voice seemed a little harsh and I wondered just how closely he'd been keepin' up with me. For a flash of a second, I saw Bridger's face and then I saw Ross's face. I tried to remain calm.

"What was there to make me think any different?" I snapped back at him.

"The fact that I love ya with all my heart . . . and ya gave birth to my babies." He whispered as he stepped closer. I could feel myself bein' pulled toward him with every step he took. He was like a magnet and I was powerless to resist him. He removed the dark-rimmed glasses and put 'em in his pocket as he slid his other arm around me.

"I've missed ya little girl. God how I've missed ya." He mumbled as his lips closed over mine. His tongue slipped between my open lips and I surrendered completely. I lost all sense of judgment and reason as he laid me back across the bed. I didn't care where we were or who might walk in the room. My love was here and for the first time in years, I felt totally alive. His kisses grew more demandin' as his hands caressed every curve of my body. It was all I could do to breathe, yet I still could not get close enough to him. I unbuckled his belt and let his clothes fall to the floor as he pushed my skirt to my waist and removed my underclothes. In a moment's time, we were one again. The familiar rhythm of our lovemakin' was as natural as ever. We couldn't kiss hard enough, we couldn't blend close enough, and our union took on the same intensity that only we had shared. We reached that heart stoppin' moment at the same time and I was sure I'd never be able to breathe right again. Chad shuddered and then shuddered again before he finally relaxed over me.

After a few seconds, he raised up on his elbow and looked into my eyes.

"I've thought of this and dreamed of this for so long, honey. There's been days that I didn't think I could make it without ya." He spoke softly as he kissed the tips of my fingers.

I laid there, lookin' into those captive blues and thought to myself, *you managed for almost four years without me. Why now?*

"Chad, I . . ." he kissed the words from my lips. Once again, I wrapped my arms around his neck.

Suddenly, we heard voices in the hall. They sounded like they was right outside our door. Startled, we thought of nothin' but gettin' our clothes back on and in order. There was a tap on the door and it slightly opened. I laid back on the bed and Chad sat casually in the chair.

"Oh, she's asleep. I'm sorry Father John, but I'm going off shift now." The nurse whispered. "Will you tell her that I told the nurse coming on duty not to disturb her? She should sleep well tonight. You seemed to bring great comfort for her Father. Thank you for coming. Can I get you some more coffee?"

I laid still and continued to pretend to sleep.

"No thank ya. I was just fixin' to leave. We'll let her rest." Chad answered as he stood up and placed his hand on my forehead . . . and just like that, he was gone again.

****

I woke up sometime in the night and I laid there in the dark and listened to the thunder roll outside. The rain pounded on the window and lightnin' lit the night sky. I sat up and stared at the door for a minute and then at the chair beside the bed. Disappointed, I realized it'd only been another nightmare, one of hundreds or maybe thousands over the last several years. But this one had seemed so real, as real as the storm that raged outside my window. I laid back down and turned over. Maybe I could get a little more sleep, and let go of the memory of that dream like I had all the others.

It seemed like only a short while and the halls come alive with activity. I suppose they was as quiet as they could be with all their noisy equipment and low chatter. I got up and went to the bathroom and washed my face and straightened my hair and clothes. I desperately needed to see my baby.

"Morning Mrs. Barrett. Did you sleep better?" The night nurse asked me as I stepped out into the hall.

"Yeah, I did. Thank you."

I slipped into Eli's still, dark room. There was a low light on over his head and the endless beepin' and sounds of the equipment. He hadn't moved an inch. I sat down beside his bed and took his little hand in mine. I pressed it to my lips and for a moment, I thought I could almost smell the cologne that Chad'd always worn. That dream had shook me to the very core of my soul.

"Baby," I whispered softly. "I dreamed about your Daddy tonight. He was here with us. He come in here and held your hand and kissed your little cheek." The tears rolled down my cheeks as I went about tellin' him about his Daddy. Of course, I didn't tell him everything in the dream. But I wanted to try to get across to him that his Daddy does love him. I know he does. How could he not?

I dozed off with my head against the crib, still holdin' the little hand. I was startled awake when the lights flipped on and the nurse come in to chart his vitals.   "Good morning Mrs. Barrett. I see you are already up and around. Did you sleep better on a real bed?" she asked.

"Yeah, I did. Thank ya for lettin' me stay in there."

"Just between me and you and Bonnie, there wasn't a bit of sense in you having to sleep on that old couch in the waiting area when there was a perfectly good bed just sitting in there. I'll change the sheets and nobody will be the wiser. Bonnie or I will see what we can do to find you a room when we can."

"Thank you. You're mighty thoughtful."

"Sure was a heck of a storm last night. Part of the hospital lost most of its power around 3:00 a.m. I heard part of the town is still without power. It sure was nice of Father John to stay with you until you went to sleep. Such a nice man and awfully good -looking for a priest. What a waste!" She laughed as she finished her notes and left the room.

Fath . . . Father John? How could that be? It was a dream. I know it was a dream . . . but, how else would she know the name he used? But where did he go and why did he leave us again? He didn't say he would be back, but surely he would. It was real, he was real, and what happened . . . that was real too!

I must've sat there for an hour or more without movin'. My mind refused to give me a second's rest and raced over the whole thing again and again. I'd been exhausted and I was still exhausted. The entire night was more than my mind seemed able to process.

I was startled when Dr. Kline and one of his nurses walked into the room. He picked up Eli's chart and studied it for some time, before he went to the bedside and carefully lifted each eyelid and shined his light into Eli's eyes. He watched the machines for a couple of minutes before he come over to me.

"How are you doing, Mrs. Barrett?" He asked.

"I'm not really sure this mornin'. I'm okay I guess. How's my baby?"

"He's stable. I don't see much change yet, but I didn't expect to this soon. We just have to give it time. You need to try and get some rest. We're keeping a very close eye on him."

"Can't ya tell me anything more than that? This waitin' is makin' me crazy." I told him as I started to tear up again.

He put his hand on my shoulder and looked me straight in my eyes. "I will tell you this. I am very optimistic at this point. He's a strong, healthy little boy and he has his Mom right beside him. Keep talking to him and encouraging him. That's the best medicine for right now." He lightly patted my shoulder and left the room.

"I know it's hard, but try and be patient, Mrs. Barrett. Dr. Kline is the best there is for these types of injuries." His nurse tried to comfort me and then she left.

I sat there quietly for a few minutes then I stood up and paced around the bed. I don't need this right now. I need to give my baby boy my full attention. Of all the times for Chad to return, and as much as I thought I needed him . . . not now! Just not now!

I set my jaw and made up my mind to focus totally on that tiny boy layin' in that bed. I adjusted his pillow and straightened the crisp white sheet that lay across him. It seemed a little cool in the room, so I unfolded a blanket from the shelf and carefully spread it across his legs. When I couldn't find anything else to do, I took a comb from my purse and carefully combed what was left of his silky blonde hair. I made a point to avoid the still-bandaged area. He never moved. He slept an unnatural sleep that didn't even begin to look normal. I leaned over and kissed his little cheek.

"Eli?" I whispered. "Eli, can ya hear Mommy? I need ya to hear me baby. Ya gotta come back to me. I love ya so much and . . . I need ya to come home and . . . and you and Jonny be the men of my house. Please, fight hard sweetie. Fight hard to come back." I sobbed.

Suddenly a warm arm wrapped around my shoulder and pulled me into a comfortin' embrace. I wrapped my arms around the warm body beside me and clung desperately. I cried for a little while before I raised my head to be sure who it was that was holdin' me. I was sure it would be Chad who had come back to be with me. It wasn't!

"I got here as soon as I heard Princess. I didn't know." Ross tried to comfort me.

There was no doubt in my head that this was somethin' I absolutely didn't need either. Not now! Chad could walk in at any given moment and I . . . oh, hell. What would I do? What in heaven's name would I say?

"Ross? What are ya doin' here? How did ya find out?" I stepped away and turned to face him.

"I ran into Floy and Toby last night at the café in Mason. I couldn't believe it when they told me. Why in the world didn't you call me?"

"I haven't had time to call anyone but Jonny. That's for just a few minutes right before he goes to bed. When did ya get here?"

"Just a few minutes ago. I almost never found a parking place. How is he doing?" he asked sincerely.

"Not much different than the day they brought him in here. He hasn't moved or opened his eyes at all. Dr. Kline says he's doin' good and it will only take time . . . but, I just need somethin' to give me a little hope." I sighed a very weary sigh.

"Let's go outside where we can talk." Ross suggested.

We went out into the waitin' room. My eyes searched every nook and cranny to be sure Chad was nowhere to be seen. I felt a little more comfortable after we got into the waitin' room and there was no one else inside.

"So why is it that you didn't take a moment to call me?" He looked upset.

"To be honest Ross, I hadn't heard from ya in quite a few days and I didn't really know why. I just didn't expect to hear from ya again." I told him bluntly.

"Lilah, I had some major problems I had to iron out. What in the world would make you think that you wouldn't hear from me?"

"The last time I called, ya were pretty short and more or less hung up on me. What was I supposed to think?" I paused for a minute. "This ain't the time or the place to talk about all that. I got a baby in there fightin' for his little life and that is my only concern right now."

I stood up and started toward the door. His hand caught my arm and pulled me back towards him. "Lilah, you're right and I'm sorry about that. I can explain it all later. Let's go back in there with Eli."

"No." I stopped at the door. "There can only be one person in there at a time. You might as well go back home and I'll keep you posted." I tried not to sound as desperate as I felt. I panicked at the thought of him bein' anywhere around if Chad should come back.

There was a shocked expression on his face and I felt really bad after I'd said it. I knew it sounded short and unkind, but what else was I supposed to do?

"I'm sorry, Ross. I didn't mean to sound so ungrateful. It's just been such a stressful few days and I'm at my wit's end with worry. I just don't need anything else to worry about right now."

"I'm not sure what you mean. I thought I might give you a little comfort and take some of the responsibility off your shoulders by sitting with him some." Ross spoke softly.

I stood there for a moment and thought about what he'd said. It was a very kind thought and I should've appreciated it, but how could I? There was no tellin' when Chad might come back and there was no way I could let 'em run into each other. My heart was poundin' in my chest and I felt a trickle of sweat roll down the back of my neck.

"That's really nice of ya, Ross, but there really ain't nothin' ya can do. I don't leave him for more than a few minutes and that's not apt to change. I have to be right there when he wakes up. He'll need to see his Mama and his Mama will be with him. There is a couple of things ya could do for me if ya don't mind."

His eyes brightened a little. "What's that Princess? I'll do anything you ask? I just want to help and be there when you need me."

"What I need right now is someone to go back to the ranch and take care of my horses and other animals. I know Dee is there..., but she has her hands full with Jonny. Besides, she doesn't know much about takin' care of a ranch. Could ya . . . would ya do that for me? That would take a lot of worry off my shoulders." I tried to make it sound like it was somethin' I really needed done, but I knew that Toby was takin' care of the ranch for me.

"If that's what you really need me to do . . . of course I will go. All you have to do is ask me and it's done." He hesitated a moment. "Are you sure you want me to go? I'd planned on staying here with you until Eli was better, but I can go if you really want me to."

"Ross, it would be the very best thing ya could do for me right now. I worry myself to death about it." I almost pleaded with him.

"Do you want me to at least stay the night?" he asked me.

I felt frustration comin' to a full boil. "No, it's not necessary. I know it's a long drive, but I would be so relieved if you went back and I knew everything was okay."

"Alright, I guess I will start back home then. Before I go, could I at least hold you for a moment?" he asked as he pulled me into his arms.

I felt sick to my stomach. All I could think about was Chad walkin' around that corner at any minute. I put my arms around him and we held each other for what felt like an eternity. Just a few days ago, I'd loved the idea of bein' in Ross's arms. It wasn't that I didn't like him holdin' me . . . it was just that, I really needed him to get the hell out of there.

As I started to step back, he wrapped his arm around my neck and covered my lips with his. For a second I wanted to pull away, but his kiss was warm, gentle, and familiar. I found myself relaxin' in his arms and enjoyin' the taste of his lips, lips I'd become more than a little fond of lately.

Reality suddenly jumped into my head and I pulled away. "I need to check on Eli. I'll try and call ya tomorrow. Be careful goin' home, Ross. I gave him a little kiss on the cheek and walked hurriedly out the door and down the hallway.

Chapter 15

I'd been two days since I'd seen Ross or Chad. There was still no change in Eli's condition and I was beside myself with worry. It seems that when worry, frustration, and exhaustion gets ya in its clutches, it just sucks the life right out of ya.

It was around 2:00 a.m., and I thought about goin' into the room that Bonnie'd told me to use, but I hesitated just long enough to lean my head against the wall behind the chair that I spent most of my days sittin' in. I must've fallen sound asleep, 'cause when my head dropped to the side, I almost fell out of the chair. I struggled to sit upright and that was when I saw the shadow standin' by the window. I stood up and quickly reached for the brighter light switch.

"Leave it off." I heard a soft whisper that I was almost sure I recognized.

"Is that you?" I asked as I stepped nearer.

"Who were you expectin'?" Chad's voice was low and I couldn't miss the coolness in his words.

"I wasn't expectin' nobody, but I'd been hopin' that ya would be back. We didn't even get a chance to talk when ya were here before."

He turned toward Eli, "How's my boy?" He asked.

"Dr. Kline says he's stable and doin' as well as he can expect." I moved closer to Chad. He walked around me and to the other side of the crib. "He ain't opened his eyes or moved since the surgery." I continued.

He stood there with his eyes on Eli and held his tiny hand as he leaned over the crib.

"He's so beautiful. I never dreamed he could be this beautiful . . . so small, so helpless, and . . ." he paused and swallowed hard. ". . . and he's ours, mine and yours, together. It just doesn't seem possible that we created these two perfect little angels." He looked up at me in the dim light and I could see the tears that filled those gorgeous blue eyes.

"I know. I still stare in amazement. They're identical and the spittin' image of you. They have your beautiful blue eyes and your perfect lips and smile. Everybody says so and everybody loves 'em so much. They've become my life." I told him.

He closed his eyes for a minute then looked coldly into mine. I noticed the muscles in his jaw flinch as he took a deep breath. It was like he held me captive with those blue eyes and I found it impossible to look away. It'd been so long since I'd been able to look at that beautiful face, the face I'd dreamed of for night after endless night. This was the face that'd filled my thoughts and fantasies for four long years. There was no way that I could've missed the bitterness that seemed to burn just below the surface.

I walked slowly around the crib to stand beside him. "Are ya gonna stay for awhile?" I asked him.

He continued to lean on the crib rail. As he leaned over and kissed Eli's hand and placed it under the sheet, my heart ached with love for him. I watched as he smoothed the few strands of silky blonde hair away from Eli's face and gently brushed his thumb along his brow line.

"Chad?" I whispered. "Are ya gonna stay here for awhile? I really need ya to be here with me. I need ya to stay." I almost pleaded.

He stood up and walked over toward the door. There was no one in the hall, only the nurses seated quietly at their desks. Chad was as breathtakin' as ever, even in his priest disguise. In fact, I thought it really looked extremely good on him. With his hands buried in his pockets, he finally turned and walked back toward me.

"I'll sit here with ya for a little while, but ya know I can't stay here all the time. I just can't." He turned and pulled the extra chair over to the other side of the crib and sat down.

There was no doubt in my mind that he was very upset about somethin' and it appeared to me that he didn't have no intention of discussin' it with me. In the past, whenever he was angry about anything, he didn't hesitate to let me know all about it. He was different somehow. The first night he showed up, he was the same man I'd fell in love with, but somethin' had obviously changed since then. It was like a wall had suddenly grown up between us and I just wasn't sure how to react to that. I moved my chair beside his and sat down.

"What's botherin' ya, Chad?" I asked him.

He just shook his head and sat starin' at Eli.

"I know ya too well for ya to try and pretend that there ain't no problem."

He turned and looked at me with a fiery blue glare. I watched as his eyes moved from my eyes to my lips, to my hair, and then to my neck and back to my eyes. They had softened a little, but I knew he had somethin' he wanted to say. I waited, but he wouldn't say a word.

"Chad? The other night was unbelievable and I was so thrilled to see ya, to be with ya again. Now you're cold as ice. What happened?" I asked him.

His glare searched my face again before he shook his head. "Nothin' . . . nothin' I shouldn't have expected. I . . . uh . . . I just . . . ." He stood up quickly and leaned over the crib. He kissed Eli on the forehead and turned toward me. "I . . . uh, I can't stay here. I gotta go. I should never have come."

With that he rushed out the door. "Chad wait!" I called, but before I could get up and to the door he was gettin' into the elevator and the door was closin'. The last thing I saw was him wipin' his eyes as the door shut.

****

It'd been three days since Chad had visited. I'd not heard a single word from him, but Ross'd called twice. I was in the waitin' room lookin' forward to Floy and Jonny comin' up for a visit. It'd been a long week and a half and I'd seen no improvement in Eli. My confidence had started to dim a little and I was becomin' somewhat more depressed.

Without any warnin', I was attacked by a tiny pair of arms wrapped around my leg. "Mommy, me miss you!" Jonny squealed, as he climbed up into my lap. "Do ya live here now? Can I live here wif you and Eli?"

"No baby, I'm just stayin' here 'til Bubba gets well. He can't stay here by hisself. I think he'd be very scared, don't you?" I told him.

"Yeah . . . he needs us to live here wif him." Jonny decided. "Can me see him and talk to him now?"

"In a little while sweetheart. There's some colorin' books over there with some crayons. Why don't ya color a picture for Eli?"

As Jonny busied hisself with colorin', Floy and I had a chance to talk. She knew about Ross's visit, but I'd told her nothin' about Chad's. I wasn't sure how she would handle it.

"How ya holdin' up honey?" She asked me. "You've lost some weight and ya just look plum wore out."

"I'm okay. I need to tell ya somethin' Floy. Ya ain't gonna believe it, but . . . I had some company last week."

"I know." She answered. "I talked to Ross when he got back. I thought he would stay a little longer than he did."

"That was all my fault. I had to get him outta here."
She frowned and looked at me with a very confused expression.

"I was afraid that . . . that Chad would see him, or he would see Chad. I don't know. I just couldn't let 'em run in to each other." I stood and went to the door and looked down toward Eli's room.

"What the hell are ya talkin' about Lilah? Are ya tryin' to tell me that Chad was here?"

I nodded without turnin' around.

"What . . . how . . . how'd he know? Who told him?" She stammered.

I simply shrugged my shoulders. She knew about as much about it as I did. I didn't have no answers. Floy come over, grabbed my shoulders, and turned me around to face her.

"Come on, cough it up! What happened?" she demanded.

I told her everything that'd happened and how strange he acted when he left.

"I think he saw ya with Ross. That would be the only explanation. He wouldn't come here and not stay 'til he knew how his son was. That's got to be what happened." Floy had a way of seein' things that I tended to let my emotions hide.

"Do ya really think that's what happened?" I asked.

"Of course it was. It's plain as the bird in that tree. What I want to know is how he knew what was goin' on with Eli. Just like he knew ya was pregnant, there's somebody keepin' him informed. I bet ya a brand new dollar bill!"

"He did ask if I really thought he wouldn't be keepin' up with me. Oh God Floy, what have I done." I suddenly felt like I was gonna be sick to my stomach. "What in the name of all that's holy have I done?"

I dropped into a nearby chair as the reality of it all hit home.

"Now wait just a minute!" Floy raised her voice a little and firmly sat down beside me. "You been waitin' on him for four years, without a word other than a one-minute phone call on Christmas Eve. Is that supposed to be your life? I know the boys are your life, don't get me wrong, but a woman needs more than a yearly call. Like I said before . . . ya know he ain't been livin' like no monk! Ya have a right to find happiness, Lilah!"

"I know. The only thing is . . . I'm never happier than when I'm in his arms. It's like my soul sings every time he touches me. Now, I have to accept that he ain't never gonna come back. He's more than likely gone for good this time."

I was suddenly interrupted by a little voice right beside me, "Mommy? Who's never comin' back? Why you gots tears? It's okay Mommy, Eli's comin' back and we take good care of ya." Jonny wrapped his little arms around my leg again and hugged as hard as he could. How could I not smile?

****

Two weeks passed, then three, then four. Doctors, nurses, and physical therapists come in and out on a daily basis. Everyday seemed to be just like the one before. Durin' the day, I talked to Eli, still read him books, and sang him his favorite songs. At night, I laid on the bed and prayed for his recovery. But always, I went to sleep thinkin' about Chad.

The pleasant, but pungent, smell of cleanin' and sterilizin' had become absorbed into my clothin', my hair, and even the pillow and blankets that I slept on at night. The daily sounds of the hospital had started to become so familiar that I hardly noticed 'em anymore. I called Jonny nightly and Ross every three or four days. I was beginnin' to miss Ross and found myself callin' more often than I had before. His deep, sexy voice was a great comfort somehow and I'd started to long for his strong arms at night.

It was Sunday mornin' and Floy, Toby, and Jonny were on their way to the hospital. I waited at the elevators so I could tell 'em that Eli was in a private room now. He was still hooked up to most of the equipment. They had removed the breathin' device and he was breathin' on his own and it seemed so much better in a room where I could have a cot and sleep right beside his little crib.

I waited down at the end of the hall by the elevators. I was watchin' out the window when the elevator doors opened. I turned to find Ross and Jonny standin' in the hall, hand in hand. Jonny ran to me and hugged my neck.

"Mommy, me and Ross come to see ya and lift ya up with spirits." He was beamin' as he kissed my cheek.

I looked at Ross a little puzzled. "Lift me . . . what?" I whispered. He grinned and shook his head. "I think that was supposed to be, 'lift your spirits'."

"Oh . . . okay. Well, sweetie, ya certainly have done that. My spirits are sure enough lifted." I told him as I picked him up and swung him around in my arms.

"What are you doing down here?" Ross asked.

"They moved Eli to a private room and I wanted to catch ya here so I could show ya the way. Did Floy and Toby come too?"

"No, just us men." He said as he winked at me.

We walked back down the hall and turned toward Eli's new room. As we neared the door, I heard the nurse speakin' to someone.

"Yes Father, I'll be sure and tell her." She said as she stepped out the door. "Oh, there you are Mrs. Barrett. Father was just tellin' me that he had put Eli on their prayer list at church. Isn't that wonderful?" She smiled as she walked past us. I froze in my tracks. There was just no way this was happenin'. This was the first time Ross'd been there in a month and now Chad shows up. What in the hell was I gonna do?

Before I could even begin to clear my mind, the door opened again and the priest walked out into the hall. I stepped back and my breath caught in my throat. I began to cough like I'd swallowed a bug.

"Are you okay, ma'am?" the priest asked as he stepped toward me.

I nodded my head as I tried to clear my throat. He turned, rushed back into the room, and come out with a glass of water. I took a sip or two. "Thank you . . . Father."

I wasn't so sure I could contain the strong desire to burst into hysterical giggles. My relief was so great to see the bald head and deep brown eyes of the man who handed me the glass of water.

We talked a minute, I thanked him for puttin' Eli on the prayer list, and he left. I turned to look at Ross. He had a bewildered look on his face. I know he thought I acted a little strange, but he just didn't have no idea at all what I'd just gone through.

We opened the door and went inside. Ross went to Eli and leaned over the crib. He brushed his hair back and spoke softly to him and encouraged him to wake up.

"Mommy, I wanna talk to Eli. Him need me, now," Jonny said as he started to attempt to climb over the crib.

"Wait Jonny, I don't know if that's a good idea." I told him as I took him off the crib bars.

"It is! It's a good idea Mommy. I branged him sumpin' and he needs it right now," insisted Jonny.

"What did ya bring?" I asked him.

"It's a secret for me and Bubba. Nobody knows. Him telled me him needs it, so I branged it to him." He clung tightly to a little bag in his hand.

I smiled at him. "Okay, let me check with his nurse and see if it's okay." I turned to Ross, "Do ya know what it is?"

"Nope, he wouldn't tell me anything about it. He just said that Bubba told him in his dream that he needed it." Ross shrugged his shoulders and smiled.

"Well, if Jonny thinks he needs it, then I'm sure he does," I told him as I started out the door.

It only took a few minutes for his nurse to say okay, and I was walkin' back in the door.

"No!" I heard Jonny growl between his teeth. "It my Bubba, and me gettin' in dat bed wif him." He glared at Ross as he jerked away.

"What's goin' on? Ya know ya can't be talkin' that loud in Eli's room." I half-whispered in an angry tone.

"Ross not let me up wif Bubba." He tuned up to bawl.

"It's okay, Jonny. He just wanted ya to wait 'til I found out if it was alright." I tried to comfort him.

"Did her said it okay? Mommy, Eli's waitin'."

"Yes, she said it'd be fine so long as it wasn't nothin' that might harm him. Now, is this a safe thing?"

"Oh, yeah ma'am. It a best thing!"

"Okay."

I took his shoes off and lifted him over the rails of the crib and sat him beside Eli. Jonny opened up his little sack and I almost cried when I saw what he'd brought. He pulled out the soft baby blue shirt of Chad's that they were both so attached to. It was so hard to believe that he was willin' to give it up to his Bubba. As I watched, he carefully unfolded it and tucked it around Eli's face and neck. He leaned in close to Eli's ear and whispered just loud enough that Ross and I could hear.

"I branged it Eli, just like ya telled me. Now ya can gets all better and come home wif me." Then he softly kissed his brother's cheek and laid his little head on the pillow beside him.

My jaw dropped when I thought I saw the slightest hint of a smile from Eli. I turned quickly to Ross.

"Did ya see that Ross?"

He took my hand and squeezed it gently. "I did, Lilah. I can't believe it, but I did."

I wasn't seein' things. It really happened and Ross had confirmed it. I rushed to the other side of the crib.

"Eli? Baby can ya hear me?" I held his little hand and kissed it. "Eli? Open your eyes, honey. It's Mommy . . . it's Mommy, baby."

There was nothin'. He just continued to sleep. I frantically pushed the nurse's button and waited. "Get Dr. Kline!" I almost yelled. "Hurry, get a doctor in here!"

****

Later that evenin', Dr. Kline told us that he'd checked the information on some of the machines and it'd confirmed that when Jonny'd put the shirt to Eli's face and laid down beside him, there'd been a definite reaction. He said it was a very good sign.

I was so excited that I couldn't hardly stand it. After weeks of not knowin', there was progess at last. Ross and I just sat and watched Eli for hours. We was lookin' for any movement at all. Jonny'd been in the crib most all of the time. He was very quiet and hardly moved. He just laid there beside his brother, clingin' to the sleeve of that shirt. I thought that it would've been wonderful if Ross wasn't there and Chad'd walked in and seen his boys like that. I knew he'd be so thrilled or at least, I thought he would. Then I shamed myself for thinkin' that way. Chad'd left so suddenly and was so cold to me. Then there was Ross, right beside me, and almost as excited as I was. I knew it'd be hard to get past what'd happened between me and Chad, but now I was fairly sure I could. I was a much stronger woman now than he'd left four years ago. Besides, I had Ross now, and we was growin' closer ever day.

"I still can't believe that," whispered Ross. "It's like he really knew exactly what Eli wanted or maybe needed. It makes you wonder doesn't it?"

I tried to ignore the little chill that ran up my right side as I nodded to Ross's question. I already suspected that Eli had some special abilities, but I wasn't prepared for Jonny to possibly have 'em too.

About the time that thought went through my head, Jonny stretched in his sleep and I caught my breath as I saw Eli turn his head toward him. Ross turned quickly toward me with a startled look on his face.

"Did you see that, sugar?" he asked.

"I did! He turned his head. Not much, but he did turn it!" I was so happy I could've cried! I started pressin' the nurse's button as quick as I could. It was only a minute and they was in the room.

"This time Ross seen it too! Eli turned his head a little. He did. He really moved his head."

The nurse stepped back out and in a couple of minutes, a doctor came in the room. He immediately checked the readout on the machines and then proceeded to check Eli's eyes. He lifted one eyelid and moved his little flashlight back and forth, then the other one. He turned to me, "I see a definite reaction to light and the read out indicates some movement. I don't want to sound too optimistic just yet, but I think he is starting to come around. I'll notify Dr. Kline and he'll most likely stop by later today or tonight."

I was overcome with joy. "Thank ya doctor. I just can't thank ya enough."

"Well, all I did was tell you what I saw. Eli is the one doing all the work," he answered.

"Ever since I put his brother in the bed with him, he seems to be makin' a lot more progress. Maybe that's what he's been needin' all this time. They've been inseparable ever since they was born. I don't know why I didn't think of it myself," I said.

He looked at me a little surprised. "Who's idea was it?"
"His brother's. He said Eli needed the shirt they always slept with and needed him to be here with him. I guess he was right." I lowered my voice as Ross put his arm around my shoulders. It'd been a wonderful day.

****

Ross had stayed the night, but I'd convinced him to leave without Jonny. I felt it was the wisest thing to do, seein' as how Eli had seemed to respond to him so well. Dr. Kline was in agreement with me. I took Jonny shoppin' with me so I'd have some clothes for him while he was there. He was so excited to get to pick out a teddy bear for Eli and a little stuffed dog for hisself. We grabbed some dinner while we was out and then headed back up to the hospital.

It'd been nice to be outside for a little while. I'd very seldom left the room, let alone, the hospital. It was good to breathe fresh air again and hear the songs of the birds in the trees in the parkin' lot. It was real pleasant just to feel the sunshine on my face and shoulders. Just as we entered the revolvin' door and stepped inside, I stopped dead in my tracks as a sudden weakness spread from my face to my feet. I'd caught a glimpse of a priest as he exited another door. I couldn't be positive, but I was almost sure it was Chad. I didn't see his face, but the long, silver-blonde hair and his distinct way of walkin' was undeniable. I ran in the direction he'd gone, draggin' my poor baby with me. When I exited the door, there was no sign of him anywhere. I'd wanted him to see Jonny too and to see how beautiful both his sons were.

Disappointed, I turned and went back inside.

"Mommy, why ya dragged me out of side?" Jonny asked in a very concerned little voice.

"I'm sorry baby. I thought I saw someone I used to know. I wanted him to meet ya, that's all." I tried to reassure him.

We went up to Eli's room and Bonnie was there, checkin' his vitals again. She turned toward me. "He's still breathing very well on his own." She said. "We're still monitoring him in case there are any problems, but Dr. Kline says that so far, he's doing great!"

"That's a good sign, right?" I asked.

"That's an excellent sign Lilah."

Jonny started to climb over the bars of the crib. "Wait! Let me get your shoes off and wash your hands. We can't take a chance of bringin' any germs back to Eli. As soon as I was finished, I lifted him up into the crib.

"Bubba? Look! Look what I buyed ya. It just for you. Him wanna be you teddy bear. Him want to sleep with ya ever' night and help ya get better." Jonny put the little bear in Eli's hand. He was rewarded with that little hand slowly pullin' the bear up to his chest. I was just stunned.

"Mommy, look, Bubba likes him . . . him smiled at me."

I'd been so surprised by the movement of his hand that I hadn't even noticed the soft, one-sided, little smile on his lips.

"I think he does, Jonny, I really think he does. You are the very best medicine for him."

Jonny and I hugged for a minute as we watched in amazement how Eli cuddled that little bear and a trace of the smile was still on his precious little face.

Dr. Kline later explained that the brain was healin' and he wouldn't be surprised if Eli just opened his eyes at anytime.

"It's a slow process. Some heal quicker than others, depending on the severity of the damage. Eli is a little fighter and even though it's taken quite awhile, we're now seeing improvement every day."

I woke up in anticipation every mornin' thinkin' that today might be the day. The boys continued to sleep in the same bed and snuggle the precious powder blue shirt, night after night. I waited and watched and prayed.

****

". . . and . . . and then him said 'my love you, my boy.' But I was asweep and not waked up yet."

"Was him us's real Daddy?"

At first I thought Jonny was talkin' to the toys in the crib until I listened a little closer.

"Yeah Bubba. Him gots you eyes and him was cryin'."

"Why?" I heard a little voice ask.

"Him say him got to go back, but him love us berry much. Him tell me, I need tell you."

"Did him weave us?"

"Yeah, but him berry sad."

It hit me like a tree limb in a storm. I was hearin' a conversation between my two babies! I sat straight up outta bed and stared in disbelief. Jonny sat up in the crib and Eli was still layin' down, but his big bright blue eyes was wide open and he was awake as he could be. I tried to control my excitement a little, but I was overjoyed.

"Eli, baby, when did ya wake up? How do ya feel?" I reached over the crib rail and hugged him gently and kissed his face over and over.

"Mommy! You cried on my face. Why ya makin' tears on me?" Eli asked.

"I'm just so thrilled that you're awake. Praise the Lord, you're awake!"

I pushed the nurse's buzzer like crazy. "Come in here . . . bring Dr. Kline. Hurry, just get in here!" I all but yelled.

When Bonnie rushed in the door, she nearly fainted. "Oh, thank God! Thank you Lord!" she said as she rushed back out into the hallway.

I could hear her in the hall as she told everybody at the desk. They called Dr. Kline and before long the room was full of nurses, aides, and doctors.

"Well, good morning young man." Dr. Kline said as he stepped to Eli's bedside. "So you finally decided to wake up and join us, did you?"

Eli looked from me to the doctor and back again. Before anyone could say anything Jonny chimed in. "Ya was dead sleepin', Bubba. Just like Mommy, but you sleeped for hundred of years like Mr. Winkle in Mommy's story. When me dream, you tell me to bring dat blue huggy and sleep wif ya. So I did, I bringed it right quick." Jonny smiled at Eli and laid down on the pillow that they shared.

"Did me sleep a hundred years? Did me Mommy?" Eli asked seriously.

"No, but it sure did seem like it, sweetie. How do ya feel now?" I asked him.

He looked around the room with big wide eyes. "Me hungry, Mommy."

Happy, relieved chuckles were heard from everyone.

****

The next week was filled with tests and physical therapy, and me bein' trained to help with his therapy. I'd sent Jonny home with Ross when he'd come back to visit. Eli was none to happy about it, but it was a lot easier on me with one less child to try to handle.

Eli'd grown stronger every day and was just startin' to eat solid food.

"I've never seen anyone recover as quickly as Eli." Dr. Kline said as he wrote in Eli's chart. "It took him awhile, but now he is progressing in leaps and bounds! Everything appears to be back to a normal level except his strength. He will require physical therapy for a while yet, but it is nothing that can't be done at home. I believe he will be ready to go home by next week."

I hadn't expected that. "That's the best news I've had in months." I told him. "I'll miss everyone here, but I won't miss this place or its food. Thank ya Dr. Kline." I said as I startled him by huggin' his neck.

"It always gives me great pleasure when things turn out like this. It's the true purpose of my calling." He smiled and walked out the door with a very satisfied look on his face.

Chapter 16

We arrived home to find that Ross had pretty much been livin' at the ranch. He'd taken full charge of the day-to-day care of the animals and seemed quite at home. Floy and Toby had come to get us and it was a good homecomin' for Eli. Dee'd spent a lot of time gettin' things cleaned and ready for the big day. It was great to have everybody together and safe at home.

I reckon the only shadow on the whole day was the never-endin' missin' of Chad. It should've been him that come and got us, and it should've been him carryin' Eli into the house. I scolded myself for even lettin' the thought make its way into my head. Chad made his choice for whatever reason, and had walked out of our lives yet again. I'd spent a lot of time thinkin' about it and decided that I was gonna work on a new life for myself. I wanted a real home for my boys and it was painfully clear that it wasn't gonna include Chad.

It was only a couple of hours and Eli was gettin' very tired. Dee and me took both boys upstairs to get 'em tucked in bed. Before we could leave the room, they'd cuddled together and was sound asleep with their beloved huggy.

"Ross has really been a huge help, Lilah. He's just took over and run the ranch like an old pro. It sure has made it a lot easier to give Jonny my complete attention. Sometimes he'd ride the horses for hours, then bring 'em back, brush 'em down, and then go into town to tend to his business. He's a hard worker. I never seen anybody so dedicated to anything in my life." Dee told me.

"That's great to hear. I knew between him and Toby that I didn't have anything to worry about with the animals. Of course, I never had to even give it a thought that you was takin' excellent care of my baby. You're like his other mother, Dee." I said as I gave her a big hug.

We went down stairs and Dee headed for her own room. "Good night, ya'll. I'm exhausted too."

That left me and Ross alone on the couch. He put his arm around me and pulled me close. "Put your feet up, honey. I know you are just worn out."

We sat in silence for a long time and I guess I must've dozed off to sleep.

"Princess? Let's go get in our bed. I'm pretty tired myself." He whispered as he lifted me off the couch and carried me up the stairs.

I didn't object and that pretty much settled it for Ross, I guess. Before I knew what'd happened, he'd moved his stuff in and stayed. At first, I wasn't so sure about the situation, it'd not settled too well when he'd referred to MY bed as OUR bed. It'd been mine and . . . well, it'd been mine for the last four years. It didn't take long for me to become fairly comfortable with it. I truly liked havin' a man around the house, especially at night when we cuddled and talked. Our lovemakin' was always wonderful. Ross was a very gentle, satisfiyin' lover, but always I'd lay there after he'd gone to sleep and wonder how Chad had known so much about my private life. It was as if he was standin' right there lookin' in the window at me. It never failed that I'd dream about him every night that Ross and I made love and I'd wake up in a quiet, withdrawn mood. Ross never seemed to notice and so it went from day to day.

****

"I'm goin' to the office, Princess. I'll be back sometime tonight." He said as he gave me a brief kiss and went out the front door. It seemed like he was just wearin' hisself out between the office and the time he spent with the horses. Dee was right, he was very dedicated to takin' care of 'em.

A knock at the door told me I had unexpected company, but before I could get through the livin' room, the door opened, and little Laurel come barrellin' in like the wind.

"Laurel Marie! I said knock!" I heard Floy scold.

"I did Mommy. I knocked! Didn't I Aunt Lilah? I knocked." She argued.

"Yes you sure did sweetie!" I told her as she gave me a big hug.

Floy come in right behind her. "I said, knock and wait 'til somebody opens the door."

"I did Mommy. I knocked and I opened the door!" She sounded a little confused about what the problem was.

Floy threw her hands in the air. "I give up!! She's just like her Daddy . . . she'll argue all day and in the end I'm not even sure what it is we're arguin' about. How are ya doin'? How's the baby doin'?" All this was said in one breath.

I shook my head and laughed. "I'm great. The boys are great, and I'm thrilled ya come to see us."

I was sure that Dee had finished with Eli's physical therapy, so I sent Laurel up to see what Dee and the boys was doin' while Floy and I settled at Nanny's old kitchen table for a cup of coffee.

I took a drink and let the warm, pungent flavor linger in my mouth for a moment. Somethin' about a cup of fresh coffee was so relaxin' and brought out my very mellow side.

"So, how is it with Ross livin' here?" Floy got right to the point. But then, that was her way and always had been. She hardly ever minced words.

I took another drink and sat there for a moment before I answered her. "It's different. It's taken a little while to adjust, but I'm likin' it more and more. I just wish he wouldn't work so hard. I told her how he worked around the ranch, fixin' fences, and everything else that needed attention. He took care of my chickens, cows, and especially my horses.

"Sounds like a good man." She replied.

"Oh, that ain't all. He still goes in regular to take care of his farrier business. By suppertime he is just wore plum out. I don't know how he does it, but when Eli's completely recovered, I'm gonna go back to tendin' to the ranch. I always enjoyed it so much."

"Well, I gotta admire him for takin' over like he has. He's been a godsend durin' all this. Now tell me, how's he doin' takin' care of you and the babies?"

"Floy, he's wonderful. I couldn't ask for nobody any better. I just wish he was here a little more."

"So, he hasn't popped the big question yet?" she teased.

"Oh, heck no. We ain't ready for that . . . not by a long shot."

"Toby was tellin' me last night that when he saw Seth last week, he mentioned it to him. He was shocked by Seth's reaction. He said he got kinda pale and then started cussin' and pacin' like a idiot. He told me he ain't never seen Seth get so upset about anything like he did when he heard ya'll was livin' together. I think Seth was head over heels for you and none of us even suspected it. I feel really sorry for him. I think that was why he was movin' back here, to be closer to you." She shook her head.

"Floy I don't know what to say. I had no idea. He never let on to me, in fact, he acted just the opposite and I didn't know he was movin' back. Where's he stayin'?"

"With us for a little while, just 'til he can find him a place. He's thinkin' of eventually hirin' on where Toby works, so maybe Toby can help him get over it. I sure hope so. Seth's a good man."

"I know. I really like him. He's not only nice, but he's a very good-lookin' man. I bet he'll find someone else in no time."

****

Several weeks passed and it seemed like I hardly spent any time with Ross. He was gone most of the time and when he was home, he spent most of his time off with the horses. He would ride one of 'em and the other two would follow him. They would be gone for hours sometimes.

One night, several weeks later, he come in really late, ate supper, bathed, and sat on the couch with me.

"I'd like to go up to our room and talk in private if that would be okay with you." He said.

"Sure," I answered as I thought to myself that it was a clever way to invite me up to bed. I was pretty sure what he had on his mind.

The boys and Dee were already asleep, so I turned out the lights while Ross locked the doors. I started up the stairs as he followed me. I shut the door and locked it without turnin' on any lights. Ross went straight to the lamp and turned it on. Okay, so he wanted some light . . . I was okay with that.

"Sit down Lilah. We need to discuss something that has really been bothering me."

He was serious about a discussion.

"What is it, Ross?"

"I've been here quite a while now. We're living like a married couple in every sense of the word." He began.

I really hoped he wasn't goin' to bring up us gettin' married. Not yet. I just wasn't ready to take that step.

"Are you happy with me being here?" he asked.

"Well, yeah. I enjoy you bein' here Ross. Why?"

"I'm not sure how to say this . . . but I would really like for it to be just the four of us. I don't see where we really need Dee here. She's really a nice lady, but don't you think that if we need a sitter, we can just ask Floy? I want us to be a real family. I feel like she is always right around the corner and it makes me very uncomfortable. Can you understand what I mean?"

"Well, I understand what ya mean, but Dee isn't just a sitter. She is a very dear friend and she's been here for years. I don't think I could ever ask her to leave." I said.

"Is she more important to you than I am?" Ross interrupted.

"No. It has nothin' to do with us. It's just that the boys wouldn't know what to do without her. She's been with 'em their whole lives."

"I feel like it's more important for their Mom to be their main caregiver. Don't you? She needs to go find a life for herself and quit expecting you and the boys to fill that void. I really want you to tell her to go." He said firmly.

I was stunned. How in the world could I just tell her to go? We'd been so close for so long and she'd always been right there when I needed her. I was very uncomfortable with the idea.

"I'll give it some thought." I told him.

"It shouldn't take a lot of thought, Lilah. It's a simple fact of who is the most important to you. Is it me or is it the sitter?"

I became very uneasy with the whole conversation.

"I said, I will think about it." I told him.

He stood up and started to the bathroom. "Well don't take too long. I'd like to see this resolved very soon." He went in and shut the door.

What I'd thought was goin' to be a very romantic evenin', had quickly turned into a bit of an argument. I had a sudden sinkin' feelin' in the pit of my stomach. It was a familiar feelin' and I didn't like it one bit.

When he come to bed, he turned his back to me and went straight to sleep. I guess I laid there most of the night thinkin' about what he'd said. I hated to tell him, but Dee was just as important to me as he was. I loved Ross, but I wasn't really in love with him. I wasn't at all sure what I was gonna do. Either way, somebody wasn't gonna be happy and I had a real strong feelin' that it was most likely gonna be me.

When mornin' come, Ross was gettin' ready to leave for work. I laid there, wide awake, with everthing rollin' through my mind for the billionth time.

Ross suddenly knelt at my bedside and right in my face.

"Princess, I'm sorry if I came off a little harsh last night. It's not that I don't like Dee, it's just that I've waited all my life to have a family and I'm so in love with you and the boys. I just want so badly to be one of the three most important men in your life. I feel like an outsider looking in." He said as he dropped his head.

"Ross, you're not an outsider."

"Then what am I?" he asked sadly as he stood up and went out the door.

What a miserable way to start the day. It'd been bad enough to have to think about our talk last night . . . but now I had to think about Ross's hurt feelings.

I got up, got dressed, and went downstairs to start what promised to be a very long day. I'd just started toward the kitchen when I heard Dee and the boys talkin'. I stopped to listen for a minute.

"Eli said ours really Daddy come to see him, Aunt Dee." Jonny told her excitedly.

"Well, I'm sure he would like to do that if he knew you were sick Eli." She said.

"No!" Eli was a little angry. "Him did, Aunt Dee. Him said him love me and Bubba and for me to tell him. Him look just like Bubba only old and bigger. He gots blue, blue eyes and him kissed me on the head, really!!"

How in heaven could Eli know all this? That was exactly what'd happened.

"Did he say anything else?" Dee carefully questioned.

"Yeah . . . him loves us and him loves Mommy wif all him heart . . . him got tears on my face, then wipe 'em off and said good-bye. Him was gone then." Eli said very sadly.

Dee put her arm around him and hugged him, "That was a very beautiful dream, honey."

Eli pushed her away and jumped down from his chair. "Dat's not a dream. Him was right there! Don't say that no more!" he yelled as he took off out of the kitchen.

I was stunned. Eli had never yelled at anyone in anger, but he was really mad. I stepped out into the kitchen and found Dee with her mouth open watchin' Eli and Jonny go across the back yard.

"What was that all about?" I asked her.

"Eli's been tellin' Jonny stories about see'n his Daddy at the hospital and Jonny is believin' it. I tried to suggest that it was just a dream, but . . . well, you heard how that went."

I stepped to the back door. "Boys!" I hollered, "That's far enough. Stay in the shade, too. Eli! Don't be out but a few minutes and no runnin'."

They stopped where they were and sat under a shade tree in the back yard. Even though the doctor had said he was fully recovered, he was weak and I still was not comfortable with a few things.

I sat down at the table with Dee. "What would ya say if I told ya that Chad really was there?"

Dee's jaw dropped for the second time that mornin'.

"What if I told ya that what Eli said really did happen . . . except the last part. I didn't see that, but I heard him tell Eli just what he said."

"Do you mean to tell me that Chad showed up at the hospital? How did he know what happened? What . . . ?"

"He did, and I got no idea how he found out. He seems to know a lot about my life."

Dee stood up and paced around the room. "I feel so bad for trying to make Eli think different. But then, how could he know what happened if he was still unconscious? Do you think he was doing that thing he does about knowing what he can't possibly know?"

"That's the only way to explain how he knows any of it. I was right there and he was still in the coma. I don't know how he does it. Jonny does it too. I told you how they communicated through dreams when Eli wanted the blue huggy. I think I'm goin' into Bigby and see a friend of mine who might be able to shed a little light on this. I'll be back after awhile." Dee agreed and I left right away.

****

Lamar was sittin' in the sun room when I got there. I walked up behind him and put my hands on his shoulders.

"Lilah. I'm so glad you came." He sounded tired.

"How are ya doin' my friend?" I asked him.

"I'm better than yesterday, but I plan on bein' even better tomorrow." He smiled. "I been sittin' here waitin' on you. Our friend said you was on your way." He teased.

I sat down on the footstool in front of him. "Why is it that you can see her and I can't?"

"Ya can feel her. I know ya can. She's with ya always. To see her . . . you just have to close your eyes and open your mind."

"Lamar, I need to talk to ya about somethin'."

"Then let's go into my room. It's much more private there. Sometimes . . . the walls have ears." He laughed.

Lamar got settled in his big comfy chair and I sat in the chair across from him.

"Now . . . what's going on sweetheart?" he asked.

"I don't know how to say this . . . but, I think my boys have the same gift that you do. I'm not sure what to do about it."

He chuckled. "Do about it? My sweet girl, there's nothing you can do about it. What makes you think they have the gift anyway?"

"They know things they can't possibly know, and they seem to communicate in dreams from long distances. Eli was the first and seems to be . . . I guess, stronger. But now, Jonny has started it, especially when it comes to things with his brother. What should I do, Lamar?"

He sat there very thoughtful for a long time. For a minute, I thought he'd gone to sleep. He suddenly looked up and reached for my hand.

"You're right, Lilah. By concentrating, I just linked with Eli in a very small way. I told him to give you something when you get home. Let me know what happens."

"How can ya do that?" I asked him.

"Nanny helped me. You have somewhat of a gift also. You have an unusual ability to sense danger. Those storms that I told you about, the ones that border on a big crisis . . . well Eli's accident was one of those, but . . . I fear a much greater one is brewing."

"Is that all ya know about his accident?" I tested him.

"He smiled an all-knowin' smile. "Do you mean . . . about Chad bein' at the hospital. Of course I know. He left for your own good or so he thinks. Lilah, he's hurt, . . . deep inside, but he loves you enough to let you go."

"How do ya know all this stuff?" I wanted to know.

"Nanny. She keeps me up to date on you because we both love you so much."

"Ya said somethin' about a bigger storm. What are ya talkin' about?"

"I sense that somethin' isn't what it seems. I'm not sure yet if it's . . ."

There was a knock on the door and it opened. Junie popped her head in the room.

"Lamar, it's time to leave for your dentist appointment." She said as she pushed a wheel chair in from the hall.

"We'll talk later sweet girl." He waved as he was bein' wheeled from the room.

I was even more confused than I had been. Now I had yet another thing to worry on. I left and started home. As I went up the mountain, I stopped by Floy's to see her for a minute. I needed her advice about Dee, as well as Ross's sudden need for her to go. I was still uncomfortable about the whole subject. Floy was sittin' outside on her porch when I pulled up to her house. She told me that Laurel was down for a nap, so I felt this was a perfect time for a visit.

"What ya doin' out runnin' around?" she asked.

"I been to the nursin' home to visit. I had a good talk with Lamar . . . before they hauled him off to the dentist."

"That's good, ya seem to think a lot of him. You've said a million times how much ya love talkin' to him. He sounds very special."

"Ya have no idea how special he really is. But that's not what I stopped to visit about. I have a big old problem and I'm just not sure how to go about solvin' it." I explained.

"What's up?"

"Ross." I said flatly. "Last night he said he needed to talk to me. He wanted to talk privately, so we went upstairs. I wasn't sure what he wanted to say, but it didn't take but a little bit and he laid it on the line."

"I bet I know what he said. He wants to get married don't he?" She grinned.

"That's kinda what I thought too. No. He says he wants Dee to move out of the house. He thinks she should get on with her own life and let the four of us live like a normal family."

Floy sat there and thought for a minute. "Maybe he's right, sweetie. I think it'd be hard to have a fifth wheel around all the time. What do you think about the idea?"

It took me a few minutes to roll it around in my head again. "Dee's always been there for me, and the boys have had her there since day one. I can't really imagine her not bein' there. With Ross gone all the time, I think I'd just be lost."

"Are ya sure she's not just stayin' there 'cause she thinks ya expect her to?" she asked me.

"No, the ranch is her home and we've all done just fine, up 'til now. I just don't understand Ross."

"I think he really loves ya and just wants a normal, average home life." She paused for a minute, "I wish I could tell ya what to do, but I think that it's just somethin' you got to figger out for yourself. I can only imagine how hard it'd be."

We sat there in silence for a few minutes before I decided to go on home.

"I don't like bein' given these kind of . . . ulti . . . ultimatums. I don't have to make no choice between the people I care about! Ross will just have to get over it." I told Floy firmly. She smiled and nodded her head and I got in my Jeep and drove away. I was determined to settle this today 'cause it was drivin' me crazy!

The dogs greeted me as I pulled up to the cabin and got out and walked to the porch. I'd just stepped in the door when I was met with two cryin' little boys.

"What's the matter?" I asked as I knelt down beside 'em. "Why ya cryin' so hard?"

"Mommy" sobbed Eli, "Tell Dee she not go!! Tell her no!"

"Her leavin' Mama." Said Jonny as he threw his arms around my neck. "Tell Ross, go home and not make Dee cry! Mommy help!"

My babies were devastated and anger started to boil in my blood.

"Where is she?"

"In hers room. She makin' a bag to go away!" one of the boys all but screamed.

I rushed through the kitchen and into Dee's room to find her with a tear-streaked face, sittin' on the side of her bed.

I tried to control myself and not upset her no worse than she already was.

"Dee?" I said as calmly as I could manage. "Tell me what the hell's goin' on."

"I need to go, honey. I probably should've left a long time ago, but I thought we were all so happy together."

"We are. What makes ya think any different?" I asked her.

"You all need your privacy. I need to go start my own life and let ya live yours."

I thought for a minute before I said anything else. "Dee, was Ross home?"

She looked at me and for a minute I thought I saw a flash of fear in her eyes.

She dropped her head, "Yeah, he was here for a few minutes."

Suddenly I was livid. It was painfully obvious that he'd already had his say before I could even make up my mind.

"Let me tell ya this, Dee. You're welcome to live here as long as ya want. This is my home and I say who comes and goes! Now unpack and forget about leavin'."

I was surprised when she just sat there shakin' her head from side to side. "I love you and these boys Lilah, but I can't stay now. It's time for me to get on with my life."

She got up, picked up a couple of bags, and started out the door. "I'll send for the rest later." She said as she went toward the front door in tears. When she reached the livin' room, Eli and Jonny attacked her. Clingin' to her clothes and legs, they cried and begged her to please not go. She got to the door and stopped. "Listen to me. I love you both so very much and maybe I can come visit with you. I just can't live here anymore . . . I'm so sorry . . . bye." She whispered through tears as she finally made her way out the door. She suddenly turned and looked me straight in the eyes. "Be careful, honey. Be very careful." And just like that . . . she too, was gone.

****

By the time I'd calmed the boys down and gotten 'em into bed, I was so mad that my heart was poundin' in my ears. How dare him! How dare him to tell anybody in my house to leave! Ross had no right and I damn sure intended on tellin' him as soon as he stepped in that door!

It was late when I heard his truck pull up out front. Usually I'd done be in the bed asleep by that time, but I was still so damn mad that there'd been no chance of sleepin', not even for a minute 'till this was settled. I was sittin' in my rocker up in the bedroom when he opened the door very quietly and slipped into the room. I flipped on the lamp once he'd shut the door. He jumped as if he'd seen a ghost.

"What are you doing still up?" He asked softly.

"Waitin' on you, Ross. Did ya really think I'd be able to sleep after what ya done?"

He slipped out of his dark gray jacket and loosened his tie. "What is it that I did?" he asked as if he didn't have a clue.

I sat for a minute just almost in shock. "I think ya are perfectly aware of what ya done! Don't act like ya don't have no idea what I'm talkin' about. Why the hell did ya take it on yourself to talk to Dee behind my back?"

He turned and looked at me as he removed his shirt. I was almost amused at the way he carefully folded it and laid it on the chest of drawers. His eyes were oddly cold and his jaw was set.

"I felt it was a matter that needed to be taken care of and I didn't see any reason for putting the burden on you."

"Ya didn't see any reason . . . I told ya I would take care of it and discuss it with her. I don't recall askin' ya to say a damn word to her, Ross."

His blue-green eyes flashed fire for an instant before he regained his calmness. He came over to me and knelt beside my chair. I suddenly noticed that I had a death grip on the rocker arms and my knuckles had turned almost white.

"Princess . . . ," he spoke softly as he caressed my cheek with the edge of his thumb. "I love you beyond anything in this entire world. I would protect you with my very life. I just want us to be a normal family. You know, a mommy, a daddy, and two little boys. I just couldn't wait to start our new life." He stood up and pulled me out of the chair and into his strong, muscular arms. "I'm sorry, sugar. Forgive me? Forgive me for just wanting to be your everything."

His lips softly covered mine and I found it impossible to still be so angry with him. His arms pulled me close against the heat of him and there was no doubt about the passion that he felt. The desire that was startin' to boil in my blood drew me into the moment and I forgot about Dee and everything that I'd been so angry about only a few minutes ago. Before I knew it, we were naked in the bed and Ross's hands and lips explored every inch of my burnin' body. We hadn't made love with that much passion in a long time. I hadn't realized how much I'd needed him until that moment of complete satisfaction. As he relaxed beside me, he gently let his fingers slide through my hair and down my neck to my throat.

"Princess?" he whispered, "Don't ever . . . I mean ever again . . . talk to me in the tone you used earlier. Do you understand me?"

His voice had taken on a cold, angry tone that I'd never heard. I suddenly became aware that his fingers were, more or less, around my throat and I felt a great uneasiness come over me.

"You didn't answer me, Princess. Do you understand what I just said?"

I wasn't sure what to say. This was not the Ross I knew. I tried to pull away, but his hold on my throat became slightly tighter. I raised my hand to push his away. His face was suddenly right in mine. His beautiful blue-green eyes were somehow different. They had a cold glare about 'em that scared the hell out of me.

"Let me go Ross! This isn't funny." I told him.

"It's not supposed to be funny. I'm dead serious. It upsets me very much when you use that tone when you're talking to me. Don't do it again."

"Don't tell me what to do in my own house!" I tried to jerk away. That was when I felt a sharp slap across my face. I was totally caught off guard. I hardly knew what to think.

"Maybe now you will take me a little more serious. I didn't do that to hurt you sweetheart . . . that was just . . . an attention-getter. I will get a little more respect around here."

He leaned in and kissed my lips, but I did not kiss him back. I was in shock and so mad I could hardly contain myself. Somehow I sensed that I should just play it cool and calm until I could get away from him.

He wrapped his arms around me and within minutes, he was sound asleep. I started to move and his arms tightened and he pulled me closer. My mind raced in confusion.

What was goin' on here? This just couldn't be happenin'.

I suddenly realized that I didn't even know this man in my bed. He was a completely different person.

I tried to turn over and, again, he pulled me closer.

I laid there for hour after long hour just tryin' to make at least a little sense out of all that'd just happened. My body was so tense that before long I started to get a terrible headache, and I could feel my heart poundin' in my throat.

If only I could get up, I would grab my babies and head to Floy's house as fast as I could. My friend Stanley, the sheriff, would help me. Toby would help me.

But every time I made the slightest move, his arms clutched me tighter.

I watched as the light outside my window started to change from the darkness of night into the slightest hint of daylight. Glancin' around the room, I wondered what the day would hold in store for me . . . for us. Somethin' caught my eye as the shadows began to lighten. I blinked . . . blinked again, and wondered if I was asleep, or maybe half-asleep. I could see somethin' in the corner beside the fireplace. It was almost a shadow, but kinda fuzzy. I blinked again and it dissolved into nothin'. What the hell was that? I bit my lip and it hurt like heck. It was a certainty that I was awake, but I'd never seen anything like that in my entire life. I lay frozen and focused on that corner for a long enough time that the room became quite light.

The alarm clock sounded and Ross sat up on the side of the bed. I closed my eyes and pretended to be asleep. I thought to myself that this might be my chance to leave as soon as he left for work.

He showered quickly, leavin' the bathroom door wide open. I could hear him puttin' on his clothes and shoes.

"Princess?" He asked as he shook my shoulder lightly.

I opened my eyes. "What?"

"I forgot to tell you that I brought my sister home with me last night. She's staying in Dee's old room. She'll be helping you with the boys for a few days while you adjust."

He leaned over and kissed me on the forehead and left the room.

A thousand more questions spun through my head as I got up and dressed.

Why would he get rid of Dee just to bring in his sister to watch the boys? It made no sense at all. I just knew that it would make it harder to get away with her bein' right there.

I went down the stairs and started into the kitchen and found Ross and his sister in what seemed like a heated conversation. They went silent just as I walked in.

"Lilah, sweetheart, do you remember my sister?" he asked. "Sivle, I'm sure you remember Lilah from when she came into the office."

"Yes, I do. How are ya doin'?" I made myself be cordial.

I couldn't help but notice the stiffness in the way she stood. "I'm doing just fine, thank you."

I took the chance to let her know just where she was. "Welcome to my home . . . Sivle? Did ya say?"

"Yes, it was my grandmother's name, and thank you for allowing me to be here." She smiled that same practiced smile from the first time I'd seen her.

"Well, you ladies have a good day. Lilah, if you need to go to town for anything, Sis was just saying she needed a few things, so she might appreciate going in with you. I'll try and be home early." He said as he went out the front door. We both stood there in a very awkward silence.

Chapter 17

It'd been a week and everything seemed to be goin' pretty good, I guess. Sivle was good with the boys and they seemed to like her okay. She was a little cool toward me and I really didn't understand it. I tried to be as nice as I could bring myself to be, but I still didn't understand Ross bein' so set on us bein' alone and then movin' his sister in the minute he got rid of Dee. It puzzled me why she wasn't goin' into work at all. I hadn't been anywhere that Sivle didn't find a reason to go along. It was startin' to wear on my last good nerve.

Ross was as sweet and gentle as he'd always been, except for that one night. I didn't understand that neither, but I decided to let it go . . . still, I knew I'd never forget it.

Floy had called to tell me that Seth was back and was still very upset that I was with Ross. I felt sorta bad, but . . . it was just somethin' that happened. I asked her how long he'd be in town. She told me she didn't know, that he was workin' on somethin' in Bigby. I told her to tell him hi for me and that I'm sorry he's upset with me. I couldn't help but wonder why her and Toby hadn't been out in such a long time but then, I hadn't been to their house lately either.

The phone rang.

"Hello?" I answered.

"Lilah? This is Dora at the center. Lamar wanted me to call ya. He's on his way to the hospital and he insists that he needs to talk to ya. It don't look good, honey. Ya better hurry."

I hung up the phone and ran into the kitchen where Ross and Sivle were havin' coffee.

"It was the center." I told 'em as I grabbed my sweater and purse. "I gotta go to the hospital. Lamar is really bad and wants to see me. Will ya watch the boys while I'm gone?"

I heard Ross answer, "Yes," as I rushed toward the front door where he caught up with me.

"Princess?" he said as he grabbed my arm. "I hope he'll be okay. Don't be long . . . I'll worry."

I left quickly before he changed his mind and drove as fast as I could into Bigby, and then straight to the hospital.

****

I rushed into the emergency room and was immediately met with that sickenin', sweet smell of disinfectant. Findin' the receptionist, I asked where I would find Lamar.

"Are ya family?" she asked.

I thought for a minute. "Yes, I am."

She picked up the phone at her desk and talked with someone. It was only a couple of minutes and Dora come to the desk.

"I'm so glad ya made it, honey. He's been beggin' for ya. Come on. I'll take ya to him."

She pulled me through doors, around corners, and past doctors and nurses. Before I knew it, I was in Lamar's small cubicle. He didn't look good. So many machines and tubes and monitors reminded me of Eli's stay in the intensive care unit.

I stepped a little closer.

"Lamar?" Dora spoke softly in his ear. "She's here sweetie. Lilah is right here."

I somehow managed to shake off the sudden shock of seein' that bigger than life man just layin' there so still. His hand moved slightly toward me.

"I'm here, Lamar. Whatever ya need my friend . . . whatever ya need, I'm right here." I told him as I took his frail, very pale, cold hand. He mumbled somethin' that I couldn't understand. I leaned a little closer.

". . . alone . . . just you." He managed to say.

"I'll be right outside." Dora said as her and the nurse stepped out into the hall.

"You're gonna be alright, Lamar. Just try and take it easy and . . ."

"No!" He spoke clearly as he grabbed my hand tightly. "Let me . . . listen to me." He coughed as he turned his head toward me. His blind eyes stared into nowhere as he struggled to find his words.

". . . danger . . . death . . . boys must . . ." he coughed again and had a hard time gettin' his breath.

"Lamar? The boys must what?" I felt my stomach rise to my throat.

". . . help you . . . we will. Chad not . . . Chad's not . . . *(cough)* Chad."

Lamar took a deep ragged breath and the last words he whispered were ". . . her and me will . . . *(cough)* be . . . right there, always . . . hi . . . hiiide." His voice was a whisper.

His precious hand went limp and I heard the same death gurgle that I'd heard when my Nanny'd passed.

I held his hand and sat there as I studied his sweet face. I was relieved when I realized that he had the most peaceful smile on his lips. Somehow I sensed that Nanny and Miss Mae was right there beside him. I stood up and tried to wipe the tears from my face as I whispered out loud, "Take care of him, ladies. Show him the way."

****

Later, I drove Dora back to the center. We'd cried all the way, but I was surprised to find we still had tears to share with all the residents there. Everyone was so upset to think that Lamar would never be back to share his beautiful laughter with 'em.

As Dora and I went into his room, I took comfort in the peace that I found there. I'd been sure that I'd find a great sadness and emptiness.

Dora opened the drawer to the nightstand beside his bed, "He told me a long time ago to make sure ya got this, honey. I want to give it to ya now before anyone else comes in here. He said ya would understand the significance."

She pulled out a small, tattered, black box from the rear of the drawer. My hand shook as I took it. I had no idea what in the world I would find inside.

"I'll give ya some privacy, Lilah." Dora said as she left the room.

I carefully opened the lid. For a minute, I was puzzled, then I realized the point of the small red ball that lay inside. It was a sign of the presence of unseen guardians. A joy filled my heart as a single tear ran down my cheek to join the smile that spread across my face.

I hugged Dora as I went out the door and got in my car. I sat for a minute and thought about all that'd happened so quickly. Takin' the box out of my purse again, I noticed that it seemed to have a little more weight than I would expect from a small rubber ball. I opened it again. Removin' the ball, I shook the box gently. There was a definite sound in the bottom. I carefully lifted the liner. In the very bottom, laid a thin, gold pocket watch. I took it into the palm of my hand and admired the beautiful detailed carvin' on the cover. Inside was a perfect, well-preserved old watch. The sun sparkled on the face of it and then I noticed faded words engraved inside the lid. *Foresight is the gift . . . accept it well.* I was certain it'd been a gift from Lamar's Grandpap . . . but I was sure that Lamar'd said that his Grandpap had passed before he'd been born. How could he have give him that watch? It must've been a gift to Lamar's Grandpap from somebody else. I closed my hand over it and wondered ... who?

****

The funeral service was held in Bigby three days later. I wasn't sure that I was up to goin', but I knew in my heart that I had to be there. I tried to get Ross to go with me, but he said he had too much to do at work. Sivle stated that she'd watch the boys while I went and I was glad for that. I still missed Dee, but all and all, things were goin' pretty smoothly.

My heart was heavy as I walked down the sidewalk to the large Catholic Church that sat on the back of three very large lots. The flowers were so beautiful and the grounds were very well kept. I sat for a moment on a small bench beside a fountain that flowed gently into a koi pond. I finally stood up and made my way to the beautiful old church. It was my first time inside. I hadn't known that Lamar was Catholic.

I signed the book and found a pew and sat down near the middle of the church. There were a lot of people already gathered and I recognized many from the nursin' home.

During the service, I felt like I was caught in a bad dream and only became aware of my surroundings as I neared the casket in front of the altar. I looked at Lamar's sweet face, a face I'd so grown to love. He didn't look right without his dark glasses on and my hand shook as I reached to caress his precious face. That face would be branded into my memory for the rest of my life . . . that face, with a peaceful, happy smile.

Afterwards, I sat by the fountain and watched the funeral procession as it left the church. I just couldn't watch my dear, sweet friend be put into the ground. There was a desperate, growin' panic in my gut and I knew I was about to lose control of my tears. I went back inside the church. It was empty, so I wandered toward the altar and knelt. I wasn't sure why I did it . . . but I felt some peace and comfort there. I prayed for a little while and then got up and started toward the entrance door. I passed the little booths that I knew were confessionals and for whatever reason, I stepped inside and closed the door. There was somethin' warm and safe about bein' in that tiny closed space. I started to relax when a little door opened and someone whispered softly, "Do you want to make a confession?"

I was so startled that I couldn't speak. What was I supposed to say? I had no idea what I was doin'!

"I . . . no, I . . . I just came in to . . . I'm not Catholic. I was just . . . I just needed a quiet place to be." I fumbled for words.

"Tell me how I can help." He whispered so softly I could hardly hear him.

It took me a few minutes to find my words. "My heart's broken . . . again. I'm confused and lost and I . . . I'm afraid . . . and I'm afraid for my babies. Now I've lost the only person I could talk to. The only one who could advise and help me. I've lost the only man I'll ever really love and now, my dearest friend. I've made a horrible mistake and I just don't know how to get out of it . . . I've lost control of my life and I'm afraid that I . . . ." I broke into uncontrolled sobs.

I heard the priest as he took in a ragged breath and whispered, "He'll watch over you and your boys . . . . The King will guide and protect you, just trust him."

The little door softly shut and I sat there for a minute before I got up and walked out into the empty church.

When I reached the entrance door, I turned and looked back at the altar. I caught a glimpse of the priest as he stepped quickly out the side door. I knew it was impossible, but I was sure I recognized the way he'd carried himself . . . and the hair! I ran down the long aisle to the back door and flew into the courtyard. For one brief second, I saw a flash of black behind the flowering bushes, but when I come around the corner . . . there was nothin'.

I sat down on another bench and just stared at the bushes. I tried ever' way in the world to reason with myself that what I thought I saw was impossible. I played them two brief glimpses over and over in my head and I thought about the voice inside the confessional. I just couldn't say for sure. He whispered so soft and low that most times I could hardly hear him. Everything I thought I'd saw made me almost sure that it'd been Chad, but why on earth would he be here and in a church. There was no way in hell that he'd heard of Lamar's death. I scolded myself and got up and headed to my car. My head was spinnin' as I sped along the highway. Tears still blured my vision and I felt sick to my stomach. I couldn't keep imaginin' that everytime I turned around I was seein' Chad. I had to pull myself together.

"Pull off on the next road, Chica."

I was so startled that I almost lost control of the car. I missed hittin' one car and almost took out a tree as I struggled to get control again.

I turned on the dirt road to the right and drove up into the deserted area. I never would've done that except that I knew that voice instantly. I screeched to a halt under some large oak trees and turned in my seat, just as Chad sat up in the back seat. His big beautiful eyes were huge and he looked pretty unnerved.

"Ya just scared the hell out of me! I thought we were dead for sure." He said as he ran his fingers through his long silver-blonde hair.

I just sat there in shock. I couldn't believe my eyes, but there he sat in the priest's jacket and collar.

"If ya wanted to give me a heart attack . . . ya just almost succeeded." My voice was shakey and I was tremblin' from head to toe. "It was you I seen in the church, wasn't it?"

"I knew ya seen me when I was leavin'. I figured I better come and talk to you."

His crystal blue eyes seemed to search my soul as he studied my face and eyes. He got out of the back seat and opened my door. I could hardly stand since my legs was shakin' so hard.

"Hi Chica." He said in a low soft tone as he bit his bottom lip and winked at me. That was all it took. I flew into his arms like a kid who'd just found his mama. He wrapped 'em around me so tight that I could hardly breathe and I knew that I was home. This was where I belonged and wanted to be more than anywhere else in this world. He leaned back and stared at me, raised one eyebrow as if to ask a question, then made a sound somewhere between a growl and a groan. One hand came to the back of my head as his lips eagerly took mine. As his kiss deepened and his tongue began to explore my mouth, I melted against him. He swept me up into strong, but gentle, arms and carried me beneath the trees. I sat on the grass while he took off his jacket and laid it down. Chad knelt in front of me, then carefully laid me down on the makeshift blanket. I looked up at him. How my heart had longed for this moment and my body'd craved this intimacy. He removed my black dress over my head and tossed it aside. With his other hand, he searched for the fastener on my bra. He slipped off my panties and I laid there as those unforgettable blue eyes swept across my naked body. His fingers fumbled as he was unbuttonin' his shirt. Breathin' heavily, I whispered, "Are ya gonna leave that collar on?"

He smirked, "Naw, I don't think any priest should be even thinkin' about what I'm fixin' to do with you. The rest of his clothes disappeared and he laid down beside me.

"When I saw ya at the hospital . . . it . . . uh . . . all just happened so fast. I don't want to just have ya. I want to make love to ya. I need to make love to ya."

He took his finger tip and lifted my chin slightly, just the way he'd done the very first time. His lips touched mine as gently as a butterfly landin' on the tip of your finger. Soft lips moved to the side of my neck and then to my earlobe. Magic sparks of electricity spread through my body. His lips moved to my breast as my breath caught in my throat. Down to my stomach and back up to my shoulders, arms, and finger tips, he left a trail of fire. Where his lips weren't , . . his hands and fingers were. Before I knew what was happenin', he was over me and inside, and my body seemed to lose control. He moved slowly at first and for a minute . . . I thought I was gonna die, then the rhythm picked up and my senses soared. As I reached that magic peak, I felt Chad tense and then groan softly, and I knew we were both swimmin' in the same wonderful sea of satisfaction.

Afterward, we laid there in each other's arms, just enjoyin' the moment. I didn't want to speak for fear I'd wake up from the most wonderful dream I'd had in years. Chad said nothin' until a small, bright yellow butterfly landed itself gently on his chest.

"Chica," he whispered very softly. "Do ya see this?"

We both watched as the fragile little critter rested quietly with its wings folded. I raised my head and rested it on my hand and the little butterfly just stayed where it was.

"My Nanny," I whispered, "always told me that when a butterfly lands on ya, that it's a passed loved one come to call. A way of lettin' ya know that they're with ya and lookin' out for ya. I wonder who this is sittin' on your heart."

Just then, as if it understood what I'd said, it turned towards me, paused, then quietly took flight again. I glanced back up at Chad and found those very serious blue eyes studyin' my face.

"My Mama used to tell me the same story. I would like to think that it was her." He closed his eyes for a second. "I love you Lilah."

My heart paused in my chest. "I love you too, Chad. In spite of everything, you're the greatest love of . . ."

He wrapped his arm around my neck and pulled me down to his waitin' lips, the lips that any woman would long for. His lips were made for kissin' and I never got enough of those kisses. Our passion for each other won out again.

****

Later after we were dressed, we walked hand in hand up the wooded trail. The brightly colored leaves began to fall when a small gust of wind came through.

"Memories, pressed between the pages of my mind." I said softly.

"Memories, sweeten with the ages just like wine." Chad sang in a whisper.

"This reminds me of the very first time we made love, Chad. Remember . . . down by the spring on the ranch?"

"How could I ever forget, honey. Why would I even want to try." He wrapped his arm around my waist and pulled me close.

"Chad, please tell me you're gonna stay this time. Tell me that you're home for good and that we can be a real family with our boys."

"I thought ya already had a family, Lilah. From what I hear, you're all but married."

"That's not the way it is, Chad. I was just so hurt when ya left me at the hospital and didn't even come back to check on Eli, that I . . . I . . . I just let myself get caught up in somethin' that I . . . I'm just not sure how to . . . ."

Chad interrupted, "Don't Chica. I don't even want to hear it. Nothin's changed. I can't stay. I love you and those boys with my whole heart, but I just cannot stay."

"I think I deserve some kind of explanation here. You just give me this 'I can't stay shit' and expect me to accept it. If ya really loved us . . . nothin', and I mean nothin', would keep ya away!" My temper was on the rise.

"You'll just have to take my word for it. I can't! Besides, I don't think you're too lonely!" He raised his voice and a coldness came into his eyes.

"That's not fair Chad, and ya damn well know it! Tell me this, how many women have ya had in your bed since ya left? Don't ya dare lie to me. I know ya better than ya think. You're a gorgeous, sexy, hot-blooded man and I know ya haven't been doin' without sex all this time!"

He turned away and I felt a stab of jealousy in my heart. I had my answer right there. He couldn't even look at me. I turned and ran down the trail as fast as I could go. I don't know what I was runnin' to or from, but I needed to get as far away from him as I could get. I saw my car in the distance and started to pick up speed when a rock rolled out from under my foot and I felt myself linger in the air just before I landed in the pile of broken limbs from an old fallen tree.

The next thing I heard was a strange rattle, like a child's toy, then a very painful burn in my left leg. Somewhere around that time, I lost consciousness.

****

I was in extreme pain as my mind started to awaken. I heard voices. I recognized Ross's bossy tone and decided to keep my eyes shut for a little while longer. I just wasn't ready to face him and try to come up with an explanation for what'd happened.

"There was a priest that brought her in and told us she'd been bitten by a rattlesnake out at the cemetery. He'd done the standard crosscut and suction to pull out as much poison as possible and then he brought her in here." I heard someone explain.

"Where is this priest? I'd like to thank him for taking care of her." I heard Ross answer.

"I'm not sure." The male voice answered. "I haven't seen him since we told him she would be okay. He may have left already."

"Did he leave a name?" pushed Ross.

"I couldn't tell you, sir. You'll just have to ask at the office."

"Is she really doing alright?"

"She's doing about as well as can be expected. Thank God the priest was there and got her here as quick as he did. She'll probably be able to go home tomorrow or the next day. We may keep her an extra day because of the hit she took to her head when she fell. We want to make sure that she doesn't have a concussion."

"Yes, thank God he was there." Ross said. "See to it she has anything she needs or wants. She's very important to me."

Very important to me . . . not I love her with all my heart . . . but . . . very important. I thought that was a very strange way to put it. Did anyone in the world really love me? The pain was not all that bad at that point. I didn't know if it was from somethin' that they gave me or if it was the fact that my heart ached so much more. I didn't know that I'd hit my head. I supposed that was why I couldn't remember anything after fallin'.

I made the decision to fake sleep for a while longer. It seemed that ya could learn a lot when people thought ya wasn't there, besides . . . I really didn't want to talk or try to explain to Ross.

I heard the doctor leave, but I sensed that Ross was still in the room. I continued a steady breathin' and listened closely. I heard him pick up the phone by my bed.

"Hey?" I heard him almost whisper. "What are you doing? No I'm still at the hospital with her . . . . Yeah, they said she'll be alright, some old priest found her and brought her in. I owe him big time, we can't afford for anything to happen to her."

I wondered who he was talkin' to in such a low voice. He sounded strange and nothin' like the man I thought I knew.

" . . . I know, just make sure and keep an eye on those brats and make sure nothin' happens to them. That could screw up everything." He continued.

It had to be Sivle. She was watchin' my babies at home. What was he worried about "*screwin' up.*" Most of all, he'd called my babies "*brats*" and that went all over me like ice water. I was just about to let him have it when I heard him say, "She hasn't got a clue about anything . . . besides, even if she did, we've got her kids. She'll do anything for those two. Alright, I need to go before she wakes up."

He hung up the phone.

I had to think about this for a while. What is it that I didn't know? Most of all, why did he say "*we've got her kids*"? So far, I didn't like what I was hearin' one bit.

I could smell his overly-sweet cologne come way too close to my face.

"Princess?" he said softly.

I didn't move and just continued with my steady breathin'.

"Lilah? Are you awake sweetheart?"

This was not even the same person I'd just heard on the phone. I didn't react to him at all.

"Good." I heard him whisper to hisself and move away.

It wasn't long before I heard the door open and his footsteps go down the hall. I still didn't trust him to be gone. I don't know how long I laid there and pretended sleep. After a while, someone come in the room.

"Mrs. Parker?" I heard a woman ask. "Mrs. Parker, can you hear me?"

I didn't make a move. She took my blood pressure and checked my pulse. In a couple of minutes, I heard her leave.

Okay, I thought to myself that was probably a nurse, or was it? Right now, I just wasn't trustin' nobody. I wanted so bad to tell someone that I didn't think my boys was safe, but did I dare do that? No. I had to keep it to myself until I knew more about what was goin' on. His conversation on the phone had sounded dangerous and threatenin'. Oh God, what had I gotten my babies into. I wondered if I dared to tell Floy and Toby. I hadn't been able to see 'em since Sivle had moved in my house. She went just about everywhere I did. The only time she hadn't was when I went to the hospital to see Lamar and when I went to his funeral. If she'd gone, I'd probably have never known that Chad was even there. In fact, if I hadn't accidently seen him, I probably wouldn't have ever known. He hadn't come back to see me or the boys. He'd come to pay respect to Lamar. If only I hadn't made a fool of myself when I pulled off the road. I didn't stop to think that he'd had no intention of me seein' him. So there I was, more than willin' to melt into his arms and give myself completely to him . . . just like I'd always done . . . and then, just like that, he was gone, again! When the hell would I ever learn? That's beside the point! I got to figger out what Ross is up to and get him away from my babies.

I dared to open my eyes. It was such a relief to find that I was alone. The lights were low and the door was closed.

"My princess, you're awake." I heard Ross's voice from the corner. "You've about frightened me to death." He said as he took my hand and leaned over the bed. His lips on my cheek made me cringe inside. "I couldn't live without you sweetheart." He whispered as he tried to nuzzle my neck. I would as soon had a rat try to nuzzle me.

Rememberin' past events in my life, I fell into what they call character very quick.

I moaned and turned my head away as if I was still groggy.

"It's okay precious, I know you're still sleepy. I understand. They say you can go home in the morning, so I'll be here bright and early to pick up my girl."

At that point, I went so far as to snore lightly to convince him I was back asleep. I heard him open the door and leave. In the hall, I heard him tell one of the nurses that he wanted no visitors in the room . . . that I needed my rest. They were still talkin' as they went down the hallway. Seconds later my door opened. I didn't even flinch.

"Honey?" I heard Floy's sweet voice. "I think she's sleepin' Toby."

My eyes flew open. "No, I was just dozin'."

"We got a phone call. They said ya was in the hospital. What in the world happened?" Toby asked.

I pondered for a minute and Ross's conversation raced through my head. I couldn't take the risk of tellin' anybody, not even my dearest friends, what I feared was goin' on.

"I think I fell and hit my head. Somebody said somethin' about a rattlesnake and . . . (*I swallowed hard*) some priest carried me up here and dropped me off in the ER. I don't remember much past the funeral. How did ya know about it? Did Ross call ya?"

"No. Somebody with a Spanish accent called the house and told us you were here." Floy answered. "Scared us to death. It was almost like the time you got hurt out in the pasture. We got here as quick as we could."

"I think I'll get to go home in the mornin', but on your way home will ya please go by and make sure my babies are okay?" I asked.

"Sure we will. Is that sister of Ross's still camped out at the ranch?" Toby wanted to know.

"Yeah, she hardly ever leaves my side."

"I bet that's ridin' on your last good nerve" he said.

I just looked at him for a minute. "Oh, you just got no idea."

****

After they had left, I thought about my decision to not tell anybody about my suspicion until I knew a lot more about it. Ross showed up just as the doctor was signin' my release papers. The minute he walked in I felt an uneasiness in the pit of my stomach, but I fell back into character and played the lovin' little woman.

The ride home seemed to take hours after we stopped at the drug store and filled my prescriptions. Ross hadn't said much of anything.

"How'd Floy and Toby find out you were injured?" he finally asked.

"When they come by last night, Floy said somebody had called 'em. They didn't know who. Why?" I asked.

"It just surprised us when they just showed up at the ranch last night. Did you ask them to come check on the boys?"

"Of course I did. I wanted 'em to be reassured that I was okay and would be home soon."

"I don't see where that was necessary. Don't you think Sivle and I are capable of handling them?"

"Why yes I do, honey. I just felt like they might need a little more reassurin'."

"I don't like it when strangers come nosin' around, Lilah." He said coldly.

"But honey," I spoke softly and very sweetly, "They're not strangers. I've known 'em all my life and so have the boys. They just wanted to help out. I didn't know it'd bother ya. I'm sorry."

He seemed to settle down a little. "Well, I don't like it and I'd rather they didn't just drop in like that anymore."

"I understand. It's not somethin' they usually do. They was just concerned is all. I sensed a real need to be very careful about everything I said and did.

We pulled up at the cabin and Sivle and the boys was on the porch waitin'. I got out of the car and hobbled up the steps.

"Mommy? Is ya okay? Aunt Floy said a 'nake bited ya." Jonny asked as he hugged my leg.

"It did, but I'm fine now."

"If me been there . . . me would smack his head and whoop him wit a big rock!" Eli declared.

I had to laugh at the expressions on their little faces as they acted out how they would've killed the snake. They looked like tiny warriors as they stomped and swung at the imaginary critter on the porch.

"Alright!" Ross's tone was harsh. "That's enough nonsense. Get your butts in the house and find somethin' to do. Your Mother just got out of the hospital and needs her rest."

"Are you okay?" asked Sivle as she opened the door for me and the kids.

"I'll be fine. I'm just tired and need a place to lay down."

I made it to the couch and laid down on some pillows that was stacked there. The boys immediately piled on the couch with me. They were excited and full of energy.

Ross come stompin' out of the kitchen. "I thought I told you two to go find somethin' to do!" he yelled as he grabbed each one by an arm an yanked 'em toward the stairs. "Now get the hell up those stairs and don't come back until you're called." He smacked each one on the butt.

I was livid. "What the hell do ya think you're doin, Ross? Don't ya ever grab or smack one of my babies again!" I screamed. "I won't have it! Do you hear me?"

Before I knew what'd happened, he grabbed me by the front of my shirt and pulled me within inches of his face. His, what I once thought were beautiful blue-green eyes were an evil green and his face was deep red. Spit was gatherin' at the corners of his mouth and he held my shirt so tight around my neck that I could hardly breathe.

"You hear me! As long as I'm the man of this house, I'll do what I damn well please. My rules are the only rules and I will not be screamed at by you or anybody else! Do you understand me? NEVER raise your voice to me again!"

He released my shirt and pushed me so hard that I fell over the coffee table and onto the floor. I looked up to see Sivle standin' in the corner with her mouth open and Ross stomp out the door. I crawled over to the couch and pulled myself up on it. Sivle looked around nervously, then come over to me.

"You okay, Lilah? I know Ross can lose his temper sometimes but I . . . he just has so much goin' on at the office and the pressure is just drivin' him crazy."

I looked at her for a minute and was surprised to see what appeared to be concern on her face.

"That's no excuse for treatin' my babies like that, and it's no excuse for treatin' me that way. Has he always acted like that?" I asked her.

She backed away, "I couldn't say. He's just Ross." She said as she turned and went to her room.

I went upstairs to see about my boys. They were on their bed and had cried theirselves to sleep as they cuddled with the soft blue shirt that they cherished. I sat down and watched 'em sleep for several minutes. I could see Chad so clearly in their tiny faces and I felt that pain of rejection from him once again.

****

It was daylight. I knew from the crowin' of that damn . . . rooster. I couldn't believe my ears as I hobbled from the bed to the window. It wasn't my imagination. There on the corral fence post, perched a very small rooster. It wasn't the one I'd loved and cussed so much, but it was definitely a crower. How I'd missed that annoyin' sound.

Ross didn't seem to have bothered to come home that night. His truck wasn't in the driveway and I hadn't heard his loud mouth at all. I put on my robe and made my way carefully down the hall to see about the boys. They was still asleep.

As I come down the stairs, the phone rang. Usually Sivle or Ross would grab it before I could even think about it, but Sivle was either still asleep or outside. I picked up the receiver.

"Hello?"

There was a long pause before anyone answered.

"Lilah?"

"Yes."

"This is me . . . Floy," she said. "Are ya alone?"

"Yeah, what's wrong?" I asked her.

"Stanley come by this mornin'." She paused and I heard her sob. "Seth went over to Bigby a few days ago. We hadn't heard from him . . . and we was startin' to get a little concerned. Lilah . . . Stanley told us they found him. They found him in that old coal mine outside of town. Somebody beat him to near death. Stan said there was no way he survived it, Lilah. Toby's just heartsick!" She was in uncontrolled tears by the time the whole story come out.

"Why? Who would want to hurt Seth? He's one of the nicest guys I've ever known. Oh God, I'm so sorry honey. Is there anything I can do?" I asked her.

"No. I just thought ya would want to know. I . . . I'll call ya when we know more."

"Okay sweetie . . . give Toby a hug and my love."

We hung up the phones and I just stood there completely in shock. I couldn't remember anything like this ever happenin' in the mountains around here. Sure, I'd heard tell of stuff that'd went on back in the wilder days but still, not a out-and-out murder! I'd forgotten Seth was still visitin' with 'em. He wasn't a big partier or a heavy drinker. He was quiet and easy goin' as they come. I just couldn't believe it. I sat down on the couch, leaned back, and closed my eyes. I could see Seth with his black hair and soft blue eyes and that Hollywood smile. I felt tears as they began to roll down my cheeks.

"Lilah? Are you okay?" I heard Sivle ask.

I opened my eyes and glanced her way. "No. Not really. I just learned of the death of another very dear friend and my heart's just breakin'. I can't believe it!"

"Oh. I'm really sorry to hear that. Is there anything I can get you?"

"No. I'll get some coffee in a minute. I just need to sit here for a little bit and try to come to grips with this."

Those Captive Blues

Chapter 18

It was afternoon before Ross found his way home. I heard him come in the back door. I later saw that he'd thrown another pile of dirty clothes by the washer. It was one of his many habits that ticked me off. Sivle did very little around the house to help. I guess her job was to look after my boys. I still didn't understand why she'd come to perch in my house.

He come through the house whistlin' and cheerful as he could be. He stopped in the kitchen where Sivle was makin' a fresh pot of coffee.

"You're sure in a better mood." I heard her say in a lowered tone.

"Yeah well, things are lookin' better. We got that situation at work taken care of and I brought some help out to look after the ranch. It's a great day in the mountains." He laughed as he come into the livin' room.

I was sittin' on the floor with the boys colorin' in their color book with 'em.

"Now that's what I love to see!" Ross grinned as he stopped short. "My beautiful Princess and her little angels having fun together . . . my family . . . what a blessing you are!

He come to sit down beside me. His overly sweet cologne, like his overly sweet words, made me sick to my stomach. I felt a chill as he put his arm around my shoulder. Somehow, there was a strong sense of danger comin' from him. I was actually becomin' afraid of him and his vicious outbursts.

There was a sudden scream from the kitchen. I struggled to get up as we both rushed to see what was happenin'.

"What the hell?" Ross yelled as he saw the look on Sivle's face.

She was pale and shakin' so hard she could barely stand.

"There . . . there was an old man in the window!" She pointed with her shakin' finger.

Ross ran out the back door. "Stay inside!" he ordered.

He come back in and looked at Sivle with a frown on his face. "What did you see?

She sat down at the table and just stared at the window.

"What the hell did you see?" he asked again as he shook her shoulder. "I went all around the house and there is no one around."

"I saw him . . . I did. He was just staring in at me!" She sobbed.

"What did he look like?" Ross asked.

" . . . He . . . he was just an old man . . . with no eyes!"

"Then how in hell was he starin' at you?" he yelled.

"I could just feel it Ross! He was watching me alright. I know he was. He was as pale as death."

"I think you need some rest. There is no one outside. I guarantee you." Ross snapped.

"Sil, did him gib ya a red ball too?" Eli asked peekin' from behind me.

We all turned and looked at him. Jonny was under my arm against me and Eli was hidin' in back of me. The hairs raised on my arms as if a cold breeze had wrapped around me.

Ross shook his head. "Shut up and go play. This is an adult conversation. Go on! Both of you get out of here."

The boys turned and ran upstairs. I stood there glarin' at Ross.

"You got something to say?" he snarled.

I ignored him and turned to Sivle. "Did anything else happen?" I asked her.

She simply shook her head *no*.

"I don't want to hear any more about this crap. Just forget about it!" Ross said as he went into the front room.

I stood there for a minute before I went up the stairs. The boys were on their bed talkin' when I went in. I sat down with 'em and asked if they were okay. I picked up one of the little airplanes they were playin' with. "Eli? Why did ya ask about a red ball?" I questioned carefully.

Eli studied my face very seriously. His brow furrowed and his beautiful blue eyes began to glisten. "Mars friend, that banana lady, sended us one. Me thanked he brought one to Sil."

"What do ya mean, *that banana lady*, honey?"

"She comes here sometimes. She telled us her was your banany and she sended us the red ball you bringed us. She friends with . . . with . . . Mar." Suddenly Eli stood up on the bed and rushed to me. He through his arms around my neck and kissed me on the cheek.

"That was sweet baby. What in the world did I do to deserve that?" I asked.

"Me almost forgot. Mar telled me give that to you from him . . . but ya got snake bited and me forgotted."

I had forgotten also that Lamar had said he'd told Eli to give me somethin' a good while before he passed away.

I was set aback with that one. How could he know about all this? I hadn't even known where that ball had come from in the nursin' home. It was obvious that he was talkin' about Nanny and Lamar. Could it've been Lamar in the window? No. Things were just gettin' out of control here. I had to pull it together and keep a wary eye on Ross and his sister.

****

The next day I called Floy.

"How're ya'll doin'?" I asked her.

She was very quiet for a minute. It was a very uncomfortable pause.

"Floy?"

"I . . . I don't know how to answer that Lilah. We're heartbroken, confused, and . . . frankly, I'm a little scared." She spoke softly.

"I don't understand. What do ya mean 'confused and scared'?"

She suddenly changed the subject and her entire tone changed. "Let's have lunch tomorrow at Shoemaker's. I'll treat. See ya then." And she hung up!

I stood motionless with the phone in my hand. I felt like I'd missed a large part of that conversation.

The next day I managed to get away from Sivle by tellin' her that I was goin' to help Floy and Toby make funeral arrangements for Seth. I guess she'd talked it over with Ross 'cause she didn't give me no trouble about it.

When I walked into the café, I didn't spot Floy or Toby. I chose a table in the back corner so we could have a more private talk. I was on my second glass of tea when Floy got there. She come straight over to where I was sittin'.

We just hugged each other for a minute and said nothin'. I could tell by the stressed look on her face that she was havin' a very hard time of it.

"Sit down and tell me everything." I guided her to a chair.

She set there with her hand over her mouth for a minute or two, then batted some tears off her cheeks. "I was afraid to talk about it on the phone, Lilah." She whispered.

I wasn't sure what she meant. "Why would ya be afraid to talk?"

"'Cause me and Toby don't know what the hell is really goin' on with all this." Her eyes were huge and she was constantly glancin' about the room.

"Okay. Start at the beginnin' and fill me in. I'm lost here."

"Alright. When Seth come down a couple of months ago, he just said that he was lookin' into a couple of deals for a man he worked with back home. Land deals, he said. Sometimes he kept some really weird hours. Leavin' in the middle of the night, comin' in at all hours, and sometimes he'd be gone for twenty-four hours or more. He didn't talk about it much at all . . . just joked around with Laurel and Toby and we enjoyed his company as always." She broke into sobs for a minute before she pulled herself together. "Toby'd just told me about three days before Seth disappeared that he was gettin' a little concerned 'cause he'd walked in on Seth loadin' a gun and puttin' it in the back of his pants. When he asked him about it, Seth just laughed and said it never hurt to be careful when ya was workin' on things at night. I didn't understand that. What kind of land deals does a person make at night?" she took a deep, shaky breath.

"But Lilah, when he disappeared and all this come up, things started really gettin' strange. When they found him and brought him in, he just up and disappeared."

I'm sure my face reflected pure shock. "What do ya mean . . . disappeared?"

"They said that when they took him over to the hospital, there was some men there who had papers and stuff that said they could take him away." She whispered.

"Take him away to where? Who the hell were they?" This was like somethin' ya would read in a mystery book.

"Didn't say. The hospital said that they was there within minutes and just took over and left with him. That's all we know . . . except, we've got a couple of phone calls from kinda rough soundin' people tellin' us that we would be very wise to keep this all to ourselves. They said it was for our own safety and that of our daughter. How did they know us or that we got a child?" she paused. "And sometimes the phone acts up and clicks a lot. It's never done that before all this happened. Maybe I'm just bein' scared, but I can't take the chance. There could be somebody listenin' in on our conversations!"

I was speechless for a minute. I caught myself lookin' around the café too. I knew pretty well everybody in there 'cept a couple of people. They didn't look like anybody to worry about, but ya just never knew. At times like that . . . any stranger becomes suspicious.

"Floy . . . I, I just don't know what to say. I didn't have no idea ya'll was in the middle of somethin' like this. I thought I had problems, but ya'll got some serious stuff happenin'. Is there anything I can do?" I asked her.

"No. I just needed to tell somebody I could trust. Ya know . . . get it off my chest, I guess. Toby won't even talk about it. Matter of fact, Toby don't talk much at all lately. We don't even know if Seth's family knows about any of it. We're just scared to even open our mouths." The tears started once more.

I glanced around again. Nobody seemed to be payin' attention to us at all.

"Okay, sweetie. For appearance's sake, let's begin to laugh and joke and make our way out and into the car. Hopefully, that will throw off anybody watchin'."

I burst into laughter and Floy done the same. I was a little concerned that hers was on the border of hysteria. We finally got outside and walked around to the parkin' lot.

"I'll talk to ya soon. Ya get on home and try and relax. Maybe Stanley will let us know somethin' before long." I told her as she got in her car. I stood and watched as she left the parkin' lot and turned west toward her house.

Walkin' back to my car and gettin' in, I sat for a minute to think about all she'd just told me. I thought about sweet Seth, who'd once called me the "belle of the ball." I recalled how he'd made me feel when I'd tripped and fell into his arms that mornin' in the kitchen. Who'd want to hurt him, let alone kill him?

A sudden knock on the car window beside my face made me almost jump out of my skin. I had to look twice before I recognized the face.

"Mike!" I was pleasantly surprised and at the same time relieved. I rolled down the window and greeted his handsome, grinnin' face.

"Hola, señorita. I didn't mean to frighten you." He smiled.

"No. Just a little startled is all. What are ya doin' here in Mason?" I asked him.

"I'm just now on my way out to your farm. You did know that Mr. Ross hired me to help with the farm and the animals, didn't you?"

I nodded. "I'd heard him say somethin' about hirin' somebody, but I didn't know it was you. I'm really happy to hear that. I was wonderin' where ya'd been. Ya used to come out a lot and see Patton and the other horses, but I ain't seen ya in a while."

"Si, I was very busy runnin' the Split T for Mr. Ross. Now he needs me to help with the farm and I am so happy to get to do that."

"That's wonderful Mike! I'll be home in a little bit, so come up to the cabin and we'll talk."

"Si. I will see you in a little while." He grinned as he turned and walked down the old cracked sidewalk.

I felt a strange, unexpected relief when he'd told me he'd be at the farm from now on. I don't know why, but I suddenly felt safer.

Chapter 19

Kyle'd taken my car and gone into Bigby to meet with Ross at the office. I was surprised seein' as how it was the first time she'd left by herself since the night she'd showed up. It'd left me without a vehicle, but that was okay. I was enjoyin' the privacy of my home for a change. The boys were down for a nap and I decided to go down and spend some time with my horses. I'd really neglected 'em for so many months. I could hardly believe how big Promise had gotten, but mostly I was shocked to see how thin they all were. I knew that they had plenty of hay and feed, as well as great pastures to graze. I didn't know what to think.

I looked 'em over and decided that I needed a vet to come out and check 'em. This just wasn't right. Then it dawned on me that I hadn't seen Boots or Roz outside either. I looked around and finally went outside and whistled for 'em. I didn't see 'em anywhere.

I whistled again. Finally, I saw Boots slowly come out from under the little cabin up on the hill. He was slowly followed by Roz. They both seemed different . . . frightened almost. I started toward 'em. As I got closer, they picked up speed and finally come runnin' to me. I was horrified. They were both skin and bones and losin' their hair. What in the name of all that's holy was goin' on? I thought Ross was takin' care of everything. That's what he'd told me. I had to blame myself! I should've been checkin' to make sure everything was runnin' smooth. I'd been so caught up in everything else that I'd just put too much trust in somebody else to take care of my responsibilities. Anger began to boil inside me at the thought of what my precious animals had been goin' through.

"Señorita?" Mike's concerned voice broke through the red rage that'd gathered in me.

I spun around. "Mike? How long have ya known about the condition of these animals?" I snarled at him.

"I only got here just now. I had to help Señor Ross at the office, so I was late. I saw you in the pasture when I drove up, so I come right here. These dogs don't look well. What has happened to them?"

"I don't know, but come in the barn for a minute." We walked in and stopped just inside the door.

Mike stood there for a long minute without sayin' anything. "Dios! What has happened here? I don't understand how this can be!"

He was as shocked at the horses' condition as I'd been.

"This must be why Mr. Ross has brought me here. He has so much to do that he needs my help. Not to worry, Señorita, I will get them all back in shape. I will stay day and night until I've gotten this under control. Si, the horses and the dogs, I will give them the best I have."

"Thank you, Mike. I know you will. I'm so glad you're here."

I couldn't bare to look at the animals another minute and I turned and went back to the house. I didn't understand how Ross could've let this happen. He was with those horses all the time. Sometimes they'd be gone for hours and hours. That's just too much exercise and I was gonna put a stop to it. No horses needed that much workout and it looked like it was killin' 'em!

It wasn't long before Sivle returned and Ross showed up a few hours later. From the livin' room window I saw him drive down to the barn and within a few minutes he took off on Patton, leadin' Pride and Promise on ropes. I jumped up from my chair and ran to the front porch, but they were already out of sight. I ran to the barn where I found Mike fillin' water containers and feed troughs.

"Where'd he go?" I said breathlessly.

"He said he was takin' the horses for a 'pleasure ride,' Señorita. I told him they didn't need to be runnin', but he would not listen to me."

I threw an empty can across the barn. "Well, he's damn sure gonna listen to me, Mike! I don't know what the hell he thinks he's doin', but I'm puttin' a stop to it!"

I turned and stomped back up to the cabin.

****

I paced the floor from the front door to the back door, nonstop.

"Lilah? What are you so upset about? I've never seen you like this!" Sivle said.

"I don't know what's goin' on here, but I damn sure intend to find out! Ross is slowly killin' my animals and I ain't gonna have it! I won't!!" I was pretty much yellin'.

"Lilah . . . you need to calm down before he gets back. Now you know how his temper is and he'll go into a rage if you yell at him like that." Sivle actually looked concerned. It would be all that I could do to pull it together, but I knew that she was right.

"You're probably right, Sivle. I'm goin' upstairs and try to calm down."

I checked on the boys, who was playin' in their room. They spent most of their time there. It was someplace they didn't have to run into Ross. I sure didn't like the turn my life was takin', but I had no idea what to do about it. I talked to Eli and Jonny for a few minutes then went to my bathroom and drew a tub of water. I knew it would help me settle down some. I poured some honeysuckle bath soap in before I slid into the hot, steamy water. The light fragrance was relaxin' and before I knew it I'd released a long sigh. Now that the anger had eased somewhat . . . I needed to make a plan. This insanity had to come to a stop. My boys wasn't gonna grow up like this . . . hidin' in their bedroom . . . eatin' early so Ross wouldn't find a reason to yell at 'em. No! I was gonna find a way out and it just couldn't be fast enough, just as soon as I could come up with a plan.

****

The next day was laundry day. I remembered when I used to help Nanny do laundry on the back porch before I'd had it redone. She'd boil water to fill the old wringer washer tub and add powdered soap. The other tub got cold water and a small amount of what she called blueing. I recall what a pretty shade of blue it made the water. This was only used for white clothes. Nanny said it was what made the whites so bright. She was right about that . . . her whites looked like snow when she was done. I'd even seen her rinse her already-white hair with a jar of water with a touch of blueing. It made her hair even whiter and shiney. I was lost in those memories as I sorted out the laundry.

Two little boys could sure dirty up a bushel basket of clothes in a hurry. It didn't help that Ross and Sivle threw theirs in with the stack. I thought it would've been nice if she'd at least done a load ever' once in awhile. I did, after all, have a new automatic washer and dryer. No matter, I would get it done eventually.

I only had a load left and was gettin' ready to put it in when I noticed some clothes that I'd missed under the little foldin' table. Of course, they was Ross's. He just tossed 'em anywhere and everywhere. He didn't have to wash 'em, so what'd he care. I unwadded a pair of dark gray slacks and a light gray shirt. I was about to toss 'em in the washer, when I noticed the amount of dirt on 'em. *Good Lord!! What'd he been doin'?* It looked like he'd been wallerin' in black mud! I looked closer as I tried to decide what I needed to do to get 'em clean. The closer I looked, the stranger it seemed. Some of the black stuff brushed off like dust, but some of it was a lot more stuborn. It suddenly clicked in my head. I'd been around this stuff all my life in one way or another. It was coal dust! Now where in the hell did Ross get into coal dust? I took 'em on the back porch and shook off as much as I could. I sure didn't want that crap in my washer. As a lot of it drifted to the ground, I could see somethin' else on the sleeve and one of the pant legs. I took it inside and tried to rinse a spot out of the sleeve. A pinkish-red color began to fade onto the light gray. I immediately stopped wettin' the spot as my hands began to shake uncontrollably. Things began to click inside my sometimes thick head. *Oh God! That looks like . . . like . . . blood! Now wait.* I told myself. *Maybe he hurt himself or maybe it's horse blood from work.* For whatever reason, I made a split-second decision to put those clothes in a plastic bag and hide 'em. It took me a minute before I decided on just the right place. Everyone but Ross was still asleep. I'd heard him leave early that mornin'. I placed the bag in the bottom of a clothes basket and took some clothes out of the dryer and stacked 'em on top. Quietly, I made my way upstairs and peeked in on the boys. They was still sound asleep. Takin' the basket into the small attic-like space where I'd stored Nanny's things, I dug to the back and put it in a little chest, covered it with boxes of her stuff, and started to leave just as a red button rolled across the floor and touched my toe. I bent and picked it up before I stepped on it. The icy coldness of it instantly told me that it was one of Nanny's signs. *Thank you Nanny.* I said to myself as I turned and shut the door. There wasn't no doubt that she was lettin' me know that she was watchin' over me and my babies.

Startin' down the hall to my room, I paused and turned back toward the room I'd just left. I checked the door. Yes, it was closed. My heart pounded in my chest as I paced the hallway and looked in at the boys for the third time.

Rememberin' the laundry, I hurried back down to the washer, filled it with soap, and turned it on again. My hands was shakin' as my head spun in confusion. I just couldn't dare think the thought that was explodin' in my head. Back in my room, I still paced. *No! No! There's no way this could be true!* I refused to believe what common sense was tellin' me. A thought outta nowhere brought me to my feet and I rushed into the closet.

The floor was littered with shoes, slippers, and boots. I searched bein' careful not to disturb too much so that Ross wouldn't know I'd been goin' through stuff.

There had to be a dirty pair of shoes or boots crammed in there somewhere, unless he'd changed 'em at the office. Just as I about decided to give it up, I saw a paper sack that I didn't remember ever seein' before. It was stuffed in the very back behind a travel bag. I pulled it out and sat there in the floor starin' at it. Somehow I knew that there was somethin' evil about that damn bag. As the sweat from my face dripped on the bag makin' tiny dark spots, my already shakin' hands slowly opened it. In the bag was a pair of Ross's boots. Just as I'd suspected somewhere in the back of my brain . . . they was filthy. I took 'em out and carried 'em over to the window on the other side of my bed where the mornin' light shined in on the floor. As I run my hand across one of 'em, it was clear to see that it was covered with coal dust. When I looked closer, I saw the same blackish spots as I saw on the shirt and pants. With cold, shakin' hands, I scratched off a big glob of it and went into the bathroom. I added a small amount of water and it started to dissolve. A tiny trickle of red made its way down my finger and when I lightly dabbed at it, I found that I was holdin' a small bit of flesh-like stuff. The hidden fears in my head come screamin' to the surface as I watched a small piece of black hair wash down the drain.

I grabbed the soap and started scrubbin' my hands. I scrubbed 'til they was raw. Then I scrubbed 'em some more.

I had to take a minute to think. What I saw was real! It wasn't no dream. *What should I do? Should I call Stanley?* No! I wasn't sure I could protect my babies. If what I was thinkin' was so, then Ross was clearly a . . . a . . . a murderer!

Those Captive Blues

Chapter 20

It was the next day and I'd found it more than hard to act normal. Nothin' was normal about my life at this point, but when I thought about it, nothin' had been normal in my world since that first trip to Lexington years ago.

I hadn't said nothin' to Ross about the horses. Mike'd promised me he would take good care of 'em and for whatever reason . . . I felt somehow that I could trust him. It was about time I admitted it . . . I was terrified of Ross. He was up to somethin' and I was sure he was involved in Seth's murder. For the life of me I just couldn't figure out how or why. Most of all, I couldn't understand what part I played in it all. What the hell did he need with me and the boys?

Sivle'd pretty much been the same quiet shadow she'd always been. More and more, I felt like her job was to watch my every move for her brother.

Me, her, and the boys had just sat down to the table for dinner. Ross was at work as usual.

I pushed my luck. "Sivle, why does Ross spend so much time at work? I thought he wanted to be able to spend more time with me and the boys. It seems like I see him less than ever now that he lives here all the time."

"He . . . he just has so much to do running the office and out with . . . with the workers . . . and all. I'm sure he'll get to where he can be here more." She answered.

I couldn't help but notice how flustered she'd gotten over a simple question.

"Maybe he needs ya to come back to the office and help out. Why did ya quit anyway?"

"He'll manage," was all she said as she got up and put her plate in the sink. Just as she turned to come back, a glass suddenly hit the floor, shattered, and a sharp piece sliced the calf of her leg open. She turned and looked at me as if I was supposed to have an explanation. We both stared at her leg as the blood gushed down to the floor.

"How did that happen?" she whispered as I grabbed a cloth and held it to the wound.

"I don't have no idea." I lied as I helped her sit down and I raised her foot onto the other chair. The fact was, I saw that glass lift up off the counter and slam to the floor. It was just a hard thing to tell somebody. I was sure that she'd think I was nuts, but I knew what I'd saw. There was a sudden, familiar chill in the room. It was a lot like what I'd felt upstairs when the button come rollin' across the floor. I glanced around the room and caught sight of the boys sittin' at the table. They was both starin' at the kitchen sink like they'd seen a . . . ghost. They looked at me with huge blue eyes and opened their mouths to say somethin'. I shook my head "no" at 'em and they turned back to the sink. I think they sensed it was better to just keep it between the three of us.

I cleaned Sivle's leg and put some bandages on it. I thought it could use a few stitches, but she refused to consider the idea. After I helped her to the couch, I went back, cleaned the glass, and done the dishes, while the boys went out in the back yard to play. I was standin' at the window when I saw Eli and Jonny both sit down on their knees and look up toward a large stump in the yard. They sat as if they was listenin' to somethin'. I watched as they paid close attention. I'd never seen 'em sit still for that length of time, so I quietly opened the back door and stepped out on the porch. There was birds singin' and dogs barkin' off in the distance, yet they both set without movin'.

"Eli?" I called. "What kind of game are ya playin'?"

Neither of 'em moved a muscle.

"Eli?" I asked again.

"Shhh." He ordered as he glanced angrily toward me. "Mar tell us 'bout him's grandpap."

"Is he here right now?" I asked as a chill wrapped around me.

"Him waaas!" Jonny scolded. "Now him not talkin' no more!"

Eli giggled. "Him say tell ya 'hi tweet girl' and 'don't worry, him take care of dis.'"

I looked nervously at the stump and around the yard, but I saw nothin'. How else could they know he called me "sweet girl" or anything about his grandpap? Just then the faint, sweet, sweet smell of Juicy Fruit gum drifted past me. I took a deep breath and felt reassurance that Nanny and Lamar were near and all would be okay.

"Don't talk about any of this around Ross or Sivle." I cautioned 'em both. They nodded in agreement.

****

The next night, Ross was home early and everyone seemed on edge. From the minute he walked in, it seemed like everybody had to walk on egg shells to make sure they didn't cross him. We ate supper and were in the livin' room. The boys were bathed and ready for bed, Sivle had just come out of her room, and Ross was on the couch readin' a newspaper he'd brought in with him.

"Eli. Jonny. Come here right now. It's time to hit the sack." I called to 'em.

Bein' the rowdy little boys they was, they ran helter-skelter around the house, squealin' at the top of their lungs. I played the chase game with 'em for a few minutes, but after I caught a couple of Ross's angry glances, I decided we'd better stop.

"Come on boys, that's enough. Let's head upstairs."

They were wound up and made another lap through the front room.

"I mean it . . . let's go . . . now."

Suddenly Ross yelled out. "Mind your damn Mama and get the hell up to bed!"

Both the boys and myself stopped short just outside the kitchen near the chair where Sivle was sittin'. I took the boys' hands and started toward the stairs. All of a sudden, we all saw Ross's head jerk backwards and pause there for a couple of seconds. He bellowed and jumped up off the couch.

"Who the hell did that?" he yelled at the top of his lungs.

We all just stared at him. Even Sivle had a stunned look on her face.

"Did what?" I asked him as I pulled the boys closer.

"Who grabbed my damn hair and tried to break my damn neck?" His voice raised even higher and louder.

"Ross, nobody was near you!" Sivle blurted out.

He shot her a look of pure fury as he turned back toward me.

"You're crazy as hell, woman. One of these damn brats did it! Who did it?" he continued to yell as he came towards us.

"They was over here by me, Ross. They neither one touched you!" I defended.

"Of course not. And you wouldn't lie for them at all now would you?" He screeched as he grabbed Jonny and pulled him away from me.

Before I could speak, he pulled Jonny over his knee and spanked my baby so hard he couldn't get his little breath.

"Let him go, you bastard!" I screamed as I slapped him across the face with all the strength I could muster.

He dropped Jonny to the floor as he grabbed me by the hair. I felt his fist as it struck my jaw and then my eye. The next blow busted my lip and I fell to the ground. I could hear my babies cryin' and screamin'. I managed to look up just in time to see him give my little Eli the same whippin' he'd give Jonny. As I tried to get to him, Ross's boot struck me in the chest and I went flat to the floor again. My little boys was hysterical and Ross was yellin' like a mad man while Sivle stood by her chair and said nothin'. I saw Ross as he carried both boys upstairs and pure fear and anger lifted me from that floor and I took the stairs, two at a time. Just before I stepped into their room, I heard a ear-shatterin' scream. *My God, what has he done?* Stumblin' in, I saw Ross rippin' somethin' to pieces. It was powder blue and I knew instantly what he'd done. He'd just broken my babies' hearts!

"This shit has to go. You are old enough now that you don't need this damn piece of crap in order to go to sleep. Now get your little asses in that bed and don't let me hear another sound out of either one of you!! If I do . . . there will be hell to pay!

"Get out!" I screamed. "Get out of this room. Get out of this house! Get out of my life!"

The next thing I knew, I was bein' dragged down the hall to my bedroom by the hair of my head. Ross threw me onto the bed and slammed and locked the door. I'd only felt that helpless once in my life and I'd said then that I'd never let it happen again. For a second, I wondered if I had what it took to put a stop to it. Once again, I felt the full strength of his fist as it caught me in the chin and I felt myself slip into darkness.

As I began to try to regain consciousness, I found myself stripped of clothin' and Ross on top of me. It dawned on me that beatin' a woman'd really turned him on. It seemed to last for hours, but I was powerless to stop him. Flashes of memories flew through my achin' head. I kept my eyes closed and offered no response at all. He finally rolled off and lay there in exhaustion, but had the nerve to kiss me on the shoulder before he got up and went into the bathroom.

I wanted to go check on my boys, but my body hurt so bad, in so many places, that I didn't have the strength to move from the bed. I felt a very cool air gather around my battered body. I opened my one eye as much as I could. There beside the bed was a very light, glowin' mist and close to my ear I heard a faint whisper. "They're fine. I'll comfort 'em. Sleep now." I could barely make out the words, but my heart knew that it was my Nanny . . . and I slept.

****

It was two days before I could make it down the stairs. I stayed in the boys' room most all the time and tried to reassure 'em that all was okay. I was only foolin' myself, 'cause they knew that nothin' was okay. Ross had been gone since that night, but Sivle come up and brought us food. I was surprised at her almost kindness. Then again, I thought, maybe her job was just to make sure we didn't die! I had to remind myself of all that I'd learned in the last few months! There was no one I could really trust.

Later in the evenin', I heard Sivle comin' up the stairs. She knocked lightly on the door and came inside my bedroom. "I have to go in for a few groceries. Is there anything that you need? I'm taking the car, but I won't be gone very long." She spoke quietly.

I simply shook my head and turned back to the window. I heard her go out the front door and watched as she got in the car and drove down the old dusty driveway. As quick as I could, in spite of the pain, I made my way down the stairs. I knew Ross was gone and there was no one in the house. I thought that if I could get Floy or Toby to come get me, it would be a perfect time to escape. As soon as I got to the bottom step, I reached for the phone and dialed their number, but there was not even a ring. There was nothin' but silence. I picked up the base and found that there was no cord connectin' it! A chill ran down my spine and I knew then that I was alone, isolated from everyone, and I wasn't sure what I was gonna do. I thought for a minute about the tractor, but on givin' it a second thought, I was pretty sure that Ross had taken the keys to that too.

There was a knock at the back door. *Maybe Sivle had locked herself out . . . or maybe it was Ross.* I thought to myself as I peeked around the corner toward the kitchen. I was relieved to see Mike standin' there at the door. When I unlocked it, I was a little startled at the way Mike looked at me . . . as if he'd seen a total stranger.

"Dios, Señorita." He almost whispered. He stepped inside and continued to stare at me with huge, shocked black eyes. "Are you alright? What has happened to you?" he asked as he rushed to get a chair for me.

It was then that I realized what I must've looked like. I dropped my head and stared at my lap.

Mike fell to his knees in front of me. "Señorita Lilah, should I take you to the hospital? Have you fallen? How in the name of all that is holy did this happen to you?"
Even though I felt such a warmth toward Mike, I wasn't sure he could be trusted. After all, he did work for Ross and all I knew about him was that he'd been so kind to Patton when he'd been hurt. Yet, I had no idea where his loyalties really were. I decided to keep my problems to myself for the time bein'.

I raised up my head and looked him square in the eye. "No, I'm fine. I . . . I fell down the stairs the other night while I was playin' with the boys. I'm much better than I look." I tried my best to give him a convincin' smile.

"I'm so sorry. No one told me about this. I'm much relieved to hear you are okay." By the smile he gave me, I wasn't so sure that he believed me. "I wanted to tell you that Señor Ross has given me permission to move into the small house in the back; however, I also wanted to be sure that it was okay with you."

I had to think quick. If he found out about the entrance to the cave and the secret that was hidden there, it could be a disaster. It was somethin' Ross could never, ever know about! I made a decision and tried to be as calm as I could be.

"I think that makes good sense, Mike. It'll save ya a lot of time and gas." I paused for a minute. "Can I ask ya a big favor though?"

"Anything . . . anything at all."

"It has always been a family place. My great grandma was the last to live there and things are as she left it, except the bathroom I had put in several years back. Would you please not rearrange the furniture? It's a very special place to me." I sighed as a memory flashed through my mind of me and Chad and the old bed that was up there.

"Oh, si. I have no need to do anything but maybe make a little to eat and shower and sleep. Thank you so much, Señorita. I will take the most best care I can of your little casa." As he started to leave, he turned back.

"Please take care and be very, very careful Señorita. If you ever need me for anything, you just let me know and I will be right here for you." He seemed so sincere that it brought tears to my eyes.

"Thank ya, Mike. Thank ya so very much."

He left and I shut the door behind him. How I wished I knew that I could trust him. But again, I had to remember that he works for Ross. Probably somebody else he's brought out here to keep me trapped . . . in my own home!!

It wasn't long before the boys discovered that I wasn't upstairs. I'd just come back in the livin' room when I saw 'em sneak to the top of the stairs. Their little eyes were big with fear as they started to tip-toe down the steps.

"It's okay, they're both gone. Come on down here." It broke my heart to see how nervous and afraid they'd become in the one place that they was supposed to feel safe and secure.

We went in the kitchen and ate breakfast and they played outside 'til they saw Sivle comin' up the drive. They both come runnin' inside. Eli was yellin' at me and Jonny, "Hurry, hurry! It's comin' back. Go up Mama, go up fast."

We quickly went back upstairs and into my bedroom where the boys seemed to feel the safest. I heard Sivle come inside and it was only a matter of a few minutes before she come into my room.

"Are you all okay?" she asked as she looked around as if she expected to find somethin' goin' on. "I saw that you came down for something to eat."

"We're fine, and yeah we did go down to eat. We're just readin' some books." I answered as I picked up another book and started readin'. I guess she got the point, 'cause it was only a second or two and she left the room.

"Mommy?" asked Eli, "when Ross die . . . can we dis fly away like birds?"

I looked at him a minute, "Why did ya say that, honey?"

"We hates him guts! Him make you cry and him broked us Daddy's blue huggy!"

Once again, I couldn't believe my ears. There'd never been mention in front of those boys as to where that huggy had really come from.

"What do ya mean about your *Daddy's* blue huggy?" I asked softly.

"Bananny told me. Him leaved it one day, but him come back and get it. Now him will cry 'cause Ross broked it up to pieces. I don't want my Daddy to cry!" His little face turned very sad and tears welled up in his beautiful blue eyes and then Jonny began to cry with him. I felt a stabbin' pain in my own heart as I snuggled my two sad babies. I think I was about as attached to that blue shirt as they'd been. I hated Ross even more than them for all that he'd done. It wasn't long before they both fell asleep on my bed. I wanted to join 'em and pretend my life was just a big nightmare, but I knew I couldn't afford that kind of luxury. I needed some time to think.

I went into the space where Nanny's stuff was stored. I was glad I'd not gotten rid of much of it. I found great comfort in amongst her belongings. I worked my way toward the back where I could lean against the wall and just sort out my mind. With my arms wrapped around my knees, I closed my eyes and tried to let my mind clear. It wasn't easy. I was in a hell of a mess and I feared for our very lives. The silence was deafenin' and I could hear my heart beat in my ears. I'd almost dozed off when I suddenly realized that I could hear mumblin'. . . or at least I thought I could. I listened more carefully and just as I was about convinced that I only "thought" I was hearin' it, I heard a voice quite clear. In a few minutes I figured out that I was right above Sivle's room downstairs. I quietly stood up and flipped the light on. I couldn't hear anything then, but when I crawled carefully back to where I'd been sittin',

I could hear the mumblin' again. With the light on, I could see clearly that I'd been sittin' beside an old pipe of some kind. Maybe it'd been a vent pipe at one time. There was no tellin' what it was meant for, but I soon discoved that it was a very good place to listen to some of what went on downstairs when they thought that I was upstairs in my room. This could be a very handy discovery!

Over the next few days, I took ever' opportunity that I found when Ross was gone and Sivle was in the kitchen or bathroom, to make my secret listenin' place better. I'd found the old hand drill that'd been grandpap's. Nanny'd held on to it and it was stored amongst her stuff. I quietly and very carefully drilled a couple of small holes in the old abandoned pipe. Very carefully, I rearranged several of the boxes so it was impossible to see the hidin' place. I'd piled pillows and blankets all around the floor and walls so that no one could here me as I quietly moved around. All in all, it'd kept me busy through the long weary days.

When the boys were asleep at night, I'd slip into this hidden little nest and listen for a little while to see what I could hear. Sometimes, but not very often, I'd heard Ross. I mostly heard Sivle hummin' to herself and sometimes talkin' out loud to no one in particular. She'd often say things like *it's just not worth it!* or *I just can't put up with much more of this!* Sometimes she sounded so angry that it didn't even sound like Sivle. Then after awhile, I'd go back to my room and try to sleep.

It was on one of those nights that I'd just dozed off when I was rattled to the bone by an earth-shatterin' scream. Before I could think clear, I ran to check on the boys who were sound asleep, then I stumbled down the stairs and into a darkened livin' room. I heard the scream again and I hurried toward Sivle's room. Just as I made it to the kitchen, I ran smack into her as she came runnin' toward the livin room.

"Sivle?" I panted, "what the hell is happenin'?"

Her face was white and her eyes were huge. She was shakin' so hard that her teeth was actually chatterin'.

"I . . . I . . . it was . . . I . . ." she stood there stammerin' and pointin' towards her room.

I grabbed her shoulders and shook the hell out of her.

"What in the name of all that's holy are ya tryin' to say Sivle?"

"That . . . that old man! He's in my room! There . . . the . . . there's a old hag with him too! Get a gun Lilah, get a gun!" She was yankin' on my arm so hard she almost pulled me over in the floor.

"Stop! Stop it now!" I jerked away and went into the kitchen. I picked up a rollin' pin and the biggest butcher knife I could find. Sivle was right behind me as I made my way to her room. I could hear her ragged breath as we both tip-toed through the open door. Ready to attack, I flipped on the light switch with my elbow. I looked to my left, then quickly to my right as I stepped in. I stood back and shoved the door against the wall to see if anyone was behind it. Nothin'. We made our way to the closet. If anyone was in that room, that was where they had to be hid out. I jerked back the curtain and pulled the string to the overhead light. Nothin'. I got down on my hands and knees and searched under the bed. Nothin'. When I stood up and looked at Sivle, there was no doubt but what she'd seen somethin'. She was scared out of her wits.

"Sivle, tell me what ya saw."

She looked around nervously before she answered me. "It was that old man . . . the one with no eyes. He blocked the door with a cane. The old hag he brought with him pulled my hair, then slapped my face. I was terrified and it really hurt. I tried to get out of the door and that old man hit me with his cane. Twice! Just look at this."

She pulled up her nightgown and sure 'nuff there was two big stripes across her leg. They was red and already had started turnin' blue. I was shocked.

She continued, "Then that old hag started laughin' . . . laughin' like a witch or somethin' . . . Ow!" she yelled.

"What?"

"Somebody just pinched the hell out of me!" She said as she turned and looked behind her. "Stop! Ow! Stop!"

I couldn't move as I watched her jump around the room grabbin' her ear, then her arm, first one and then another, and yet another. Finally I grabbed her and pulled her to the light where I could see better. Sure as anything, she had bright red pinch marks all over her. I pulled her out into the kitchen.

"Lilah, I think it was some awful ghosts!" she whispered loudly. "I really do!"

I looked her in the eye and answered as sincerely as I could. "No Sivle . . . there are absolutely no bad ghosts in this house. I think ya are just stressed out and had a bad old dream. Here, take these asprin and go back to bed."

"But you saw, it was . . . I was . . . maybe you're right. I'm sorry." She said as she turned and headed to the livin' room, "but I'm sleepin' in the livin' room for the rest of the night."

I turned and headed up the stairs. I had to smile a little at the thought of what I'd just witnessed. There was no doubt in my mind that Nanny and Lamar were to be held accountable for all the fuss. Just as I come to the door of my room, I looked down. There on the floor, up against my door, was my bright red scarf. I hadn't seen it in years. I knew it was Nanny lettin' me know that I'd been right about her and Lamar.

****

It was a week later when Ross finally returned from his unexpected trip to Texas. I felt a lot healthier and I was gettin' around so much better. Still, I preferred to stay upstairs with the kids more than anything else. I had, however, slipped down to the barn a couple of times to see my horses and dogs. Mike seemed to be doin' a good job with all of 'em. The horses looked much better and the dogs were back to their old selves. I got the chance to visit with him for a few minutes and I found myself strangely comforted when once again, he got very serious and told me that if I ever needed him for anything at all . . . he'd be right there.

I was also a little concerned when I found that the phone had been removed from the hallway and keys to the car and even the keys to the tractor was nowhere to be found. I was totally isolated. It concerned me a lot that neither Floy nor Toby'd been up to even check on me. I just couldn't have imagined that they hadn't noticed that I was not around or callin' or nothin'. We'd been so close for so many years and it was really strange that they wasn't at all worried. Then I reminded myself that they still had a lot on their plates with what'd happened to Seth. My guts twisted in a knot at the thought. I knew that they needed to know about what I'd found, but I was terrified for my boys. Knowin' what I knew, Ross might do just about anything if he even suspected that I knew what he'd done. A cold chill ran down my spine at the very thought.

It was after midnight when I heard Ross drive up in front of the cabin. All the lights were out upstairs 'cause the boys was asleep and I'd gone to bed about the same time. I quietly got out of bed and tip-toed to the door. I heard when he come in the back door and shut and locked it. I prayed to myself that he would just sleep on the couch. He done that sometimes and I was glad 'cause I couldn't stand the thought of bein' near him. After a few minutes, I heard Sivle's voice and it sounded like they was fightin' about somethin'. Curiosity got the best of me and I slipped down the hall to the storage space. I carefully crawled into the cubby hole that I'd made and settled in my little spot.

At first I didn't hear anything but mumblin', and I got a little scared that Ross might be comin' upstairs. I didn't want him to find me out of my room. Just as I was about ready to leave, I heard them loud and clear.

"Did everything go okay?" Sivle asked him.

"Like clockwork." He answered.

"This is the last time isn't it, Ross? I can't handle anymore of this. The stress is really getting to me."

"When this is done, the only stress you'll have, my dear, is where and how to spend all that money." I heard him laugh.

"What about her and those little boys?"

"She won't be any the wiser. She's dumb as a box of rocks. Just a little longer and we'll clear out." He told her.

"I can't do this any longer, Ross. You don't understand. Things have been happening here that I don't understand. The stress is making me crazy. There's ghosts here Ross. You're gone all the time, but I have to stay here. They've attacked me! I gotta get out. Now!"

"You'll be fine . . . now shut up." He snapped.

I heard somethin' break and just knew that he had hit Sivle too. I scurried from the storage and quickly, but quietly, made my way down the hall and stairs. I knew that somehow I had to stop him.

As I come through the kitchen, I picked the rollin' pin up off the counter and stopped in front of Sivle's door. I didn't hear anything. *Oh God, what if he's killed her? Would he kill his own sister?* I stepped back and got the big butcher knife from the drain tray. If he'd killed her, then he wouldn't hesistate to kill me and my babies.

I listened at the door again. I heard a slight moan. I was sure it was her and I knew that I had to do whatever I could to save her. She moaned again only louder. She was wakin' up! I had to go in there.

I chose to keep the rollin' pin and laid the knife on the table by the door. My hand was shakin' and I knew the familiar taste of pure fear in my mouth when I grabbed the door knob. I turned it quietly, hopin' to catch him off guard. Silently, I eased the door open. I tried to be prepared for whatever I found inside. No amount of preparation could have prepared me for what I saw in that room.

Both Sivle and Ross were completely naked on the floor. They were so involved in their act of incest that they never heard the door open. I froze where I was, and the rollin' pin dropped loudly from my hand to the floor.

They both immediately turned and looked at me. Time seemed to stop for an eternity as we all seemed helpless to know what to do. With a great effort, I backed out of the room. Once my feet moved, I ran to the stairs and rushed up to the boys' room and locked the door. I didn't have nothin' to protect us and no way out without runnin' into Ross. I heard him when he come up the stairs and when he opened my bedroom door. When he come to the door to the room where the boys stayed and found it locked, he hammered on it with his fist. We didn't move to open it. He hammered again and when I didn't open it, he kicked it so hard that it broke off the hinges and fell to the floor.

I could tell by the look of him that he was insane with fury. He stalked across the floor like a crazed man, grabbed me by my arm, and yanked me to my feet.

"You stupid, sneaking bitch!" He yelled. "Who in the hell ever told you that you could just walk in someone's room like that?"

"It's my damn house and I'll go wherever I want!" I screamed back. "You and your sister are sick! Sick perverts! I want ya both out today!

"You're not even close to knowing what you're talking about you ignorant bitch." He growled as he got so close to my face that I could've counted his nose hairs. He pulled back his fist as his other hand grabbed the hair on the back of my head.

"No!" screamed Eli, "you not hit my Mama!" Both boys jumped from the bed and wrapped theirselves around Ross's legs and began to chew on 'em.

"Damn you little bastards! I'll beat the hell out of both of you!"

He let me go long enough for me to pick up a hardback book and pound him in the face with it. "Run, boys! Go hide in the woods! Go! Now!!" I screamed!

I glimpsed the boys as they flew out of the room. I could only pray that they was clever enough to find a good place to go. As I tried to run from the room, Ross caught my foot and I fell. He stradled across my stomach and clenched his hand around my throat. It was all I could do to breathe. I swung at him and slapped him several times until he ducked back and I kneed him in the back of the head so hard that he let go. It was just long enough for me to start to roll away. I was almost on my knees when he grabbed my hair again and started slammin' my face into the floor. I could taste the blood from my nose and lip as it ran into my mouth. He pulled me up like a rag doll and I felt his fist slam into my face and I had no doubt that he was goin' to beat me to death. I guess I passed out for a couple of seconds. I woke up to several more slugs to my face, then I heard him stand up, and walk out the door.

"Sivle!" he yelled. "Go find those damn kids and haul their asses back in here. She told them to go to the woods. Find them, now!"

I somehow managed to crawl down the hall to the top of the stairs before Ross saw me. I had to get to my boys before anyone else did. My eyes were swollen shut and all I could see was a bit of light, but I was determined. Then I heard Sivle's voice comin' from downstairs.

"I was in the bathroom, Ross. What did you say?" she asked.

"You're as stupid as that bitch! I said go . . . ." He paused mid-sentence. "What the hell! Where do you think you're going, you ignorant slut?"

I knew he had to be talkin' to me, although I couldn't see him at all. Just as I felt the top of the stair and raised up on my knees to stand, I felt a boot kick me in the back so hard, it knocked the breath out of me. I could feel myself floatin' for just a second and then I landed on the hard floor at the bottom of the stairs. There was a crackin' sound just a second before my head hit the table beside the couch.

Swirlin' stars and then nothin' but blackness and silence.

Chapter 21

"Honey? What do ya think of this one?"

"Oh, it's perfect! I love it. I bet there's not a prettier one on this here mountain!"

I staightened the tarp out as Chad chopped the tree that would be our very first Christmas tree. I could smell the sweet scent of the freshly-chopped wood and the snow was beginnin' to come down quite heavily. I shivered.

"I just love Christmas." He said softly as he wrapped his arms around me. The warmth of his body and the scent of his cologne made my heart sing with joy.

I could hear children playin' and laughin' in the background and there was the smell of a good campfire. Someone was talkin', but I couldn't understand a lot of what they was sayin'. Maybe the terrible headache I had was why.

"It ain't over yet. I just wished I could've avoided this." I heard a man say. I suddenly remembered some of what'd happened. Was it Ross that I was hearin'? What did he mean . . . it wasn't over? Was he plannin' to do somethin' to my boys? At that minute, I heard kids laughin' and a dog barkin'. That was the sound of my own precious babies. They was okay, but where were we? I knew I had to lay still and listen until I knew what was goin' on. At least I knew they both seemed to be alright for the time bein'.

They was quiet for a little while, then I heard a familiar voice.

"Niños? Come and eat now."

"Is Mama dead, Mike? She sleeped like she's dead." I heard Jonny ask?

"No, she is not dead. She is better today. Not to worry little one."

I was right in what I'd suspected. Mike was in on this whole thing. I still wasn't sure what it was that they was up to, but now, I knew at least part of the truth.

I felt a cool wet cloth go over my eyes with a gentleness that I hadn't expected and I dozed off tryin' to listen to whatever I could pick up on.

I heard a moan and quickly recalled what I'd seen in Sivle's room. I suddenly felt nauseated and could feel bile rise up in my throat. A hand helped me to turn over as I heaved and heaved, but nothin' would come up. I laid back and drifted off again.

I was back in the cave. I knew the smell only too well. I watched as Chad lay unconcious at the feet of that mad man who kicked him in the stomach yet again. Then I heard the moan again and realized that it was me and not Chad. I'd been dreamin' again. I tried to open my eyes, but they were swollen shut. I heard the men talkin' again.

"How'd ya get 'em in here, Mike? It took some doin' to not get caught."

"It was the niños, Señor. They came to the little house cryin' and told me that their Mama was being killed and she told them to run and hide. I wasn't sure what to do. It was them who showed me the secret passage behind the big cabinet. I don't know how they knew. I got them inside and quieted so I could go see about the Señorita."

"How did ya keep from bein' seen?"

"There was no one there. I guessed they were searching for the little ones. So I went inside and found her like this on the floor. I quickly wrapped her in a blanket and carried her through the edge of the woods to my cabin and in here."

"But, how did ya know who to call? How did ya go to town without the kids?"

"They are very smart Señor. I asked them to watch her very closely so no one could hurt her again. I brought them their dogs so they could feel safe and they promised to be very quiet and stay right beside her. That is when I went to town and called him. He is also my amigo. Then you came in the night to my cabin, thank God, and brought everything we needed to keep her comfortable and fix her wounds. I know he must have sent you."

"Yeah, we've been in constant contact for some time now. He knows how to get things done, that's for sure. The main thing now is that they're safe. We'll figure out later how to get 'em away from here."

I was confused. I was in pain and yet somehow, I felt strangely safe. I let myself drift off to sleep again. Maybe, just maybe, I'd dream of Chad again.

****

I felt a tiny hand very softly touch my face. "Mommy?" a little voice asked. "Mommy are you alive yet?"

"Yes baby." I managed to barely whisper.

"Yea Jonny, hers alive now. Mommy, we gots to tell ya what Bananny and Mar telled us. She say we be safe soon and she can sleep and hers loves us all bery much."

"Yeah," I heard Jonny chime in, "and Mar said to say that yous home is where yous heart is."

I smiled and wondered what all of it meant. My mind just couldn't begin to understand any of it. I heard footsteps.

"Niños, let your madre rest. Do not wake her up just yet. She needs much sleep."

I heard the boys scamper away. "Mike?" I managed to whisper.

"Dios, Señorita, they woke you up anyway. I'm so sorry I let that happen." He answered.

". . . Where?" I whispered again.

"We are safe in the cave behind the cabin where the niños showed me. Ross will never hurt you again. This I promise you on mi madre's grave."

I smiled and relaxed for the first time in many, many months.

I was later awakened by voices.

"Are ya sure, Mike?" I heard the man that I'd first thought was Ross, ask.

Mike sounded terrified and yet very excited. "Si. I saw with my own two eyes. If I hadn't, I would never believe such a story."

"Okay. Calm down and tell me from the start," the man said.

"Si. I was going down to the barn to tend to the horses like I always do when Señorita Sivle yells at me and tells me Mr. Ross wants to see me. I knew he'd been searchin' like a crazy man for Señorita Lilah and the children. He had questioned me several times, but I always pretend that I know nothing about what he is saying. He believes me because he has talked before about the dumb Mexicans who are uneducated and barely speak American.

So I go up to the big cabin to talk to him yet again. I can see he has also struck his sister in the face . . ."

"No," the man interrupted. "She's not his sister. We recently learned that she's his wife of several years and also in on his scams."

"Dios! I had no idea." Mike was shocked.

"Go on with your story."

"Yes, and I could see that she was very frightened. There was much damage to the things in the house and I could hear Mr. Ross as he cursed and stomped around upstairs. I called out to him as his sis . . . wife and I go into the living room. He quickly appeared at the top railing of the stairs and said, 'Mike, have you seen any sign of that bitch anywhere? There is no way that her and those little bastards just disappeared by theirselves. She was in no shape to go very far! If you lie to me, so help me God, I'll kill you where you stand. Do you understand me?' I told him I had seen nothing. I was just tending to the horses. That is my job, is it not? Mr. Ross then said, ' I think you're lying to me. You're both liars! I'm going to kill you both' he screamed as he raised a pistola and aimed straight at the woman you say is his wife. That is when it happened."

"What did ya see?"

"Awww, I still cannot believe what my own eyes have shown me. There was suddenly a thin cloud, like fog, that surrounded him. The look on his face was of a man being crushed by a bear or something. He lifted up off the floor into thin air and was hurled to the floor below. He landed on his head and I heard the loud crack and saw his head twisted to the back. He never moved again. I looked back to where he was standing and saw what was left of the mist rise up through the ceiling. When I looked at his . . . wife, she was sitting in the floor and looking in a way that I have only seen those who have lost their minds look. I left and took the truck into town and called mi amigo to see what I should do. Then I went back to the ranch and continued to tend to the horses. When the sheriff came, I did exactly as I was told to do. I became just what Señor Ross believed me to be, a stupid Mexican ranch hand who only knew that the Señorita and her children had left several weeks ago to go to a country I did not know. I pretended great shock when they told me what had happened at the cabin. Señorita Sivle was taken in handcuffs and I heard Sheriff Stanley tell her she was under the arrest for suspicions of murder. She mumbled something about the ghosts doing it and I heard the officers snicker as they left."

"Ya done good Mike. We couldn't have pulled this off if it hadn't been for you and him.

"Thank you, Señor. But could you please expain again what this was all about."

"I can't go into all the details, but I'll tell ya what I can. I've been an FBI undercover agent for many years now and this is one of the roughest bunches I've ever personally been involved with capturin'. They damn near killed me and I was really scared for my family, but I knew I had to get Lilah out of this mess she'd stumbled into. Without goin' into detail or all the legal terms, I'll just tell ya this. They was stealin' thoroughbred horses from Texas and several other states, bringin' 'em here to the far back edge of Lilah's isolated ranch and breedin' 'em. Not just with the studs they'd stolen, but with Lilah's high-dollar thouroghbreds too. They was sellin' the unbranded colts with forged papers and was also takin' semen from the studs and sellin' it to breeders all over the country. We think that they had plans to go world wide eventually. Thanks to you, and a lot of other people, includin' Sheriff Stanley, we're roundin up the whole bunch right now. They'll be gone for a long, long time.

"That is very good to know Señor Seth. I think we can all sleep a little better now."

My heart skipped a beat when I heard Mike call the man by name.

"Seth?" I whispered.

I felt him take my hand. "I . . . I thought ya was . . ."

I squeezed his hand to let him know how happy I was that he was okay. "Seth . . . thank you." I sighed.

"Here Lilah, take this. It will help you with the pain. I'll give ya a shot too."

****

I could feel the softness of a real bed and hear a distant hummin' like that of a motor before I really woke up. I tried to open my eyes and to my surprise, I could see. It was blurry, but I could see. Even though one arm was now in a cast, I caressed the beautiful royal blue blanket that covered me. I closed my eyes for a minute, then turned my head, and rested for a few more minutes before tryin' to open 'em again. When I finally did, I was greeted with a sight I'd been sure I'd never see. Across from me, seated in a large royal blue chair were my two beautiful little boys. They were sound asleep in the arms of their sleepin' Daddy. I couldn't believe what I saw. The three most important people in my life, together at last. Chad, with his beautiful silver blonde hair and full pouty lips, cuddled his blonde-headed twin boys. As I watched, he opened those unforgettable blue eyes and looked straight into mine. "I love you, Chica." He whispered. "I'll never let ya outta my sight again."

The Final Chapter

Sometime later, I opened my eyes again. I'd been sure that what I thought I'd saw was only another dream. My head pounded and every inch of my body hurt, so I knew that I was awake. I glanced around and found that I was still in a room with an oval ceilin', but there wasn't no sound. I turned and looked to see if my babies and their Daddy was still sittin' in the chair where I thought I'd seen 'em earlier. The royal blue chair was still there, but nobody was sittin' in it. I wondered where in heaven's name I was. When I started to sit up, my world spun so much I had to give in and lie back down. While I laid there, my mind started to remember the horrible things that'd led up to that minute.

How could all of this have happened? How could I have been so wrong about Ross and Sivle, and why oh why had I let 'em into my home?

Then it struck me . . . where in the hell was my baby boys? I tried to sit up again, but it was more than I could handle.

"Somebody help me!" I cried out.

A young man come right in. "What can I do for ya ma'am?" he asked very politely.

I looked him over, but couldn't recognize him. "Who're you?" I asked very nervously.

"I'm Danny. I was told to stay here with ya 'til they could get things ready."

"Ready for what?" I asked him. "Have ya seen my babies?"

"No ma'am, I just come on duty, and I'm not sure about the rest. I was just told to look out for ya. I'm sorry. Is there anything I can get for ya?"

"Yeah, somebody to tell me what's goin' on." I answered.

I'll tell the boss that ya wanna see him." He told me as he left.

I felt like I was in another nightmare. This room was small and yet very fancy, and I knew right off that it was someplace really special.

It was only a few minutes after I closed my eyes that I felt the presence of somebody in the room with me. I opened my eyes slowly and my breath caught in my throat. Standin' there in a blue shirt that matched his unforgettable blue eyes was the reason my heart still beat. Chad sat on the edge of my bed and took my hand.

"Uh . . . ya alright Chica? Danny said you were upset." He spoke softly.

I could barely bring myself to speak. This was real. It wasn't another dream. I could feel the warmth of his hand as I held to him tightly. My heart beat so loudly in my chest that I was sure he could hear it. His silver-blonde hair glowed in the dim light and his slightly-crooked smile once again captured my heart.

I swallowed hard. "Ch . . . Chad? What . . . how . . .?"

"It's okay, baby girl. It's all over and you're safe."

"My babies! Where are my boys?"

"*OUR* boys are fine. They're safe and bein' well fed. I'm gonna get ya off this plane in just a couple of minutes. There was a couple of things I wanted done for ya first."

He knelt down beside my bed and leaned toward me.

"Honey . . . I should've took ya with me the first time, but I just didn't want . . . well . . . you'll come to understand 'cause I'm never lettin' ya go again. You're with me from now on. You, Eli, Jonny, and me . . . together forever . . . in my world. I love you more than I could ever have imagined and I come so close to losin' ya. Never again!"

As those full pouty lips neared mine, the scent of that wonderful cologne he always wore drifted across me and my arm wrapped around his neck while I melted into the heat of that breathtakin' kiss . . those kisses that I never wanted to be without again.

It wasn't long before I was helped from the plane and found myself sittin' on a landin' strip in a wheelchair. It was pitch black except for only enough lights to see some people around me. I only recognized Danny as he wheeled me toward a helicopter that was nearby.

"Danny? What are we doin' now?" I asked him.

"It's all good ma'am. The boss and the kids went ahead to wait for you. We're headed home now." He said cheerfully.

I wasn't sure what that meant. I was dizzy, unnerved, and confused as Danny and another man lifted me carefully into the helicopter. As soon as we took off, I noticed that all the lights around the plane went out and it sat in pitch darkness. It seemed that we moved almost silently into the night.

It wasn't long before we landed on a well-lit concrete pad that again was surrounded by the dark. I was gently moved from the helicopter and placed in what I thought was a limousine beside Danny. When we drove away into the dark, all the lights where we'd just landed also went out. It wasn't very long before we pulled up to a large, ornate gate with security guards armed and ready. We went up a beautiful drive that wound around for the longest time before we stopped in front of a large white plantation style house complete with the large white columns. Standin' in front of the huge double doors was my beautiful boys and their Daddy. My chest tightened with the need to break into tears of joy. Their little faces shined with pure happiness as they each held on to their Dad's hands. Chad stood there in white slacks, the beautiful blue shirt he'd worn earlier, and a white jacket. It was about the most beautiful sight I'd ever seen.

In a flash, I found myself bein' wheeled across what looked like a white marble front porch and into the waitin' arms of my boys and the love of my life.

"Hi Mommy! Guess what? We finded ours Daddy!" Eli jumped up and down in excitement. Jonny just stood holdin' onto Chad's hand and lookin' up at him with so much love and wonder on his little face.

"I see that baby . . . I see that."

"There's just one more thing I want . . ." Chad started to say.

"Daddy, let me tells her," whispered Jonny.

"No, no." squealed Eli. "Let me, let me."

Before anything else could be said, someone come out of the door behind Chad and stood grinnin' at me.

"It ours Aunt Dee, Mama! She comed to live wif us forever!" Jonny announced with pure delight.

My breath caught in my throat and I couldn't believe my eyes. Tears flowed down my cheeks as Dee ran to hug me. How I'd missed her!

"I sure hope those are tears of happiness . . . 'cause I didn't know what else to do. I just know that I can't live any longer without ya and without our boys." Chad said as he knelt beside my chair. "When I heard about what Ross had done to Dee, I contacted her and offered her the opportunity to join us here. After all, she is a part of this family, too."

"Do ya see this smile underneath these tears? Of course I'm happy, I just can't believe that after all these years . . . we're finally together . . . all of us . . . forever . . . I hope."

"No, don't hope . . . know . . . its forever." He whispered as he put his arms around me and kissed my neck. "Welcome to my world, honey."

****

It'd been two weeks and it seemed like I was gettin' better by the minute. I'd been able to get up and walk around . . . slowly, but at least I was movin'. As I explored the huge house, I was surprised at the beauty and elegance of it. It seemed like the whole place had white marble floors and huge tall ceilings. I was sure there was at least 20 people that worked there: some were housekeepers and some were cooks. I'd seen a huge amount of groundskeepers. They all referred to Chad as "boss," but with very deep respect. All of 'em seemed to be Hispanic and spoke a small amount of English. I don't think I ever knew anybody as kind and carin' as this group of people. It seemed that they all loved and admired Chad almost as much as I did. I thought it was strange that when I called him "Chad," they would often look at each other and smile.

There was maybe four Americans that was always there. It was a long time later before I learned that all of those people lived on this property . . . this remote island that apparently, Chad somehow owned.

It was a wonderful place for the boys to grow up. They had the ocean and beaches and pets of all kinds. Mostly, they had their Daddy and that made 'em happier than anything.

****

I was sittin' on what they called the patio, drinkin' iced tea, when Chad come walkin' out of the rose garden.

He stopped and leaned against a tree. "My Mama loved the roses." He sighed as he reached down and picked one from its bush. He was beautiful in his white slacks and black shirt. I felt like he was studyin' me as much as I was admirin' him.

"Hi baby girl." He little more than whispered as he walked toward me and handed me the beautiful red rose. "How ya feelin'?"

I hesitated for a minute. "Like I'm livin' in a dream that I never want to wake up from."

"It's a dream for me too, havin' you and the boys here with me. I can't help but wonder though . . . how long it will last?" He said as he looked down at his feet.

"What . . . what do ya mean by that? I thought ya said it was forever?" A pain shot through my heart like an arrow.

He sat down at the table beside me and leaned over on his elbows. For a minute, he just looked at the glass surface of the table. Then he looked up at me with a painful look on his face. His piercin' blue eyes explored every inch of my face. I felt like he could almost see my soul.

"I . . . uh . . . I just meant that I can't help but wonder how long you'll be happy here, livin' like this. This is my life now . . . this island . . . this perfect paradise. Ya know, it's truly perfect now that you and the kids are here with me. But how long 'til ya want to go back?"

I thought a long, tense minute before I answered him. "I don't know Chad."

He looked as if I'd slapped him, his eyes filled with tears, and he suddenly stood up and quickly walked out into the garden and out of sight.

****

It'd been several days since I'd seen him or even heard his voice. I'd often heard him play the piano, but I hadn't even heard a note.

The boys ran and played nonstop and were always watched, cared for and cherished by our beloved Dee. It was so good to see 'em happy and healthy, and actin' the way little kids should be allowed to act. It was very different from the hell that Ross had created back at the ranch. A chill ran down my spine as I recalled ever'thing that'd gone on there. They always found time to come to me for a kiss and a hug, but they somehow seemed different. Before, they'd clung to me like little vines and now they seemed to be able to let go a little and feel free to enjoy life.

The boys had just gone down for the night and I wandered out on the patio. The moon was full and the sounds from the jungle that was outside the walls seemed calmin' in a strange kinda way. I lay down on the huge lounge and tried to relax. I found my mind wonderin' back to Kentucky and back into the mountains where I'd lived for a short while with Bridger. It was hard to imagine him sufferin' all he had in a jungle that probably sounded a lot like this one. He was such a beautiful man, both inside and out. I could easily have fallen in love with him, except for the fact that my heart belonged to only one man. As much as I'd sometimes fought it and thought I'd won, my heart belonged to only Chad. I caught sight of a sudden fallin' star and whispered out loud: "Aw, Chad, I need to tell ya that there's nothin' that could make me leave ya now. All I want is to spend the rest of my life right here . . . with you."

A shadow suddenly fell across the lounge. I looked up in time to see Chad step around one of the huge white columns.

"Is that true, Chica? Is that what ya really want?"

I smiled at him and before I could say anything else, he lay across the lounge and took me into this arms. Those full, hot pouty lips covered mine and his tongue slipped between my teeth. It was the first time he'd kissed me with real passion since I'd arrived at the plantation..

"Chad . . . all I want is you . . . all of you," I whispered breathlessly as his hands slid under the pale pink nightgown I was wearin'. As he softly caressed my breast and kissed my neck, it was all I could do to breathe. He carefully slid the gown over my head between kisses as I unbuttoned his shirt and ran my hands across his chest and the muscles of the back that

I'd dreamed of for so very long. It was only a matter of moments and we were lyin' naked in the soft moonlight that swept across our bodies.

Suddenly Chad raised up on his elbow. "You're mine Lilah. You're mine and I'm yours. This is the beginnin' of forever and there'll never be another man or woman in our lives. I want you, I need you, and I will love you for eternity. We start new . . . right here . . . right now." He whispered breathlessly.

I smiled and nodded as he rolled on top of me. My heart beat frantically and I shivered with the anticipation of becomin' one with Chad for now and for always. My breath caught in my throat as he slid between my thighs and we fell into the magic rhythm of love. As I reached that magical moment, I cried out against his neck and I felt him shudder as he groaned in total satisfaction. It was only the beginnin' of a night of magic . . . the magic that was us.

The next mornin' I opened my eyes in the arms of the man I loved more than life. The room I'd been stayin' in was actually his, but he'd let me recuperate in it and he'd been sleepin' in another room. Now, it was *our* room!

I glanced up at his gorgeous sleepin' face just in time for him to open those beautiful crystal blue eyes. I smiled at him. He bit his bottom lip and winked at me and my heart skipped a beat.

Those Captive Blues

Epilogue

Dear Floy, my lifelong, beloved friend,

I know there's probably a whole slew of questions that ya still have. I felt I needed to write and let ya know what Chad and me have agreed would be for the best. Me and you have been through so much together and I'm truly not tryin' to keep secrets from ya. We know that Seth has told ya some of what happened, but we believe it would be best to wait awhile before we can tell ya Chad's true identity.

I'm pretty sure ya are aware that Miguel, or Mike as we call him, is livin' at the ranch. Chad arranged to have papers wrote up that will let him live there and run it as he sees fit. He also got the papers delivered from France, seein' as how ever'body believes that me and the kids are now livin' there.

For awhile, Chad had thought on shippin' the horses and dogs here, but we decided that they was happy where they had always lived. Besides, it might be way too hard on old Boots and Roz. Mike loves them animals almost as much as we do, so we know he'll take care of 'em like they was his very own.

We plan on gettin' more horses here and Chad's already got the boys some more pups. I sure wish ya could be here and see 'em playin' in the yard and runnin' on the beach together. They are happier than I've ever seen 'em.

Ya know Mama and Daddy think we're livin' in Paris and are very happy for us. It's also been well over a year now, so Chad said he'll make plans for me and the boys to come back to the States soon. Then we'll come back about once a year and spend some time with our family, friends, and the animals. I can hardly wait to see ya. It seems like a lifetime since all that stuff with Ross and Sivle. It's hard to believe it all happened and we survived. Ya know, since I met this man of mine, my life has been upside down. A whirlwind of the likes I never even heard of. But . . . I understand he was famous for just that!

I would sure love to tell ya where we live and how unbelievably beautiful it is here. It's like a dream come true. It's everything I never knew I wanted.

After all those years of confusion, I finally understand Chad's need for complete secrecy. It's not somethin' he wants to do . . . it's just somethin' he was forced to accept in order to have a fairly normal life.

The other day I remembered somethin' Lamar had told the boys to tell me, "Home is where the heart is, sweet girl." I know now that without any doubt that my heart is with Chad and our boys . . . I also know that I am truly home!

I hope to be able to come to visit in April sometime. I can hardly wait to see you and hug your sweet neck. Please give Toby a big hug and tell my little Laurel that Aunt Lilah will see her soon. Also, please remember to burn this letter as it is extremely important that nobody sees or finds it.

From Paradise, I send ya much love and many hugs.

Your forever friend,
Lilah

P.S. One last note. We have a new little one on the way due in late summer, around August 16th. We are really hopin' for a girl this time.

Those Captive Blues

About The Author

Linda Holmes-Drew grew up in East Texas and later returned to her home state of Oklahoma. Retiring after 34 years as a barber/stylist and shop owner, she decided to fulfill a lifelong desire to write novels. She and her husband, David, live in central Oklahoma with their Maltese puppy, Chelsea. She and David have four children and twelve grandchildren. Her latest novel, "Those Captive Blues," is the sequel to "Unforgettable Blues."

Made in the USA
Lexington, KY
01 September 2017

Made in the USA
Lexington, KY
01 September 2017